BOY
UNDERGROUND

Also by Catherine Ryan Hyde

Seven Perfect Things

My Name Is Anton

Brave Girl, Quiet Girl

Stay

Have You Seen Luis Velez?

Just After Midnight

Heaven Adjacent

The Wake Up

Allie and Bea

Say Goodbye for Now

Leaving Blythe River

Ask Him Why

Worthy

The Language of Hoofbeats

Pay It Forward: Young Readers Edition

Take Me with You

Paw It Forward

365 Days of Gratitude: Photos from a Beautiful World

Where We Belong

Subway Dancer and Other Stories

Walk Me Home

Always Chloe and Other Stories

The Long, Steep Path: Everyday Inspiration from the Author of Pay It Forward

How to Be a Writer in the E-Age: A Self-Help Guide

When You Were Older

Don't Let Me Go

Jumpstart the World

Second Hand Heart

BOY
UNDERGROUND

A Novel

Catherine
Ryan Hyde

LAKE UNION
PUBLISHING

Published by Lake Union Publishing, Seattle

www.apub.com

Amazon, the Amazon logo, and Lake Union Publishing are trademarks of Amazon.com, Inc., or its affiliates.

ISBN-13: 9781542021555 (paperback)
ISBN-10: 1542021553 (paperback)

ISBN-13: 9781542029971 (hardcover)
ISBN-10: 154202997X (hardcover)

Cover design by Shasti O'Leary Soudant

Printed in the United States of America

Part One

1941

Chapter One

The Wrong End of the Telescope

Here's a story, told by a person curiously old. And when a person is curiously old, as I am these days, looking back at youthful times feels like looking through the wrong end of a telescope or a pair of binoculars. The subject of your gaze seems impossibly distant and small, unnaturally so, as though the very fabric of space-time had been stretched. That's the way I'm seeing the day I met the boys. Suki, Ollie, and Nick.

I met Suki first, and I thought he was going to change my life. And he did, in some very real ways. Mostly by introducing me to Nick, but in many other meaningful ways as well. But I didn't see the Nick connection at the time. I saw only him.

So many times in life we think we see what we want. That we know what we want. Looking back through the wrong end of that scope, I sometimes wonder why we still believe we know anything at all.

It was the fall of 1941, early in our first semester of high school. I was at a tryout for the baseball team. I didn't play baseball, nor did I want to. I was there because I had promised my father I would go. I knew I wouldn't make the team, and that would solve everything. On the very off chance that they were desperate enough to take everybody, even me, I could always lie and say I hadn't made the cut.

I was sitting on the bleachers awaiting my turn when I first saw Suki. He was warming up by swinging three bats around. His hair was jet black and straight, a little longer than most boys wore their hair in those days. He gave the impression somehow that he simply had better things to do than cut it. He had this air of confidence that surrounded him, as though he had far weightier things on his mind than a haircut. He was Japanese. On the tallish end of average, with lanky arms and legs that he seemed challenged to control. It gave his whole body a loose feeling, which made him seem relaxed. I had always envied people who could be relaxed. I don't believe I'd had a relaxed day in my life to that date.

He seemed to be considering the weight of the bats carefully as he swung them. His face was oddly tilted, looking up and to the left, as though reading something only he could see. His black hair fell slightly over one eye as he swung.

Then he set down two of the bats and aimed his view down along the remaining one. Almost as though he could determine the perfect angle.

I thought, *This boy really knows baseball.*

I didn't think, *This is the perfect boy.* I felt it, but I didn't think it out in those words. My feelings for other boys were present by that time. Of course they were—I was fourteen. But to say I looked away from that truth in my head and asked myself no questions about it would be understating the thing.

At the time I can only describe it as a feeling like a big gaping hole in my gut suddenly being filled. Truthfully, people and things moved in and out of that dark abyss all the time, yet somehow I always thought the latest one, the current one, would be my permanent salvation.

Suki stepped up to bat.

It was funny how everything about him changed in that moment. I don't mean funny as in strange. I mean literally comical. He stood at home plate with his rear end too far out, his upper body bent too much over the plate, the bat cocked at a ridiculous angle, almost as though he were purposely choosing to lampoon the concept of a batter.

A pitch whizzed across the plate. Suki simultaneously leaned back to get out of its way and swung wildly. He missed by the proverbial mile.

I heard a bit of rude chuckling from some boys behind me, but I never turned to look.

Another pitch. Another big miss.

In between the second and third pitches, Suki stood up straight. He brushed his hair away from his eyes, as though that had been the only problem. But his hair wasn't *that* long. Then he took his wild stance again and stared the pitcher down.

The windup. The throw. The ball came whistling across the plate. Suki swung. And missed it by a mile.

By this time the chuckles had morphed into full-on laughter. I felt my face go hot and red, thinking how embarrassed he must be. How embarrassed I was about to be, in just a few minutes, over my own batting. But I swear it was less about my own baseball shortcomings and more about his. I was trying to feel his embarrassment for him. I did that in those days.

As it turned out, I was the only one feeling his discomfort. His face still looked perfectly relaxed. He looked up at Coach, who was standing vaguely at a forty-five-degree angle to first base. To my surprise, Suki burst into a grin.

"See?" he called to Coach. "Told you I was no good at it."

Then he dropped the bat and walked away.

Me, I dropped the idea of tryouts for my father's sake and ran after him.

"Hey," I said, when I had almost caught up.

He cocked his head in my direction but didn't stop walking. He might have slowed a step.

"Yeah?"

"If you don't mind my asking . . ."

On that note, he stopped. We stood mostly facing each other, and looking down at the ground. Well, I was looking at the ground. Now that I think about it, I have no idea where he was looking.

"Yeah?"

"Why did you try out if you knew you can't play?"

"My dad wanted me to."

"Oh," I said.

We started walking again. Side by side. Slower. I had no idea where we were going. But in that moment I'd have followed that boy through the gates of hell without ever wondering why.

"That's interesting," I added.

"Why is it interesting?"

He had no accent at all. I figured he had been born here. Most of the Chinese and Japanese boys at my school had been born here. Now, looking back, it seemed wrong that I was expecting an accent, but I was only just learning my way around at the time.

"Oh. Because that's why *I* was trying out, too. My dad made me."

I wondered if that was a notable coincidence between us, or if all fathers forced baseball on their sons.

He stopped again, and looked at my face, and I looked away in shame. Why shame, I don't know. It was just my fourteen-year-old default.

"Shouldn't you go back and try out, then?" he asked.

"Nah. I'll just tell my dad I did."

We walked again. We were heading vaguely in the direction of the main school building, but at an angle toward the playground in the back. For a full minute or so, neither of us said a word.

"Steven," I said, the short version of introducing myself.

"Itsuki."

"Oh," I said, which was an intensely stupid thing to say.

It was a hint that I found the name potentially tricky, though now I don't know why. Maybe it just seemed a bit . . . foreign. I never wanted to be a person who thought that way, and I was destined to stop thinking that way very soon. But there you go. We all have to go from not knowing to knowing. If you have shortcomings, I fully believe it's better to look them in the eye. Pretending otherwise gets you nowhere.

Most of my Chinese and Japanese classmates were named George, or Daniel, or Betty, or June, or Gordon.

"You can call me Suki," he said, unfortunately reading my meaning perfectly. "Under one condition. You can never, ever call me that in front of my father."

"Okay," I said. "Promise."

Since I had never met his father, it seemed like an easy promise to make. But then I was struck by an uncomfortable thought: Maybe I did know his father. Maybe I saw his father every day. A lot of Chinese and Japanese men worked on our farm, along with Italians and Irish, usually new to the country and needing work. Maybe he already knew my family. Knew a little about who we were.

That would not have been a good thing.

"Does your father work the farms?" I asked him.

"Yeah."

"My dad's farm?"

"Who's your dad?"

"Marvin Katz."

"Oh. No. He works for Joe Wilson."

"Oh. Good."

He stopped again. I averted my eyes as I had before.

"Why is that good?"

"I'm sorry. I didn't mean that the way it sounded."

"How did you mean it?"

"I just thought, if we were going to be friends, the less you knew about my family the better."

He laughed. Openly, and completely without reserve. It was a relief. I hadn't meant to blurt out that I wanted to be his friend. I was expecting him to push back against that, but he didn't seem to mind.

We walked again. Under the ring of trees that surrounded the school. It was a hot and windy day—the kind of hot wind I always associate with the valley where I grew up. That agricultural wasteland— at least in 1941—between Fresno and the Sierra Nevada range. The wind made the leaves of the trees shimmy over our heads. I could hear it. And the ground seemed to shimmy, too, as the shadows of the leaves did their little dance under our feet.

"He might *end up* working for your dad," Suki said. "He doesn't like Joe Wilson. At all. Says he doesn't respect his workers. He'll hire anybody, but then he won't treat them with that basic respect."

We passed out from under the trees and stepped onto the hot tarmac of the playground. We seemed to be headed in the direction of a picnic table where two boys sat. Why they were not in class, I didn't know. Then again, neither was Suki. Neither was I.

"Oh," I said. I had already known that about Joe Wilson. About most of the farm owners in that valley. There was a lot of that going around. "Well. I don't think he'd like my dad much better."

I was a bit curious as to what his answer would be, but I never heard it.

We arrived at the table. At the two boys.

"Steven," Suki said, "this is Ollie and Nick. Ollie and Nick, this is Steven."

And *that* was the moment my life really changed. I just didn't know it at the time. Looking back, I guess we never do.

———

Suki was sitting on the picnic table—not on one of the benches, but on the actual table—the heels of his sneakers hooked on the edge of the boards. He was eating ice cream from a small carton with one of those thin little wooden paddle spoons they gave you for free in the ice cream shops. One of his friends had handed the carton to him, and I peered in once to see if it was frozen. It seemed to be. I had no idea how it had been kept cold until that moment when Suki took it and ate it. I never asked, so to this very day I don't know.

I also didn't know at that point who was Ollie and who was Nick.

One of them was an oddly little guy with dark hair slicked back with some kind of product. The wet look. The other, the one I would later learn was Nick, was over six feet tall and built like a tank. I thought maybe he was older, but his face didn't look it. He was just huge. He wasn't overweight. Neither was he built like a weight lifter, with perfectly defined muscles in his arms, or showing through the chest of his T-shirt. He was just built big and solid.

They were talking about going camping up in the mountains.

At first I only listened, wondering over the fact that I had barely been up there. It seemed sad, like living near the Grand Canyon or Niagara Falls all your life and not even being able to say you'd seen them. But I didn't want to say any of that out loud.

Then, when a lull fell in the conversation, I said the dumbest possible thing I could have said. "Aren't you guys supposed to be in class or something?"

I immediately felt like a total idiot and wished I could take it back.

They laughed. Not *at* me, exactly. Just a spontaneous reaction. Merry. As if I'd told a good joke. I realized in that moment that these guys' lives weren't like mine at all. I wanted to be like them, but I wasn't. I was a stress machine, worrying and panicking over every subtle aspect of my life, while these guys were living life as if it were manageable and fun.

I dedicated my life, as of that moment, to hanging as close to this group as possible in an attempt to learn what they seemed to have been born knowing.

The little guy—Ollie, I would later learn—was the one to answer. He had a voice and a way of talking that let me know he was unusually smart. Actually, just his eyes gave that away. He had a way of looking at everything as though it were a butterfly he could pin down on a board and study until he had mastered everything there was to know about it.

"We're in lunch," he said. "That's a class. Sort of."

I looked at my watch. Then I felt embarrassed because nobody else had one. Most guys my age didn't have one. You couldn't buy them for $14.99 at a drugstore back then. I shifted my wrist around so it rested against my pant leg.

"I thought first lunch started at eleven thirty," I said.

"Lunch can be anytime you want it," Ollie said, without missing a beat. "You just have to be hungry."

"Don't they call your parents if you miss class?"

A silence fell, and I knew I'd said something wrong. But I had no idea what it was. Maybe they hadn't known it could happen and were worrying about it now? Maybe I shouldn't have been such an obviously nervous type, telling them everything that could go wrong?

It was Suki who finally opened his mouth and straightened me out. "Where we live," he said, "we don't have phones in our places."

My face went hot and probably red, realizing what a huge mistake I'd made. I had been guilty of assuming that every family had money and modern conveniences, the way mine did. It felt like the worst thing I could possibly have done, and I wasn't sure if we'd get through it.

Meanwhile Nick hadn't said a word. I literally had not yet heard the sound of his voice. Strong, silent type, I figured.

Suki scraped the bottom of his ice cream carton with the wooden spoon and turned his head to address his two friends. "Steven here is the son of a *landowner*," he said.

Silence reigned for a long time. Or anyway, it felt long.

Desperate to move into new territory, even territory I'd previously wanted to avoid, I said, "I've never been up in those mountains."

They all looked at me as if I'd just said I was born on Venus and swam here through space.

"Have you lived here all your life?" Suki asked.

"All my life."

"And you never once hiked up there?"

"Once my dad drove us up that dirt forest road to the end, and we had a picnic. But that's not really up in the mountains. I mean, it's not very high."

"No," Ollie said. "It's sure not."

"Come with us," Suki said.

I was amazed, because I had assumed they wanted nothing more to do with me after my ridiculous gaffes.

"Really?" I asked. But then I talked fast, before they could tell me, "No, not really." Why press my luck? "Maybe I will."

I assumed they were going soon. Because it was fall. Snows come early up in the high mountains. Nobody really trekked up there in the winter except the odd rugged outdoorsman on snowshoes.

I had no idea how wrong I would turn out to be.

———

"I want to go camping with my friends," I said at the dinner table.

Then I just waited, to see how my parents would react.

Nobody so much as looked up from a plate. It left me wondering if I had even spoken out loud at all.

I pushed my food around with my fork. My mom had made this one-skillet sort of meal. Ground beef with macaroni and something that gave it a tomatoey look. It didn't taste bad, but it didn't taste like much. And it looked unappetizing.

None of this seemed to stop my older brother. He was shoveling it into his mouth like he hadn't eaten for a week.

"Did anybody hear what I just said?"

Bizarrely, that question was followed by more silence.

A feeling crystallized around my gut and made me keenly aware of it, though at the same time I could feel that it was nothing new. Somehow being with my family felt like living in some kind of sound-proof glass booth. I could see they were right there, yet, in another way, they felt utterly unreachable.

"I heard you," my mother said, setting down her fork. "I was waiting to hear what your father had to say."

Another unbearably, unfathomably long silence.

It was so important to me to go with Suki and Ollie and Nick that my face was tingling and my stomach was tying up in knots waiting for the answer. In fact, it was so important that I knew I might go anyway, even if my parents told me not to. Whatever kind of trouble would rain down on my head as a result, I knew I might just defy them and take my lumps for it.

"Going to the lake?" my dad asked, his mouth distressingly full.

We lived about twenty miles from a lake. A hot, flat road map of water with shallow fingers that dried to sucking mud in the nonrainy seasons, and banks that filled your nose and lungs with dust.

"No," I said. "The mountains."

He gave me a curious look. Even my brother, Terrence, shot me an odd look. Which was surprising, because I hadn't even guessed he was listening.

"First snow could be anytime," my dad said.

"I know it."

"What do you know about camping in winter conditions?"

"I didn't say we had to go up *that high* in the mountains. I mean, you can go up about two thousand feet, and usually the snow doesn't come down that low." I waited, wondering if I had just given hopelessly false information in the tone of an absolute expert. "Right?"

Nobody answered the question.

My dad scratched his scalp, causing a wild cowlick, and shoveled in a huge forkful of the suspect dinner. Yes, he actually purposely filled his mouth before answering.

"Still gets cold up there at night."

"I figured that's what sleeping bags are for."

No one answered. Dinner seemed to go on as if my request had never existed.

Then, a good two or three minutes later, my dad spoke again, out of nowhere. It startled me a little. "I just think you don't know that much about getting around up in those mountains."

I said, "But my friends do."

I closed my mouth again, and silently cursed myself. Because I might have just let it slip that I was talking about an entirely new set of friends. I watched my dad carefully, but he seemed to let it go by.

Then, just as I thought I was out of the woods, my mother chimed in. She caught what my dad had missed.

"You said those boys hate the outdoors. You said all they ever want to do is go into the city and find some trouble."

I said nothing for as long as I thought I could get away with it. Then I figured the truth was going to come out sooner or later, and that it might be better to just get it behind me.

"I have new friends," I said.

We seemed to have lost my father entirely. He had disappeared into the silent world behind his glass walls. I didn't even know if he'd heard me.

"You don't see the Moore boy anymore?" my mom asked. "Or the Waterson twins?"

"Not really."

"What brought that on?"

The truth was out of bounds. I danced around it.

"I don't know," I said. "I'm in high school now. You meet a lot of new people."

"But you were friends with them your whole life. Since kindergarten."

"Maybe that's the problem. Maybe I was friends with them *too* long. You change when you grow up. Maybe it was just time for something new."

She opened her mouth to answer me, but my dad cut her off.

"Don't argue with the boy, Beth. Let him go. It'll be good for him."

"How will it be good for him, Marv?"

"It's rough country up there, and he doesn't get that yet. He hasn't had much in the way of hardship. It'll make a man out of him."

"Unless he dies first."

"He's not gonna die, Beth. Stop mollycoddling him. You're making a mama's boy out of him, and that's one thing I won't have."

I looked down at my plate and realized I had lost my appetite in a big way. "Can I be excused?"

"*May* I be excused," my mom corrected.

"Fine. *May* I be excused?"

"No," she said. Flatly. Simply. "Not until you've eaten something."

I put away as much of the bland-tasting mess as I could.

———

I tried to slip away to my room after dinner, but my mom was gunning for me and I could feel it. She grabbed me by the back of my shirt, just below the collar, and tugged me backward again.

"Help me with the dishes," she said. "I'll wash, you dry."

I desperately wanted to get away, because I had my yes answer. I didn't want to chance having it revoked.

"What did *I* do wrong?"

"Nothing. It's not hard labor or punishment to dry the dishes for your mom."

But I knew there was some kind of agenda in her asking, because she almost never did. She seemed to enjoy getting off into the kitchen by herself after dinner. She acted as though she couldn't wait to get away from us.

I tried one last desperate ploy. "I have homework."

"Fifteen minutes. Twenty, tops."

I sighed and followed her into the kitchen.

The kitchen was the only room in our sprawling one-level farmhouse that seemed to have been designed with my mom in mind. The rest of the house was decorated in masculine dark red and hunter green, with the taxidermied heads of dead animals gazing blankly from the wood-paneled walls. But the kitchen sent a clear message that kitchens were for womenfolk. White lace curtains over the sink. Brightly colored sprays of flowers on the wallpaper.

I watched my mom roll up the sleeves of her blouse and run steaming hot water into the sink.

"These boys . . . ," she began.

I felt my stomach do a little flip. I thought, *Here we go.*

"Which ones? The old ones or the new ones?"

"Well, I know all about the old ones. There's nothing to ask because there's nothing more I need to know. And therein lies the problem with the new ones."

"There's no problem with them. They're not a problem. They're just some guys. They're just nice guys."

"What do their fathers do?"

In the silence that followed, she turned off the water and began to clean a dish with a sponge-on-a-stick contraption. I watched the side of her face as she worked. She had a pretty face with a long, straight nose. Tapered. Her honey-colored hair had been done up in a bun, but long tendrils of it had fallen onto her forehead, cheeks, and shoulders.

She handed me the clean plate to rinse and dry.

"I think it's very telling that you won't answer the question," she said.

"What difference does it make what their fathers do?"

"Oh, it makes a great deal of difference. I know it doesn't seem to, for a boy your age. You just see that they're nice boys. And I'm sure they are. But people judge you by the company you keep."

"What do I care what people think?"

"And then they judge our whole family by what you do. And I *do* care."

We washed and dried in silence for a full minute or two. My stomach was doing those flips again.

"Look," she said at last, her voice soft, but full of gravity. "I'm not literally going to tell you who you can and can't be friends with."

I let out a long breath that I'd apparently been holding. I had thought she was about to do exactly that.

"Thank you," I said.

"But I *am* giving you a warning. I know you think social status is meaningless, but it's not. People believe in it, so whether *you* do or not, it's going to affect you."

"I don't even know what you mean by 'social status.'"

But I more or less did.

"Like if your family owns land and other families work that land. It makes them different from us."

I took a deep breath and got brave. "Well, I don't think it does," I said.

"Of course you don't. You're fourteen. Like I said, I'm just warning you. I'm not literally saying you're never to see them again. Unless . . . on one condition. They *are* American, right?"

Flip-flop went my poor exhausted belly.

"Of course they're American. This is America. What else would they be?"

But I knew exactly what she meant. I may have been a kid, but I had lived in that valley for fourteen years, and I knew how certain people felt about certain other people.

"Well, I'm certainly relieved to hear *that*," she said.

Then we finished the dishes with no more invasive questions asked. But I had skated all too close to something radioactive. And I knew it.

Chapter Two

First Snow

Suki's father drove us to the trailhead in his 1937 Ford pickup. It had running boards, and long tapered fenders. It seemed to have been light blue at one time, but the patterns of rust made it hard to be sure. More notably, it had one replacement fender that had not been repainted. Part of the truck was a dark maroon.

He was a quiet man who only flashed me a bright smile and nodded his head when I greeted him. Then he indicated the bed of the truck with a sweep of his hand.

Suki, Ollie, Nick, and I heaved our heavy packs in, then climbed over the tailgate after them.

Ridiculously, it had taken us so long to choose a weekend we all found suitable for our trip that it was now the first week of December. To be exact, it was early Saturday morning, December 6, 1941.

And, you know, I wonder about that, too. Looking back. The strangeness of those two enormous, life-changing events happening while we were away, blissful in our ignorance. Is it purely coincidence when that happens? Or does some invisible universal intelligence rest its thumb on the scale?

I still don't know the answer to questions like that. I go back and forth.

But I don't mean to digress.

We bounced along on that rutted dirt road, saying exactly nothing. It was cool, and just after dawn, and the sky was clear but no color at all. Like steel. I had my back up against the tailgate, facing the mountains, watching them grow closer as we bumped along. They had always been there, as long as I had been alive, but only as background for my world. They had never seemed entirely real. More like a movie set, or one of those theater plays with a painted backdrop to make it seem as though the stage has the depth of a real outdoor scene.

My stomach jangled with fear about going up there on foot. They looked big and powerful and unforgiving, and that made me feel small.

I thought about what my father had said. How it was rough country up there, and how I didn't get that yet. How I hadn't had much in the way of hardship. It gave me a chill.

Then I remembered the words that came right after.

My father saying "It'll make a man out of him."

My mother countering with "Unless he dies first."

It brought a shiver that I think the others might have seen if they hadn't been watching the view.

Still, I knew that whatever awaited me, there was no backing down now. And I wasn't sorry about that. I was scared. But I was still ready.

———

We piled out at the trailhead, pulling our ridiculously heavy packs after us. Suki's dad had his driver's side window rolled down, with his elbow resting on the top of the window well, and he flashed us another of his bright smiles.

Ollie and Nick both said, "Thanks, Mr. Yamamoto," at almost exactly the same time.

"Yeah, thanks, Mr. Yamamoto," I said, like an afterthought.

He made a three-point turn in the rutted road and headed back toward town.

We all four stood and looked at each other. Then we shrugged into our packs.

Back then we had those external-frame packs, with a horizontal belt across the bottom to rest against your lower back. I had a rolled-up rubber pad strapped to the bottom of mine, to cushion the ground under my sleeping bag, and a heavy jacket—an old army peacoat—hanging off the side. Everything I was carrying was borrowed from my new friends or their families.

We all looked at each other again, knowing there was nothing left to do but start hiking. Ollie and Suki moved out first.

Just for a moment Nick and I stood there, and he flashed me a smile that I felt all the way from my belly button, down the inside of my thighs, to my knees. I had no idea how he meant for me to take that smile. I had no idea whether he meant anything more than friendship by it. But he might have. And it was the first might-have situation of my life. And I had no idea what to do with it. It was fascinating and energizing, and not the least bit unwelcome. But it was excruciatingly uncomfortable.

It would not be an overstatement to say that it altered my life in that moment. Suddenly something that I had kept at arm's length for as long as I could remember moved front and center in my world, and I could not get over, under, or around it. It was just there, needing to be dealt with.

"Well, come on," he said.

We turned up the trail and followed our two friends, who were ten or more steps ahead. I dropped in behind Nick and trudged along, watching the back of his head. Wondering how I was supposed to live with all these doubts and feelings now.

—

The trip started out like hell before it turned into heaven. I point that out because I've come to think life might be like that straight across the board.

We hiked for hours. Literally. Hours. Somehow I hadn't anticipated that.

In my head we had just walked to a nice spot and set up tents. But now that I was up there, I began to realize why that wasn't possible. You don't pitch your tent at a thirty-five-degree angle on solid shale on the side of a mountain. The trail was almost entirely composed of rock, threading its way around switchbacks between scattered boulders—some the size of cars, some the size of cabins. Scrubby little pine trees somehow managed to grow around—or even seemingly right out of—the stone.

The sky turned from steel to robin's-egg blue as I contemplated the simple fact that all the ground I had walked on in my life had been more or less flat.

I watched Nick's back as we climbed, searching for some sign that he also found this hard going. Though, in retrospect, I'm not sure what I thought his back would tell me. My calf muscles seemed to be contracting into tight little balls of spasm, and the straps of my heavy pack cut painfully into my shoulders.

To make matters worse, I was developing a blister under the toenail of my right little toe that stung with every step.

I couldn't even see Ollie and Suki. They had moved out ahead, and the trail was too twisty. But somehow I was determined not to say that any of this hurt unless someone else said it first. I felt like enough of an outcast in my new group already.

In time the trail straightened—though it did not level off—and I saw Suki and Ollie up ahead, sitting on a rock, drinking water from canteens.

I limped along behind Nick to the spot where they sat, wanting to say "Ouch" with every step but not saying it. The last steps felt like the longest steps I'd ever taken in my life.

We shrugged out of our packs and sat, and Suki handed me a candy bar. I was ridiculously grateful for it. He could have handed me a hundred-dollar bill and I doubt I could have been any more excited.

"Thanks," I said.

He looked right into my face. I looked away to hide whatever he was trying to see.

"You doing okay?" he asked me.

"Yeah. Fine."

Then I ate my candy bar and watched Nick take off his right boot.

He was wearing a pair of battered leather work boots, but one of them had a broken lace. I had noticed him stopping to tie the lace on the trail, but I hadn't noticed that it had broken. He had retied what was left of it, but it was too short, and the boot couldn't really lace up. Not properly.

I knew what that meant. Just because I hadn't walked up a mountain before didn't mean I was unaware of what happens when you walk in an improperly laced shoe. Your heel is loose inside, and it shifts up and down. And it rubs.

The thin white sock underneath was soaked through with blood. When he pulled it off, I saw that the whole back of his heel had formed a blister that had since broken, leaving a frightening amount of skin hanging down.

He absentmindedly pulled it off. I winced just watching it.

Then he put the sock back on without any kind of dressing on that open wound. Maybe nobody had any dressing for broken blisters.

I had a thought in that moment. I had been trying to emulate these boys for a couple of months, because they didn't seem to get too upset about anything. Now I wondered if their secret was simply to keep quiet about everything that hurt.

If so, I had a good head start on their program.

"How much farther are we going?" I asked. I asked Suki, since he seemed to be leading the way.

"We're about halfway there," he said.

I kept quiet about my pain.

———

The sun was almost directly overhead when we arrived at the little mountain lake. I took one look at it, and I would have sworn it was almost worth what I'd been through.

It was on flat ground with stony banks, and snowcapped mountains framing the background. The sky had gone a deep blue, half covered with popcorn clouds. The surface of the lake was so clear and so perfectly still that it mirrored the sky, so I saw the mountains and the beautiful patterns of clouds twice, the bottom image upside-down. I stared at it for a long time, wondering if I had ever seen anything so beautiful. Coming from a hot, dusty, unremarkable valley, it's possible that I never had.

There was no one else camping there. And it made sense that there wasn't. It was December. We were headed for a cold night.

Nick dropped his pack and, much to my amazement, began to peel out of his clothes.

"Aren't you cold?" I asked, because it was probably in the forties up there, even in the middle of the day.

Meanwhile I did my best not to look, though I did steal one quick glance at his broad, hairless chest.

I was relieved when he left his underwear on.

"It's good for you," he said. "In Finland, the Finns sit in a sauna until they're all sweaty, and then they go out and throw themselves into a snowbank and roll around."

I was left unclear as to how that was "good for you," but it was my first clue that he planned to jump into that freezing water.

I looked around to see what the other boys thought about this. Ollie was setting up what I would later learn was our one and only small tent. Suki was standing behind me. He smiled his nicely crooked Suki smile and shrugged.

"It's just what he does," Suki said.

Nick took off running, hollering unintelligible sounds. He ran barefoot up onto the scattered stones of the bank, where he launched himself into the air. He seemed to fly for a surprising length of time, drawing his knees to his chest and catching them there with his arms.

Then came the splashdown.

When the water settled again, I saw nothing. Just ripples on the surface of the lake. Then Nick flew straight up into the air, breaking the beautiful—if now disturbed—reflection of the sky. He let out a scream that one might expect from a person being murdered.

Then he treaded water for a moment or two, a wild and silly grin on his face.

I shook my head at him in disbelief.

"Come in," he called to me.

"You've got to be kidding."

"No, really. Try it. Come in. It wakes up your nerves in a way you never felt before. Everybody should feel this at least once."

I looked around at Suki, who gave me a wry raised eyebrow.

"Did you ever try it?" I asked him, quietly.

"Yeah. Once."

"How was it?"

"I haven't tried it since. That should tell you something."

Still, my life was teetering on a balance point in that moment. Nothing was more important than earning the respect of my new friends. Especially Nick.

I began to strip out of my clothes, already shivering. The three boys neither stared nor looked away. They had no need to be awkward about it.

And I didn't feel ashamed of my body around other boys. I wasn't built big and solid like Nick, but I had a build that I felt good about. Slim, but with ropy, wiry muscles. Farmwork for extra money will get you that much.

What I failed to consider in that moment is that Nick's delicate internal organs were wrapped in a lot more insulation than mine.

Of course, I left my underwear on.

I walked to the perfectly clear water. At the shallow edge I could see brightly colored stones on the bottom. Other than that thin little sliver, it looked as though I were about to step into the sky.

I raised one foot to test the temperature, but Nick corrected me immediately.

"No, not that way, Steven. You can't do it that way. It won't work. You'll never go in if you try to do it a little at a time. You just have to *do it*. All at once."

I pulled a big, deep breath, knowing in the moment both that it was a terrible idea and that I was about to do it anyway. I thought it would feel about as bad as a thing can feel. Turns out I had underestimated the badness of it.

I didn't cannonball in the way Nick did. I was a diver. My father had taught me diving the previous summer at the hot and dusty lake, and I was pretty good at it. I stood there, still for a moment. Then I raised my arms over my head. Bent my knees. I pushed off hard and cleanly, sailed forward, and cut the water at a shallow angle with my hands first.

The rest of the disaster happened very fast.

The cold was indescribable. It felt like being dunked into a vat of ice water. I swear if there had been miniature icebergs floating in that lake it couldn't have felt any colder.

It plunged my body into a physical state of shock, and I sank like a boulder.

I couldn't help myself. I couldn't move. I had been lifted out of my body. I still felt the intense pain of the cold, but I was unable to command my muscles. The pressure of airlessness built in my lungs, adding a whole new, second form of pain. I felt my feet touch the bottom, but my legs folded like cooked noodles. I couldn't even use them to push up toward the surface.

My brain, which seemed to be located several feet away from my head, registered a muddy thought. *What a strange way for it all to end.*

I took a deep "breath" of water. I couldn't stop it. The pressure was too great. I had given up, anyway. It was over. Everything was over.

A huge, solid arm wrapped around my chest.

My arms were up, floating toward the surface, but I hadn't even known it. As the strong arm pulled me up, they drifted down over it, a weak attempt to hold the arm in return.

My head broke the surface, and I was vaguely surprised to still exist in the world. I couldn't feel my body at all. I wanted to take a breath but my lungs were full of water.

Next thing I knew I was on my hands and knees on solid ground, Nick's arms around my chest and belly, holding me up. In a motion nearly strong enough to crack ribs, he yanked up on me, compressing my body between his arms and torso. A double lungful of water splashed onto the stones and I gasped air, sputtering and coughing. I coughed so hard that I threw up, then coughed some more.

I felt myself being wrapped in jackets, my body convulsing in spasms of shivering, my teeth chattering uncontrollably.

That's all I remember for a time.

Suki made a roaring fire, and Ollie made soup on its heat. It was just a pot of boiled lake water with a lot of bouillon cubes and some chopped vegetables and dry noodles he had brought from home. Truthfully, after my exhausting and traumatic day, I could have used something more substantial. But it was hot. And hot was good.

I was wearing all four jackets wrapped around my shoulders like blankets. Which meant the other boys had no jackets, and the sun had gone down. We all hunkered close to the fire and sipped our soup from metal cups and did our best not to mind the cold.

To say I had not recovered from my lake experience would be to ridiculously understate the case. I was shaking so hard and so uncontrollably that Ollie had to hand me my soup in a series of half-full cups. Otherwise I would have spilled it everywhere. My teeth were chattering so hard that I knew everybody could hear it. The cold felt like it lived in the very core of me. As though the center of my gut was made of searing dry ice. The fire barely seemed able to touch it, and the hot soup helped to a barely noticeable degree.

"You know what we need to do for him," Ollie said.

I wanted to ask, but I couldn't speak in such a way as to be understood.

"What?" Nick asked. It was clear he was drowning in guilt. Had been all afternoon.

"We need to get him into the tent and get all around him and sandwich him in and warm him up with our body heat."

"Yeah," Suki said. "That's good. That might help."

We finished our soup, and they helped me walk to the tent.

I learned later, when I was able to talk, that it was a four-man tent. At the time I didn't realize that a four-man tent was more or less the size of four people lying in a row, very close together, and with barely an inch to spare between or on any side.

Ollie ducked in first and opened out the sleeping bags so we could have two on the ground and two over us like blankets. We all squeezed inside, and they took off the jackets and laid me down. Nick got on one side of me, and Suki on the other, and Ollie covered us up.

They pressed in close to me.

Of course, this was a complicated development for me, emotionally speaking. I had never had the body of another boy pressed close to me, and I already had a pretty good crush going on Nick. Well, on both of them. And it meant more to me than just an act of warming.

And it was essential to me that they not know.

We lay quietly that way for a long time. Many minutes. Could even have been half an hour. It was fully dark outside the tent, and time was hard to judge.

Then Suki said, "I don't know, Steven. I'm still worried about you. Your heart is going a mile a minute."

I knew that had nothing to do with cold, but I couldn't say so.

"I'm warming up, though," I said. I realized, hearing myself say it, how true it was. Because the chattering of my teeth had calmed just enough that I could be understood.

Nick said nothing. Just held me wrapped in his great bulk. I knew that if Suki could feel my racing heart, so could Nick. But he had chosen silence. Maybe he had simply seen no reason to comment. But I was haunted by the thought that he might know why it was hammering so hard in my chest.

I knew I could speak and be understood now, so I said what I'd been wanting to say to Nick all afternoon. "You saved my life."

"Oh," he said. "That's a pretty nice way to look at it. See, I was thinking I almost got you killed."

———

I woke in the night, in the dark. Nick was gone. Suki was asleep beside me, but he had rolled away. Ollie was snoring loudly on the other side of him.

I thought maybe Nick had just needed to step outside to relieve himself. I lay awake waiting for several minutes, but he didn't come back, so I sat up quietly and wiggled into my borrowed peacoat.

It was cold in the tent. Bone cold. But it was nothing like the cold following my lake experience. This cold was outside me. I could fend it off. It didn't emanate from the very core of my being. After the experience I'd so recently had, it felt strangely tolerable.

I moved over and unzipped the tent flap. It took some doing. Every muscle in my body screamed with tight soreness. I had to ease into motion carefully. I had to go slow.

I stepped out—and was bowled over by more beauty than I had experienced in my life. People say that all the time, but I mean it literally. Ever. In my life.

The stars were half in and half out. Clumps and trails of clouds spotted the sky, but in between them, the stars were fierce. They were so bright that their light reflected in the still surface of the lake.

It was snowing lightly.

I'd rarely seen snow before. Oh, I had seen it regularly from a distance, lying on the mountains above the horizon. But I had never watched it and felt it as it swirled around me, cold flakes settling on my shoulders, sticking to my eyelashes and hair.

As my eyes adjusted to the light, I saw the soft, dim shape of Nick's back. He was sitting halfway between our tent and the lake, apparently just gazing off into the distance.

I picked my way to where he sat, and he turned his head when he heard me. I sat by his side, easing my crampy legs into a new position in the midst of all that magic. For a time we said nothing at all.

Then he said, "Glad you're okay."

He put his big arm around my shoulder. It was a thing like the smile he flashed me before we set off hiking. It was a might-be. I wanted to answer, but I had no idea what to say.

"Have you ever seen anything more beautiful?" he asked.

"Never," I said. "Not once in my whole life."

We sat a while longer. The clouds moved off in the direction of home, leaving the stars brilliantly clear. Of course they took the snow with them, but by starlight I could see a faint dusting of it all around our crossed legs, and sugaring the banks of the lake and its perfect reflection of the universe.

"I'm really sorry about yesterday," he said.

"Not your fault. I was the one who decided to go in."

I waited to see what he would say, but he seemed to have lost himself in the magic again.

"Know what's weird?" I asked him.

"No. What?"

"Yesterday the whole trip seemed so terrible. The walking was really hard, even though I didn't want to say so, and then I was so humiliated that I couldn't even jump into some cold water without drowning. Everything just felt so miserable. And now I wake up, and it's the most perfect experience I've ever had. And I already know that when I look back on it, all I'll remember is this. It's just strange to me how things change so fast."

He only waited when I was done. Maybe to see if there was more.

Then in time he said, "Yeah. Life changes fast."

Looking back, these were oddly prophetic sentiments. But we didn't know. In that brilliant and memorable moment, we didn't know.

Now I know that, very soon, right around the time the tavern closed in town, Nick's father would get into a bar fight that would leave a man in a coma and hovering at the edge of death.

Now I know that, as we sat gazing into heaven, Nick's arm draped around my shoulder, Japanese planes were on their way to their surprise attack on Pearl Harbor, drawing our country into the war and turning Suki's life on its head pretty much forever.

Now I know that in a few months' time construction would begin on a camp called Manzanar—in a spot we would have been staring down on if not for the higher mountains in our field of view—to intern the Japanese who were no longer welcome in free society anywhere in the western states.

At the time we honestly believed everything was perfect.

Chapter Three

Climb Down in Darkness

Ollie had a flashlight.

We knew we'd need one hiking home, the days being so short and all. If not for the flashlight plan, we'd have had to leave the lake before noon to get down to the valley while we still had enough light to see our own feet on the trail.

The return hike didn't quite work out as planned.

We were about halfway down, walking close together. Ollie was bringing up the rear and shining the light forward onto our path.

The beam flickered and failed.

"It's okay," Ollie said. "Don't worry. I was prepared for this. I brought extra batteries."

We stopped with him in the dark while he found the spare batteries in his pack and replaced them by feel. He turned on the flashlight again, but it still did not produce light.

"Uh-oh," he said.

"Think it's the bulb?" Suki asked him.

"Must be the bulb."

I waited for him to announce that he'd brought a spare bulb, but he never did.

"What do we do?" I asked, trying to keep the panic out of my voice.

I could hear the sounds of movement in the brush near the trail. Probably only deer, but there were also plenty of coyotes and bears in those parts. I could feel an iciness forming in and around my gut.

"We still have to get down," Ollie said.

Then everyone fell silent for a time.

"We'll just have to feel our steps," Nick said.

Suki said, "But what if we lose the trail?"

"Does it really matter?" I asked. "We can see a few lights from town. As long as we head toward them, we'll get there." A pause. No one commented. "Right?"

"No, it's not that easy," Nick said. "You don't want to lose the trail. You could end up at the edge of a cliff. Last year some guy tried to shortcut down and ended up stranded on a ledge, and they had to send a rescue team for him."

We all stood a moment in silence.

Part of me knew in that moment that we had lost all of our magic—that we were descending into some kind of darkness. More than just the literal variety.

Although, maybe "knew" is the wrong word. I felt it but I didn't believe it.

I was standing close to Nick, and he seemed to know I was scared. I was embarrassed and relieved at the same time when he spoke, and let on that he knew.

"Grab the back of my pack," he said. "I'll get you down."

He led the way, and I held a strap of his pack—the trailing end of the strap that wrapped around his rubber pad.

My eyes adjusted to the lack of light more than I would have thought possible, but I still don't quite know how he got us down. We lost the trail three times, but he always managed to backtrack and find it again.

I was petrified, but I put all my faith in him.

Really, what other options did I have?

—

Eventually we ended up with our feet on relatively flat ground, though it seemed like an eternity. In truth, we were probably feeling our way through the darkness for about two hours.

We were likely delayed, yet Nick's father was not there to pick us up as planned.

"He's just late," Suki said. "I'll bet he's just late."

Nick did not answer. There was something heavy in his silence, but I couldn't quite place it. A worry or a fear. He was afraid his father was more than just late. I could feel it.

In the few months I had known these three boys, I had learned almost nothing about their families, and told them nothing about mine. It was a deal we had never spoken out loud, but it seemed to be understood. Now I knew a little about Nick's father—more than just the fact that he drank at the tavern, which I'd seen on my own. Maybe those were the only things I needed to know.

"We'll start walking," Ollie said. "And he'll be along."

It was a good twelve miles into town. I could only hope the second part of his proclamation would prove correct.

We trudged down the dirt road in the darkness.

I was exhausted, and more miserable than I was willing to say. Probably more miserable than I could have found the words to say, even if I'd been compelled to try.

For ten or fifteen minutes we saw nothing and no one on that deserted road, save for a black bear lumbering across, skittering away when he saw us.

Then we were blessed by headlights.

"There he is!" Nick cried out, his voice so full of relief that I hurt for him. Then, a second later, I hurt for him even more. "Oh," he added, more quietly. "No. That's not him."

I don't know how he knew so soon. Must have been something about the shape or pattern of the headlights.

They shone on us now, bathing us in the light that had been absent from our lives for so long. I turned my head to keep them from blinding me, and got a quick look at Nick's face. I saw his eyes. This was not a small thing to him, that his father had not shown up as planned. He was deeply scared. It shook me to my core, because I thought Nick was never scared of anything.

Looking back, I wonder why I ever believed that about anybody.

Suki stepped into the middle of the road and waved his arms to flag the driver down, and the man was nice enough to stop for us. He was an older Japanese man, driving an enormous flatbed truck with a single layer of hay bales strapped down to the bed. I wanted to believe he was our salvation. But, of course, he was headed the wrong way.

Suki had a short conversation with the man in Japanese, through the truck's open driver's window. I hadn't known he spoke it, and it reminded me how new I was to these boys. He was obviously perfectly fluent in two languages, and I hadn't known, or even thought to wonder.

Then he stepped back and the man drove on.

My heart felt as though it was falling into my shoes.

"He has to go up the road and feed his stock," Suki said. "He'll pick us up on the way back and give us a lift into town."

I was hoping we would sit on the side of the road until he came back for us, but the boys started walking again. I kept my mouth shut about my misery and trudged along.

It was at least twenty miserable minutes later when we saw his headlights light us up from behind.

He pulled over, and we threw our packs up and then climbed onto the now-empty bed of his truck. My muscles were so cramped and sore that I almost fell onto the road again as I tried to hoist myself up, but Nick grabbed my shirt and pulled.

I flopped onto my back and stared up at the stars as the truck bounced over the dirt road, rumbling toward town. They were brilliant, though not quite as beautiful as the ones I'd seen up in the mountains. But it was definitely a riot of stars. In any case, they failed to move me. I was only exhausted, and wanting to go home. They only reminded me that we were still in the middle of nowhere, and still without light. I had never appreciated light before. I made a silent vow never to take it for granted again.

"I didn't know you spoke Japanese," I said quietly to Suki. Then I hoped it hadn't been a stupid thing to say.

Probably it had been a stupid thing to say.

"Oh, sure," he said. "I have to be able to talk to my grandmother." We fell silent again after that.

In time the world around my eyes grew lighter, fading the stars, and the truck rumbled to a stop. I sat up to see that we had reached the business section of town.

It's almost laughable to call it that. It was nothing more than a wide spot in the road. The businesses consisted of a tavern, a tiny post office, a branch bank, two feed stores, a general store, an insurance office, and a land office. It was Sunday evening, and only the tavern was open. The other businesses were locked down and dark. But the light was more than just that which spilled out through the tavern windows.

On the other side of the businesses, on both sides of the road, lay dense residential areas. Massive flat dirt lots sprinkled with shack-sized dwellings. Some had electricity, others shone with the light of lanterns. But it was clear that hundreds of people were awake in there.

I assumed this was where my friends lived, but I had been careful never to ask.

The boys jumped off the truck. I tried to climb down, but my sore muscles had stiffened into a nearly locked position. The driver waited patiently, watching me in his rearview mirror, until I had lowered my pack and then myself into the dirt.

We set off walking. I didn't ask to where. One of the boys' houses, I assumed. Somehow one of them would get me home.

Ten or so steps later we heard the driver call out through his open window.

"Itsuki san," he shouted.

We all stopped and turned around.

"Hai, Ito san?" Suki called back.

"Ki o tsukete, Itsuki san," the man called.

Suki just stood frozen a moment, almost as though he didn't understand. Then he nodded gravely, and we started off walking again.

I trotted a few steps to catch up to him. It was hard. I hurt.

"What did he say to you?" I asked, because I had sensed a deep gravity in those words. Both in how they were spoken, and in how they were received.

"He told me to be careful," Suki said.

"Why?"

"I don't know."

Looking back, Mr. Ito must not have realized how long we had been gone. He must have thought we already knew.

"All of us?" I asked. "Or just you?"

It was a stupid question. Because Mr. Ito had ended his sentence with the name "Itsuki san." "Ki o tsukete, Itsuki san." Not "Be careful, boys," or a vague "Be careful" thrown in our general direction. "Be careful, Itsuki san."

Suki was polite about it to me, though. He did not choose to point out my stupidity.

"Sounded like he just meant me," he said. "But I don't really know."

I could feel his worry and confusion. I couldn't miss his distraction. He was locked into some flurry of thoughts spinning in his head. I could almost see and hear them. I could tell he was doing his best to talk around them.

"We'll go to my house," Ollie said, "and I'll borrow my dad's truck and drive Steven home."

I stopped dead on the board sidewalk between the land office and the tavern. "Wait," I said in Ollie's general direction. "You drive?"

He didn't answer. It was Nick who said, "Ollie's older than we are. He's seventeen."

"Oh," I said.

I didn't dare say more. I didn't want to insult Ollie by letting on that he not only looked younger than seventeen to me, he looked younger than we were. He was built small, as I think I mentioned, and he had a baby face.

Meanwhile, as these thoughts ran in my head, we passed in front of the tavern.

Suki missed a step. His body, his stride, seemed to hang up over something he saw.

I looked at his face, and I can't even describe the dread I saw there. Then I looked past his face to see what had so disturbed him.

On the inside of the window of the tavern a handmade sign had been posted, crudely taped to the glass. It was made with a panel of a shipping carton. It was huge, with rough letters a foot high.

It said: **JAPS KEEP WALKING**.

That's when I knew we had reached our new era of darkness. Not *why* we had, but *that* we had. We kept walking, the words tingling in my belly like electricity.

Or anyway, we tried.

But there was a man standing in the shadowy entryway of the tavern. He stepped out into the light. And into our path. We were walking four abreast on the wooden boards of the walkway, but he ignored the rest of us and stepped right in front of Suki.

I could hear my friend draw in a sharp breath.

He was an older man, maybe in his sixties. Maybe even in his seventies. He wore a grizzled white beard and a face tanned leathery by outdoor work. He was chewing something. Maybe gum or maybe tobacco. I could see his jaw working in the spill of light from the tavern.

He wasn't a tall man, but he was built solid. He had seen a life of hard work.

But the strangest aspect of the moment was that we knew this man. I didn't know his name, but I knew where on the road he stood to hitchhike to his job in the morning, and whose land he worked. We had passed him in town half a dozen times in the couple of months I had known these boys, and he had never given us a second look.

I knew even more surely that something had changed, but I only felt it as a nagging sense of a missing puzzle piece.

I turned my head to look at Suki, to gauge his reaction. His eyes registered a deep alarm, but he held very still.

Beyond him I was able to see—without fully absorbing the sight— that the tavern was packed with patrons. I had been by before on a Sunday evening. We all had. Sunday was not a big night for drinking in these parts, because everybody worked in the morning. But that night every stool was taken, and men stood two and three deep at the bar. Yet it was eerily silent. There was no music. No camaraderie. The gathering had all the enthusiasm and merriment of a funeral.

The man took a step closer to Suki, who instinctively took a step back. It's always a bad idea to draw an aggressor in that way, but Suki didn't have much choice. He had to be polite to the white men in town, or there would be hell to pay.

The man took another step in.

Suddenly Suki was whisked away by Nick's two strong hands on his shoulders, and Nick stepped in to fill the empty space. He stood boldly upright, his chest blown up with air.

The old man took another step in, but Nick did not yield. He didn't give an inch.

They stood nose to nose—as much as that was possible given that Nick was a full head taller—for a few tense seconds.

Part of me wanted Nick to knock the man down, or at least push him out of the way. And yet, another part of me admired that his stand was a nonviolent one. He was simply communicating to the old guy that to get to Suki, the guy would have to go through him. And that going through him would be no easy trip.

I honestly think that was the moment I fell for Nick, completely and helplessly. And for the right reasons. Not because he was handsome and not because he maybe—just maybe—had the same kinds of feelings I did. Because of who he was on the inside. Because of the parts of him that mattered.

The man spoke a few words quietly into Nick's face. I was standing close, but I couldn't hear him. I couldn't make it out. Then the old guy took one step back and spat a disgusting wad of chewed tobacco onto Nick's boots.

The man cut around us and teetered away, and only then did I realize that he was hopelessly drunk.

We walked on, as we had intended to do all along. I could tell it took several beats, several steps, until we were all breathing normally again. I could hear Nick banging the toes of his boots against the boards to shake off the mess.

"What did that man say to you?" I asked him.

"I don't want to repeat it," Nick said.

Those were the last words we spoke to each other that night.

———

Ollie dropped me off at the main gate of our farm in his dad's pickup, and I limped down the dirt road to the house.

When I stepped inside, I expected my parents to be frantic. I expected to be grilled about my lateness and then grounded.

Instead there was no one in the living room, though all the lights were burning.

According to the grandfather clock it was only a little after eight o'clock.

I stepped into the kitchen. My mom was sitting at the table, drinking what looked like a water glass full of amber-colored alcohol. And she was crying. She was leaning her forehead onto one hand, and it blocked her eyes from my view.

"Where's Dad?" I asked, even though it wasn't the most important question. Or maybe I asked it *because* it wasn't the most important question.

"He went to bed."

I should have known without asking, because my dad normally went to bed about eight. Farmwork starts early.

I took a deep breath and tackled the thing.

"Why are you crying?"

"All those people," she said. "All those innocent people."

"Wait. All what people?"

She never answered.

She took her hand away from her forehead and wiped her nose on a lace hankie she kept stashed in her dress sleeve. Her eye makeup had streamed down in black icicles onto her cheeks.

"And now we'll go to war because we don't have any choice, and I worry about Terrence. He'll be eighteen next year and he'll have to go and fight."

"Wait," I said again. "It's time for somebody to tell me what I missed while we were away."

She told me what I had missed while we were away.

Well, anyway, half of it.

She didn't tell me that Nick's father was now in jail and that his mother had left them years earlier, leaving Nick effectively alone. And that this turn of events was only the beginning of Nick's troubles. Because she didn't know.

For about another day, neither did I. For one more blessed day I thought my world was in the thrall of only one major disaster instead of two. In this case ignorance was not exactly bliss, but it was better than what followed.

Chapter Four

He'll Ask the Questions

It was the following morning, and we were in math class together. Three of us, not all of us. Ollie wasn't in any of our classes, because he was a senior.

Suki was sitting in the back row, and Nick was one row over from me, on my right, and one seat forward.

I was having trouble not looking at him.

I couldn't see his face—which in one respect was good, because that way he wouldn't notice how I couldn't keep my gaze from jumping back to him. But I could see him tapping his pencil against his thigh, against his clean slacks. Nick always came to school looking put together, which I now realize was quite an accomplishment with no mother and a father who barely handled things at all.

In time the teacher stopped speaking and turned to stare at Nick sternly, and he stopped tapping the pencil.

He set it in the little pencil groove of his wooden desk, and placed his big hands on his thighs, and tried to hold still. But every few seconds I could see two fingers of his left hand twitch.

I purposely hadn't asked him about his father. I think we were all curious as to what had happened to him. But I wanted Nick to talk about it if he wanted to and not if he didn't. I hadn't even asked if the man had eventually shown up the previous night.

The classroom door opened and two men stepped in. They were not teachers. They were not the principal. They were not men I had ever seen in that town before.

One was a tall, thin man in a tan suit, his dark hair slicked back with some kind of pomade. The other was shorter and wide around the middle, with a plain white shirt and no jacket, and with a bald pate. They stepped over to the teacher's desk and spoke briefly to her in a whisper.

Then they stood facing the class, and the thin man spoke two words that briefly stopped my heart.

"Nicolas Mattaliano?"

I actually saw a jolt hit Nick's body, the way his muscles might react if he'd stuck his finger into a live electrical socket. I could feel my heart begin to hammer.

Nick stood and followed them out of the room.

I looked around at Suki, who was quick to meet my gaze. We asked each other a lot of questions with our eyes.

Nobody had any answers.

———

It was more than half an hour later, and I swear it was the longest half hour of my fourteen-year life. I know exactly how long it was because I kept staring at the clock, waiting for the second hand to tick forward. At least a dozen times I was positive the damn thing had stopped. Positive. Then . . . impossibly . . . tick.

The door opened. I craned my neck, wanting to see Nick come in. But he never did. It was those two men again. The thin man scanned around the room with his eyes, as though our names might be written on our foreheads.

Then he called out another name.

"Steven Katz."

My stomach went cold and numb, as though that organ, all by itself, had jumped into a mountain lake.

I rose to my feet and followed the two men out of the room.

As we walked down the hall together—if you can call slouching after them like an old dog "together"—I calmed my poor gut by deciding this was actually good. This was the good news. They were talking to a bunch of students. It wasn't really anything about Nick at all.

I followed them into the principal's office.

I have no idea where the principal was in that moment, but it was only the three of us in the room. The bottom half of the window was open, spilling cool air in to where we stood. I looked out and saw the same trees dappling the ground with the same shade as that first walk I took with Suki. I just kept looking at those trees and not at the two men. Probably I was trying to transport myself away.

The shorter, rounder guy leaned in the corner and said nothing. And did nothing.

The thin man took off his jacket and draped it over the back of the principal's chair. I was shocked to see that he had a holstered revolver at his shoulder.

"Sit down, son," he said to me.

I did as I'd been told. He had a gun, for cripes sake.

He came around to my side of the desk and leaned on the edge of it, crossing his arms in front of his narrow chest.

"Where were you this weekend?" he asked me.

"Oh," I said. And then I paused. I sensed I was not getting off to a stellar start. "I went camping with my friends."

"And which friends would those be?"

At the edge of my field of vision, I saw the man in the corner poised to take notes.

"Suki, Ollie, and Nick," I said.

"Can you be more specific?"

I had no idea how to be more specific than to name them, so I said nothing. And I guess my confusion showed on my face.

The wide man spoke up. It was the first time I'd heard his voice. "Full names," he said.

"Oh. Okay. Itsuki Yamamoto. Oliver Franklin. Nicolas Mattaliano."

The man in the corner scribbled. The man in front of me asked more questions.

"Where exactly did you go?"

"The mountains."

"You misunderstood me, son. The question was where *exactly* did you go?"

"Oh. Right. Exactly. Well, we got a ride all the way up to the end of the road, where that trailhead starts. And then we hiked up to this mountain lake."

"And what's the name of this lake?"

"I don't know, sir. If it has a name, nobody told it to me. I could describe it to you. I can see it perfectly when I close my eyes. But I don't know the name of it."

"And you were away how long?"

"We left real early Saturday morning and came down last night."

"Anybody see you up there?"

"No, sir. Not up in the mountains. There was nobody else up there because it's winter."

"If it's winter, what were *you* doing up there?"

That was a good question. And with a sharp pang in my chest, I realized that my answer would sound painfully inadequate. I couldn't exactly tell them that I would have followed either Suki or Nick to the ends of the earth. That whatever they did, I wanted to do.

I gazed out the window for a split second or two. Watched the leaves on the trees shimmy in the wind.

I remembered what my dad had said. And I picked it up and ran with it.

"I heard my dad say that I hadn't had much in the way of hardship," I told Mr. Thin. "I wanted to show him I was a man."

It was a lie. I couldn't have cared less what my dad thought of my manhood. I *had* cared, at one time, but I had long since given up chasing a stamp of approval that would always be withheld from me. But the thin man seemed to accept my explanation. Funny what makes sense to people and what doesn't.

"Can anybody else confirm this?"

"Well . . . ," I said. ". . . Suki's father dropped us up there. You know. With our packs and everything. And then when we got down, Nick's dad was supposed to pick us up, but he wasn't there for some reason, so this man named Mr. Ito gave us a ride into town on his flatbed truck."

I watched him trade glances with his colleague in the corner. I had no idea what to make of that silent exchange.

"Great," Mr. Thin said. "Two people can confirm it, but they're both Japs."

I was shocked. Literally. I could feel the shock in my belly and brain.

"If they know we were there . . . ," I began, ". . . if they saw us there, what difference does it make? Who cares if they were white or Japanese? We can all see, right?"

He narrowed his eyes at me, and I regretted having confronted him.

"I'll be the one asking the questions, son."

I clamped my mouth shut. Much as I hate to admit it, I felt chastened and afraid. He had a gun, for cripes sake. But I guess I mentioned that before.

"We prefer white witnesses. We understand their loyalties better. Now. Any chance Nicolas could have gone down into town on Saturday night without your knowing it?"

"No, sir. That would've been impossible."

"You're sure of that."

"The hike took hours. Hours. And I was up with him in the middle of the night looking at the stars. That's how I know he was there."

I regretted my words immediately. Because that moment with Nick by the lake was precious to me, and I hated to sully it by letting these men see that it had existed. But the conversation had taken a turn. And this did seem to be specifically about Nick after all. And I would have protected my friend Nick at any cost.

The man leaned forward, threatening me with his body language.

"Just one more thing, son. I just want to make sure you know that we're the law. We are asking you these questions in the name of the law. I know it's tempting to lie to cover for a friend. But you would *not* want to do that in this situation, okay? That would go down very, very badly for you. So let me just confirm. You're sure everything you told us this morning is one hundred percent true and correct?"

"Yes, sir," I said, ignoring the fact that my face felt hot. "I'm not lying. Everything I just told you is true."

"Go on back to class then, son."

And I did.

—

I didn't see Nick again until first lunch. Then, when my eyes fell on him, I was so relieved I almost cried. I stopped myself, of course. I held it in. But it was a close call.

We drifted into the cafeteria lunch line together without saying a word. At first.

"What did you tell them?" he said after a while. His voice was quiet and low.

"Just the truth."

"Okay, good. Sorry you got dragged into this."

I waited in silence for him to tell me what "this" was. But there were other students all around us. Realistically, I knew I had a pretty good wait on my hands.

We took our lunch outside and sat on the picnic table where I had first met him. Ollie didn't join us, because he had third lunch, and had just been issued a stern warning about skipping class. Suki didn't join us, which was a harder guess. I wondered if he was being grilled by the law, and I figured Nick must be wondering it, too.

I took two bites of my tuna sandwich, hoping Nick would start talking without my having to ask. Then, before I could take a third bite, he spoke up.

"My dad got into a bar fight in town on Saturday night. Well, early Sunday morning, really. The tavern had closed and there was hardly anybody around, and I guess my dad hurt this guy real bad."

"Oh," I said. I didn't know what else to say. I looked down at my sandwich, but I could no longer imagine eating it. I could no longer imagine eating anything. Then I asked, "How bad?"

"He's in a coma," Nick said. He picked at some stew on his plate without actually eating any. Then he added, "They think he might die."

We sat for a minute without talking. Literally a minute. I remember thinking it felt strange that there were two boys I truly loved, and both of their lives had just fallen to ruin.

"Why do they need to know where *you* were?" I asked after a time. "I mean, what does it have to do with *you*?"

A long silence.

"Promise you won't tell anybody else this," he said. His voice was heavy with shame. His face was heavy with shame. "You can tell Suki and Ollie but nobody else."

"I promise. And I'd die before I'd break that promise."

"Okay," he said. "I believe you. I trust you. When they arrested him, he was still really drunk, and he admitted it. He confessed to having beaten the man. But then in the morning he sobered up and said I did it. That a guy he knew, a guy who was there when the fight happened, ran to the house and told him what I'd done, and he only went to the tavern to get me. And that he only confessed to protect me."

We sat for a long time. He said nothing more. I said nothing in reply. What do you say to a guy when he tells you his father just sold him out? It's really hard to know. I knew he was humiliated, and that telling me had been hard. I didn't want to make it worse in any way.

As if to underscore my thoughts on this, he picked up his head and asked me a question.

"Why did you drop your old set of friends?"

It may sound like a thing out of place. An odd request. It wasn't. None of the boys had asked me, because they knew it might embarrass me. It might be too personal. We all did that for each other. We left each other alone when we knew alone was what the other wanted. Now Nick had trusted me with a difficult, enormous truth. He wanted something in return. He wanted our playing field level again.

I gave it to him. I leveled it.

"They just kept talking about 'faggots' and 'queers.' And not even really only if they thought somebody actually *was*. It was just their way of saying something was bad. Like if a boy had some kind of sad feelings about something, he was queer. Or if they didn't like the way he looked or dressed, he was a faggot. It was their insult for everything. I took it as long as I could. Then I couldn't take it anymore."

My face burned, waiting to hear what he would say. He could have leveled my whole world with the wrong reaction. It was a vulnerable moment.

"I get it," he said. "Thanks."

Then I breathed again, and we allowed another long silence. I knew there was something else. Something more he wanted to say. I waited for it. I didn't push.

"I hope it's okay," he said after a time. "I hope you're not mad about this. I told them I could stay with your family."

"Those two men?"

"Yeah. Otherwise they would've tried to get me somewhere. They would have done something. I don't know what, but something. Sent me to an orphanage or something. Unless they could find my mom. But I have no idea where to tell them to start looking. Or if she'd even take me."

"I'm not mad," I said. "But my family is sort of . . . I'm not sure they'd help."

"No, they don't need to. I just said that so they wouldn't put me someplace. I'm fine at the house on my own. As long as they don't check."

We looked up to see Suki walking over to join us. He wasn't coming from the school. He was coming from the direction of town, such as it was. From the general store, I knew, because he had a pint carton of ice cream in his hand.

He looked shaken.

I learned something about Suki in that moment. I learned that ice cream for lunch meant he had just lived through something he wasn't admitting was hard to swallow. Like baseball tryouts. Or being questioned by two cops who want white witnesses only.

He sat on the edge of the picnic table, the heels of his sneakers tucked firmly underneath his buttocks, and dug into his snack without speaking.

"Was that really bad?" Nick asked him.

Suki only shrugged and ate ice cream. It looked like vanilla to me.

"I'm sorry," Nick said.

"Not your fault," Suki said, his mouth full.

I went back to eating my lunch, even though I didn't feel hungry at all. We all ate in silence for a few minutes. The cool breeze on my face felt good, and I was intensely aware of it, because nothing else in my life seemed good in that moment.

That's a bad moment when a cool breeze is all you've got.

"They told me something," Suki said, scraping the bottom of the carton with his wooden paddle spoon. "But I don't know if it's true. They might've said it just to scare me."

I didn't ask. I didn't dare. Nick didn't ask. We just waited.

"They said . . . I don't think this is true. They said they think all the Japanese are going to be rounded up and . . . I'm trying to think of the word he used. I think it was 'relocated.' They said it's too soon to know for sure, but they've already started hearing the first talk about it."

"Relocated where?" I asked. I couldn't help it.

"They didn't say."

"I don't think that's true," I said. "That can't be true. They can't do that."

"Why can't they?"

"You're a citizen."

"Yeah. Maybe they can't do it to me. But my parents aren't citizens. Or my grandmother."

"They're not? Didn't they want to be?"

He looked at me for the first time since joining us. Really looked into my face, and my eyes. To see where I was coming from, I guess.

"Did you really not know? They don't get to be. Japanese don't get to apply for citizenship."

I hadn't known. I should have known. How could I not have known? I felt so stupid. I wanted to disappear.

I said nothing more on the subject, because what I'd already said was bad enough.

It was Nick who spoke up.

"If it's true . . . and I agree with Steven it's probably not, but if it was true, would they take them and leave you?"

"I have no idea how it would go," Suki said.

I looked at my shoes for the longest time.

Then I looked up and said something I hadn't known I was about to say. It just came out of my mouth. "I could hide you," I said.

At first, nobody said anything.

Then Suki said, "Are you talking to me or to Nick?"

"Either of you. Both of you. If you were in trouble. There are lots of places on our farm. There's an old outbuilding that nobody uses for anything anymore, and it has a root cellar. I used to go down there and play when I wanted to get away from everybody and everything. I swear I'm the only person who's been down there in all the time I've been alive."

"If my parents had to go somewhere, I'd go with them," Suki said. "Besides, it won't get that bad." He jumped off the table all in one big movement, startling me. "I'll be back. I have to go ask the principal if he knows anything about this."

We watched him walk away until he swung the back door of the school open and disappeared inside. Nick turned his face to me.

"No, Suki's right," he said. "It won't get that bad. That guy'll come out of the coma, and then he'll tell the police it wasn't me."

Or he'll die, I thought. *And the truth will die with him.*

I didn't say that. It was too horrible a thought to dump on poor Nick. But even more of a pall fell over us, and I think it's possible that we were both thinking it at exactly the same time.

Instead I said, "And that other guy. He might tell the truth."

Nick said, "What other guy?"

"You know. He said some guy he knew came and told him . . ." I never finished the sentence. I had begun to realize my mistake.

"But none of that ever happened. So he probably just made the guy up."

"Right," I said. "I was being stupid."

"No, you're fine, Steven. It's just all weird. It's kind of a wild story. I doubt the police'll believe it. Thanks, though. It means a lot that you would at least offer."

And that's how the whole thing started. That's how we got ourselves into that.

Chapter Five

Moon Shadows

It wasn't the next night when it happened. The next night I lay awake halfway to morning, feeling like I was at the very pinnacle of a wildly steep mountain, on a sled. Teetering. Knowing that at any minute I could be in for the ride of my life. But, right in those moments, there was no movement happening at all.

Which was almost worse.

Waiting for the fall is almost worse than the fall sometimes.

It was the night after that.

I was fast asleep and dreaming when it happened. I was dreaming I was up at that mountain lake with Nick, sitting under the stars. Except the stars were . . . different. I'm not sure if I can explain it. They were brighter and more alive somehow. I got the sense that they were aware of me. In a good way. That they saw me and my struggles, and it was okay now.

And then a noise propelled me out of sleep.

I sat up fast, and gasped in a noisy breath of air.

In the dark I could see someone standing outside my bedroom window, looking in. I was petrified with surprise and fear.

My first thought was to run to the closet and get the bat my father had given me for Christmas. But the hand of the person outside came up and lightly, almost politely, knocked on my window.

By then my eyes had begun to adjust, and I saw that it was Nick.

I got out of bed and crossed to the window, my heart still pounding. I slept wearing only pajama bottoms. I found the tops too uncomfortable. Actually I found the bottoms too uncomfortable, too, but there were other people in that house, and I had to walk out into the hall to use the bathroom. Compromises had to be made.

My window was constructed with two vertical sections that locked in the middle and opened outward. Of course I was on the ground floor. Everything in my house was. There was nothing but an attic above us. It also had a wooden window seat, so that when the windows were opened out, I could easily step up onto that and step out the window. It was the perfect setup for a guy who liked to sneak out at night. But I wasn't that guy. Yet.

I opened the window, and we stood looking at each other in the dark.

"Everything okay?" I asked, quietly, because it didn't seem as if he planned to say anything.

"No," he whispered. "Nothing is okay."

"What can I do?"

"Show me where that root cellar is. Where you said a person could hide."

I stepped out the window without even taking the time to put on a shirt or shoes, and we walked together across the dirt of my father's farm. Between parked tractors. Between the fields of crop rows. Alongside irrigation ditches. Out into nothing. Into a place that looked as though human beings never bothered to seek it out.

That night we sought it out.

I could see a halo of light over the mountains. See the sky glow around it. For a moment I thought it was something magical. Then I worried it might be a fire.

"What is that?" I asked Nick, and pointed.

"The moon is coming up," he said.

It's not that I'd never seen a moon come up before. It's just that this seemed so much brighter than any moonrise I could remember. Maybe it was a weirdly clear night, or maybe my senses were just more fully alive.

He'd barely had time to finish the sentence before I saw the sharp arc of its top edge break over the mountain. It was huge and coming up fast. I wondered if the moon always came up that fast. I figured it must, but I'd never bothered to watch before.

As the sky grew lighter I glanced over at Nick. He was wearing the same big backpack he'd used on our camping trip, and it looked full. It had a sleeping bag and pad strapped on the outside. It was clear he had taken some time to pack his belongings.

I wondered how long he planned to be in hiding. I wondered how long I could hide him before somebody saw me coming or going, and caught on. I wondered what would happen to us if we were discovered.

I wondered what I had gotten myself into.

But it didn't matter, really. I was irreversibly in it by then. I would do anything and everything I could for Nick.

"What happened?" I asked.

"Somebody came to the house and told me they were coming to arrest me in the morning, so I took off and found your house. I sort of knew where it was. Everybody sort of knows who owns what farms."

The words buzzed and jangled in my belly. This was trouble on a level I'd never before experienced, even secondhand. But I spoke only of more peripheral topics.

"Who told you that?" I asked, though that was probably the least important part of the whole thing.

"I promised I wouldn't say."

"Oh. Okay. How did you know which bedroom was mine?"

"I didn't. I just had to go around real quietly and look in a few windows."

"The police believed your father? I'm not sure why they would believe your father."

"Here's the thing," he said.

But then, for what felt like several minutes, he didn't tell me the thing.

I was beginning to regret walking barefoot. I kept stepping on sharp little pebbles, and wanting to say "Ouch," but not saying it. The moon was partly visible and its glow was just unearthly. Well, I guess that's a stupid way to put it, because of course the moon is not earthly. But it seemed almost supernatural to me. It reminded me, in a weird way, that the universe was bigger than these enormous problems.

My bare torso was cold, and I crossed my arms to try to hold in my body heat.

He started up again on his own. "Remember how he told them there was another guy there who saw the thing? Who saw me do it? He said some guy saw it and came running to get him and told him what he'd seen me do. Well, anyway . . . that guy showed up at those detectives' office yesterday and told them it was me."

I stopped walking. When Nick realized I had stopped, he stopped too. He turned, and we faced each other in the growing moonlight.

"But that guy doesn't exist," I said. "Nobody ran to tell your dad what you did, because you were up in the mountains with us, and your dad was already there."

"I know," Nick said.

We stood helplessly in the moonlight for a few moments more.

"Who is this guy? And why would he say that?"

"All I know is that his name is Roger Steadman. I have no idea why he would say it."

We walked again.

I could see the little outbuilding in the distance. It threw a moon shadow across the field.

As we walked to the door of that shed, as I reached out for the handle, he said something odd.

He said, "I really was up at the lake with you. Right? I didn't just dream that?"

"No, you didn't dream it," I said. "You were there."

I pulled the door open and we stepped inside. The dark air within was dank and humid, and smelled vaguely of mold.

"I knew that," Nick said. "I'm not crazy. It's just that . . . everything feels strange right now. Like maybe none of this is real. Like the things I always thought were real might not be."

"I understand," I said.

But I didn't, entirely. Maybe nobody could without being in his shoes.

The trapdoor into the cellar was on a hinge in the wooden-board floor, and it had a thick, knotted rope attached. I pulled, and flipped the heavy door up and over, exposing rough-hewn wood stairs that were almost as steep as a ladder.

"Take your pack off," I said. "Go down without it. I'll hand it down to you."

"You're coming down, though. Right? Just for a minute, I mean. Just to talk for a minute, and then maybe I can even sleep a little."

"Sure," I said. "I'll come down."

I handed his pack down after him, then climbed in.

The outbuilding and the rough cellar underneath it were about twelve feet wide and maybe twenty feet long. The sides of the cellar were nothing but cool, damp dirt, though there were beams in place to shore it up properly. The floor was only hard-packed dirt.

I sat cross-legged, still trying to hug myself against the cold. Nick noticed, and took a jacket out of his pack and put it around my shoulders, and sat next to me.

"Thanks," I said.

We sat in silence, and I began to worry about the wisdom of this plan. I would have to sneak him food, or he would starve. I would have to bring him water. He wouldn't be able to come out at all except in the dead of night. I would have to get him some kind of pot that he could use as a toilet in daylight hours.

He spoke, jostling me out of my thoughts.

"You can't tell anyone," he said.

"Of course I won't."

"Anyone at all."

"Not even—"

But I never got to finish the sentence.

"No. Not even Suki and Ollie. It's not that I don't trust them. It's just too many people. For a secret this big, it's too many people. See, you were going to keep the secret, but you just had those two people you thought it would be okay to tell. Everybody has one or two people they figure it's okay to tell. And then, after a while, too many people know. No, when you have a secret this important, there should just be one guy who knows your secret." Then he paused. Then he added a truly life-changing kicker of a final sentence. "And you know his."

So there it was. He had heard my message correctly when I told him why I'd dumped my old circle of friends. Or maybe he had already known by then. It was hard to say.

I sat on that cold dirt floor, shivery and tingling with the gravity of the moment, just feeling how much had changed. For the first time in my life, somebody knew. I couldn't imagine how anything could ever be the same again.

"Tell them you saw me," he said. "No matter who asks, tell them you saw me. Tell them I came to your window tonight and said good-bye. Told you I was running away."

"Okay. Did I ask where you were going?"

"Yeah. You did. And I wouldn't say. No. Not that I wouldn't say. Tell them you asked and I said I didn't know. That I just told you I was going to pick a direction and start going, and see where I ended up."

"Okay," I said. "I won't let you down."

"I know you won't."

"Are you hungry? Do you want me to sneak something down here?"

"No, I'm okay. I had dinner. And I brought what I could from the house. Some canned beans and some cheese and a couple of apples. I'll be okay tomorrow, too."

"Good," I said. "Because I think the only time I dare come out here is when everybody is asleep at night."

"I understand."

We sat in silence for a few minutes more.

Then he said, "You can go back and go to sleep. I'll be okay."

"You sure?"

"Yeah. I'm fine. Just . . . maybe check in on me tomorrow night."

"Of course I will."

I shook his jacket off my bare shoulders and handed it back to him. "Won't you be cold?"

"Doesn't matter," I said. "I'll run back. You need it, and besides, I don't want anyone seeing your coat in my house."

"Smart," he said. "Good thinking."

I crossed over to the ladder stairs.

I was one rung up when he said, "See if you can find out who this Roger Steadman is. Because I sure would like to know why he did that."

"I'll find out," I said.

And, just like that, I had a mission. Something tangible I could do for Nick. Beyond what I was already doing. And I knew it would be my new obsession, and that I wouldn't stop until I found out who Roger Steadman was and why he'd lied.

I climbed out into the night and ran home.

I could see my shadow, running in the moonlight. And I knew that I was alive in that moment. Alive in a way I had never been up until then. And I knew, as I had known sitting on that dirt floor with Nick, that my world would never be—*could* never be—the same.

———

I sat in math class in the morning, and I swear my eyes flickered over to Nick's empty seat more than they had when he was sitting there.

Once, I turned and glanced at Suki over my shoulder. He met my eyes immediately, and asked me a question with his. And I caught it. And, above and beyond everything else that was going on in that moment, I felt surprised and pleased that we knew each other well enough to communicate without words.

He asked me if I knew anything about that empty seat.

If I'd wanted to say no, I could have just shrugged. But I had a specific lie I was charged with telling him. And it pulled my mood down—almost violently so—realizing I had to lie to Suki. Not that I hadn't realized it before. I just hadn't realized it and looked at his face all at the same time.

I marveled over how easy it had seemed to promise Nick what he'd asked for the previous night. I was so intent on being what he wanted—needed—me to be that I hadn't spent much time registering the gravity of lying to such good friends. But it was crushing me now.

I offered what I meant to be a sad little smile, but I think it came out more like a grimace. Then I turned away and looked back to the blackboard.

———

We walked together to our usual lunch spot, passing under the shimmery tree leaves in the warm wind. It was hot in the sun for winter, but that's a California interior valley for you.

I was surprised to see Ollie off in the distance, sitting at our regular table. I'd thought he was in too much trouble over the classes he'd skipped to join us anymore.

"What happened?" Suki asked when he was sure we were within earshot of no one.

"They were going to arrest him this morning, so he ran away."

I purposely didn't look at him as I spoke, so I didn't know how he was taking the news. But I could imagine. It was bad news, no matter how you sliced it.

"And you know this how?"

"He came to my bedroom window last night. Told me to say goodbye to everybody for him. He said he was just going to pick a direction and see where he ended up."

Silence.

I never dared look over at his face.

When we reached our picnic table, Ollie took one look at Suki's face, and I could see the reflection of Suki's upset.

"What happened?" Ollie asked.

"Steven will tell you all about it," Suki said.

Then he walked away.

I watched his retreating back and was haunted by a sense that he was upset by more than just the loss of Nick. That he was angry at me somehow. But I wasn't sure how to sort out his reaction. Especially when I couldn't bring myself to look at his face.

Was I that bad a liar? Did he know?

"Start talking," Ollie said.

I told him the same short, false version of events I had told Suki.

We sat without talking for a minute as that news settled. I looked down at my tray. I had gotten a sandwich, an apple, and an orange. I was hungry enough for all of it. But I had to save half the sandwich and one of the pieces of fruit for Nick.

I picked up the orange, because I wanted it more than an apple. But then I remembered Nick saying he had brought a couple of apples from home. I set the orange back down again to save for him.

I took a big bite of apple and, my mouth still rudely full, said to Ollie, "Where do you suppose he went?"

"Well . . . has to be north or south. He doesn't want to cross those mountains alone in the winter. And the ocean would stop him soon enough to the west."

I swallowed before correcting him. "Actually, I meant Suki."

"Oh. Suki. He probably went out for ice cream."

"Okay. Right. Because he's upset that Nick's gone."

"Maybe partly. But I think he's also upset that Nick came and told *you* he was leaving. He's known Nick for seven years. You've known him for a couple or three months."

"Oh," I said. "Right. I guess that *would* hurt."

Ollie never answered.

I took a bite of sandwich and said, "I think it's because I have that big sprawling house. I haven't seen Suki's house, but if it's one of the small ones like most of the workers live in, I expect it would be hard to wake Suki up without waking up the whole family."

Ollie seemed to chew that over for a moment. "Tell Suki that," he said.

"Yeah. I will. When he gets back. Hey. You know a guy named Roger Steadman?"

His head came up, and he looked me straight in the eye. "You *don't?*"

"No."

"He was right in our faces on Sunday night."

"Sunday night? The only person we saw on Sunday night was Mr. Ito."

"Keep thinking," Ollie said.

"Oh. Wait. There was that guy standing in the doorway of the tavern."

"Bingo."

"That's Roger Steadman?"

"The one and only."

I sat with that new information for a time, so full of questions that I wasn't sure which to ask first. But in time, I settled on one.

"He wouldn't lie about Nick just because Nick was defending Suki, would he?"

"No idea," Ollie said. "I don't really know him much. I just get the sense that he's kind of mean."

"Tell Suki what I said when he gets back. About the houses."

"Where're you going?"

"I have to go find something out."

I took my lunch back inside and wrapped most of it up in some clean newspaper. Stashed it in my cubby till I got back.

Then, for the first time in my life, I skipped part of an afternoon of school.

———

I walked to the farm where I knew the guy worked. Joe Wilson's farm, same as Suki's dad.

I found Mr. Wilson leaning on a parked tractor, smoking a cigarette. Vaguely watching the action in his fields.

"I'm looking for Roger Steadman," I said. My voice sounded surprisingly strong. I hoped I could be every bit as brave when I was staring Steadman in the face.

"He took off early. Said he didn't feel good. Not sure I'm buying it, though. Ever since he got that new truck, it's hard to make him hold still in one place."

"He got a new truck?"

"Yeah, and I'm not sure what to make of it, because he never has two nickels to rub together. But he thinks he's the big man now. If you find him, and he's not at home sick, tell him he'd best be careful. He could end up with a truck, but no job. And you can't eat a truck."

"I'll tell him," I said.

But I knew I would feel funny telling a grown man that you can't eat a truck. Besides, we'd have more important things to talk about by then.

———

My plan was to walk through town and see if I could find somebody who knew which shack was Steadman's. But that's not the way it worked out at all.

Instead I walked past the tavern, and there I spotted Nick's father's truck. I stopped dead and just stared at it for the longest time. It seemed like a thing out of place.

How did I know it was Nick's father's truck? Because four times we had seen it as we walked by the tavern in the afternoons. Nick would stop on the board sidewalk and stare at it. Then he'd look through the tavern window at his dad, who'd be sitting at the bar, more or less surrounded by no one.

That's how I would know Nick's dad if I saw him—at least from a distance. He looked a lot like Nick. They were the same size and weight. They had the same hair. The same square jaw.

Maybe that was why the lie about who committed the crime was working.

I walked to the tavern window and looked in, my fingers on the glass. I figured they must have let him out of jail. But I didn't see him. All I saw was the bartender gesturing wildly to me to get my fingerprints off his windows.

And Roger Steadman. Sitting all by himself at a table.

I took my hands off the glass of the window and moved to the tavern door, swinging it open and stepping inside. The bartender met me halfway. He was heavy and big, and he had one hand extended to hold me back by my chest.

"Out you go, son," he said, his voice hard. "You're underage."

"I need to talk to *him*," I said. And I pointed.

"Steadman!" the bartender shouted, hurting my ear. "Somebody here to see you."

"Tell him to get lost," Steadman called back.

"You heard him, son."

"I'm not leaving till I get to talk to him."

"Steadman!" the big man shouted again. "Get over here and talk to this kid outside before I lose my liquor license!"

"I don't want to talk to no kid," Steadman called back.

"Do it or you're cut off. Permanently."

We waited. Watched.

Steadman sighed, and teetered resentfully to his feet. He joined me near the door of the place and we stepped out onto the board sidewalk. I watched the old man squint against the sun as though he had never seen daylight in his life.

"What?" he said, and spat onto the sidewalk, narrowly missing my shoe.

"Why did you lie about my friend?"

"Now how am I supposed to even know who your friend is?"

"Well . . . how many people have you lied about in the past few days?"

I was being brave, and I knew it. I was flowing over with adrenaline, and it made everything feel unreal. Somewhere in that foggy background I knew there was potential physical danger in what I was doing. But nothing was going to stop me.

"No idea what you're talking about, kid."

"I'm talking about the trouble with Mr. Mattaliano."

I watched his eyes. His face twitched slightly.

"Oh, that. I just said what I saw."

"No you didn't."

"I don't recall you being there."

"I wasn't. But I was with his son. Somewhere else. So I know what you said wasn't true. Why would you do that? Just because he stood in front of Suki and wouldn't let you hurt him or embarrass him? Who does that? Punishes somebody just for taking a stand for his friend?"

For possibly a full minute my words just sizzled in the air. It seemed as though Steadman never planned to address them.

Then he pushed roughly by me. But not back toward the bar. The other way. Into the street.

"You may find this hard to believe, kid," he shot over his shoulder, "but I don't care enough about you or your little punk friends to make up any lies. I just said what I saw."

Then he got into Nick's father's truck, started it up, and drove away.

I stood on the boards a moment and watched him go. Maybe it was the adrenaline that made it hard for me to put it all together, but right in that moment it was slow math, confusing to add up.

In time I got there.

Roger Steadman had said one true thing to me. He didn't care enough about the four of us to plan any harm to our situations. No, the reason for his false testimony had been much simpler. It was transactional. He had wanted something of value. Now he had it.

And all Nick had was a root cellar, and anything I could manage to save from my lunch.

———

I trudged back to school, wondering if I had been gone long enough for someone to call my mom. Not that I hadn't thought about it before

I left. Just that the potential consequences hadn't been enough to stop me.

Judging by the length of time I'd been gone, I figured my chances were good.

I stepped into the hallway just as the bell rang the end of a class. Students spilled out into the hallway and teemed in my direction, making me feel as though I were swimming upstream. I arrived at my cubby just in time to run into Suki. Almost literally.

"Hey," I said.

"Hey," he said back. He sounded down, but not angry.

"Did Ollie tell you what I said? About the difference between our houses?"

"Yeah."

"So . . ." I almost couldn't bring myself to ask it. If his answer came back bad, I knew it would be devastating. I knew it could break me. ". . . are we okay?"

"I wasn't mad at *you*," he said. "It's not *your* fault. It just hurt."

"I know," I said. "I get it."

We stood a moment, looking down at our respective shoes. It felt as though the entire population of the planet was swarming by us.

Well . . . *our* planet, anyway. We lived on a small planet.

We began to walk down the hall together, side by side.

"You never told me what you heard from the principal," I said.

"About what?"

"The other day. You heard that . . . rumor, I guess it was . . . from those detectives. And you went off to ask the principal about it."

"Oh, right. That. He said he didn't know, but he hoped so."

I stopped dead in the hall, and other students adjusted their paths and streamed around me.

"Wait," I said. And Suki physically stopped and waited. "He said he hoped it *was* true?"

"Yeah. He said the West Coast is a war zone now, and Japanese are notoriously unassimilable, and you can never be sure of people's loyalties, and blah, blah, blah. Some other stuff, but that's what I remember. He said if my family was loyal, they could prove it by going along cheerfully. Or maybe he said 'cooperatively.'"

As he spoke, I realized my mouth was hanging open.

"To *your face* he said all that?"

"Yup."

"That's terrible!"

Suki only shrugged. It wasn't the shrug of someone who hadn't decided if a thing was terrible or not. It was a shrug that conveyed that this brand of terrible was nothing new in his world. I was the only one who was surprised.

We walked again.

Looking back, I'm fairly sure we didn't talk any more about it for a long time. Until it began to take on a tangible form, and could no longer be ignored.

Chapter Six

The Great Starry Hunter

I lay awake in bed for a long time, listening for my mom to stop rattling around in the kitchen and go to bed. Then I waited a while longer to make sure she was genuinely asleep in there.

What felt like a minute later I bolted out of sleep, sitting upright and waking up at the same time. The alarm clock beside my bed— the one I didn't dare use because it was too loud—said it was nearly 1:00 a.m.

I scrambled out of bed and slipped into my shoes. I didn't have to get dressed, because I had never gotten undressed.

I pulled my school book bag out from under the bed. In it I had packed the half sandwich from lunch—I had purposely gotten peanut butter so it wouldn't spoil—the orange, and a tin can of soup I'd quietly swiped from the kitchen cabinet, plus an old pot I'd found in the barn and a very heavy gallon of water in a glass jug. I slipped its strap across my shoulders.

I opened out my window and vaulted off its window seat and into the night.

I ran by the light of the moon.

The mountains looked spooky to me, like a place I would never dare go. I remembered having camped up there. I just couldn't remember how I'd gotten so brave.

I sprinted until the little outbuilding came into view, the heavy load bouncing uncomfortably against my hip. Then I sprinted until I got to its door.

I stopped. Panted. Placed my hand on the knob and threw the door open, stepping inside.

The trapdoor into the root cellar was standing open.

"Nick?" I asked quietly, squatting above the stairs and waiting for my eyes to adjust to the light. "Nick?" I asked it a little louder this time.

Nothing.

I climbed down the steep ladder steps, leaving the heavy load up above.

I could see Nick's sleeping bag and pad spread out on the dirt, but empty. I felt around a little in the dark.

"Nick?" I asked again.

But Nick wasn't there.

My heart began to hammer in my chest as I wondered what had happened to him. I tried to convince myself that he had just stepped away from the cellar to relieve himself, but my mind filled with horrible thoughts. What if he had been discovered? Arrested? What if he had run away for real?

I climbed up the stairs and stepped outside. Looked around as much as I could in the moonlight. All I could see was flat, dusty land.

Then I felt a hand on my shoulder, and I let loose a shriek. I couldn't help it. It was like having something jump out at you in a haunted house. I was primed to be startled.

Good thing we were a long way from the house.

"Shhh," a voice said. I could hear that it was Nick.

I breathed for what felt like the first time in a long time.

"You scared the living daylights out of me," I said, my voice a whisper. "Why did you grab my shoulder like that?"

"I was trying to be quiet."

We stood casting side-by-side moon shadows for a few beats. Then I laughed out loud. What else could I do?

"I was back behind the shed here," he said. "I was looking at the stars."

He led me around to the east side of the outbuilding. The mountain side. We sat in the dirt with our backs up against the board siding of the shed.

"I brought you some food and water," I said. "But I left it inside."

"Thanks."

I waited, but he said no more. And he made no move to go get what I had brought.

"Sorry I'm so late getting out here," I said. "I was trying to wait up, but then I accidentally fell asleep."

"It's okay. I knew you would come. Sooner or later."

We sat in silence, staring at the stars. It was a perfectly clear night, but the moon washed them out some. They were not as dazzling as that night up at the lake, when the moon had not yet risen.

"I have an alarm clock," I said. "But I was afraid I'd wake up the whole house if I set it."

I knew I was talking too much. I knew Nick was happy enough to watch the stars together in silence. But I couldn't seem to stop myself.

"You should use the poor man's alarm clock," he said.

"What's the poor man's alarm clock?"

"Before you go to bed, you drink a whole bunch of water. Like, quarts if you can manage it. You'll be up again before morning."

"That's really smart," I said.

"My dad taught it to me."

The mention of his dad seemed to stop the conversation in its tracks. But this silence felt heavy and uncomfortable. Nothing like before.

I didn't dare say more, so I just waited. In case *he* wanted to.

"How could he *do* that to me, Steven?" he asked. His voice sounded as though he was teetering just at the edge of breaking down. "What kind of a person could do that to his own kid?"

"I don't know," I said. "I can't imagine."

I wanted to put my hand on his arm. Or put an arm around his shoulder, the way he'd done with me up at the lake. But I froze in my unsureness, and couldn't bring myself to move.

"I know why Roger Steadman did it, though," I said.

I could feel his attention perk up at that.

"You know? You talked to him?"

"I did." I felt proud and unusually brave to be able to say that.

"How did you find out who he was?"

"Ollie knew him by name. He's that old man who spit tobacco juice on your boots that night we came down from the mountains."

A brief silence. I could practically hear him thinking.

"Is that why he did it? Because I stood up to him?"

"I don't think so. Not the biggest reason, anyway. Your dad gave him his truck. You know. To lie for him."

"He *told* you that?"

"No. He didn't admit to it. But then he got in your dad's truck and drove away. It was the only thing that made sense."

"It kind of *does* make sense. Because now that I know who that guy is . . . he probably *was* there. He stays till closing time at the tavern almost every night. He probably saw what my father did, and maybe he went to see him in jail and made a deal with him. Unless my dad sold the truck to him. To pay for a lawyer or something."

"Except Joe Wilson said this Steadman guy never has two nickels to rub together. I was thinking maybe I could go find those two detectives. Tell them why I think the guy lied."

"Think they'll believe you?"

"I don't know," I said. "I just figured it was worth a try."

"Thanks for going and finding that out, anyway. Whether they believe you or not."

I sat for another quiet moment in the dark with him, proud of what I had done. Proud of who I had become when I knew he needed me to become it. And I made up my mind that I would try to answer his more recent question, too. If I could find Nick's father, I would try to learn why he had done what he had to Nick.

I knew the answer would probably be less cut and dried, and less satisfying. I wouldn't learn that he had done it for some clear external gain that I could see with my own eyes, like a truck. It would likely turn out that he simply wasn't a good enough or decent enough man to take responsibility for his own actions, and of course it would be no comfort to Nick if I passed such a reason along.

I figured I would try to find him anyway.

"You think he's still in jail?" I asked Nick, because I wanted to know where to find him. "Or do you think they let him out when they decided you did it?"

"No idea," he said. "But if you find out, let me know."

We sat for a time. Long enough that I thought we might have nothing left to say.

"Orion is my favorite," Nick said, surprising me.

"The constellation, you mean?"

"Yeah. The hunter."

"I never know which one it is."

"Really? I think it's the easiest one to find. Look, it's right up there over the mountains. You see those three stars that go at an angle?"

I followed his pointing hand, and did indeed see the three stars.

"Yes!" I said, thinking it was a bit exciting now. "I do see it!"

"That's Orion's belt. And then see how, there on the low side, there's that smaller line of stars hanging down?"

"I've seen that before. I always thought it looked like a kite with a tail."

"That's Orion's sword. Now you see that really bright orange star higher up on the left? That's Betelgeuse. That's his left shoulder. His right shoulder is pretty much across from that. And it's a little bit fainter, but in front of all that there's a line of stars for his bow."

I saw the bow clearly. And his shoulders seemed tilted in a way that matched with the bow just right.

"I see it!" I said, nearly shouting. Then I lowered my voice, even though there was nobody anywhere near. "I see his bow!"

"And that bright star is his right foot," he said, pointing. "Well . . . wait. It's on the right, but I guess if he was facing us, that would be his left foot. Anyway, it's called Rigel. And the other foot . . . darn it, I knew that, but now I don't remember."

"I see the whole hunter!" I just stared at the constellation for a moment, inordinately buoyed by the way it had come alive as a figure in front of my eyes. "How do you know all this?"

"My mom had some books about the stars."

The mention of her stalled the conversation, much the same way the mention of his dad had. So I just sat there beside him, staring at the great starry hunter and feeling how easy it would be to fall back asleep.

"If we had a telescope," he said, "or even a really good pair of binoculars . . . there's this nebula in that sword. Right in the middle. Even if you don't have anything to look through, on a really clear night you can sort of see it. It looks like a star that's kind of glowing and fuzzy. But if you had a telescope . . . man. That thing is so beautiful. It would just knock you down."

I didn't really know what a nebula was. I'd heard of them, but I couldn't remember what I'd heard. But I made up my mind to quietly research the word on my own, rather than confess my ignorance.

"There's probably a telescope in Fresno," I said.

"You mean like a public one? Like an observatory?"

"Maybe. It's worth finding out, anyway. Or there's that one they built in Los Angeles."

"The Griffith Park one? I sure would like to see that."

"Maybe we'll go," I said.

It was an audacious thing to say. But I said it.

"You and me?"

"Why not?"

"All the way to Los Angeles?"

"I don't see why we couldn't."

Actually, I could think of lots of reasons why we couldn't. I just didn't want to believe in any of them, or say them out loud.

"Right now I wouldn't dare go anywhere," he said. "I wouldn't even dare walk out to the road."

"But it won't always be like this."

"No, you're right. It won't always be like this."

And, just like that, we had some kind of a plan for a future beyond this terrible era. Something we would do together. *We* would do it, which almost meant there was an *us*. It was so overwhelmingly exciting that I could barely contain myself.

"I'm thirsty," he said. "You said you brought water, didn't you?"

"Yeah. I left it inside."

"I'm going to go get a drink. You should go back to the house and get some sleep. So you won't be dead for school in the morning."

"Okay," I said. But I was disappointed.

I got up and dusted off the seat of my pants.

Just as it had seemed we were making a real connection, he'd cut things off. Maybe it was too much connection for him, or just too much too soon. Or maybe—just maybe—*he* was so overwhelmingly excited that *he* could barely contain it, too.

I ran home, choosing to believe the option I liked best.

———

In the half-dark morning I was trudging down the dirt road toward school, still buzzing with the developments of the previous night. I was exhausted, and my eyes felt grainy, as if someone had thrown a handful of sand into them. And my stomach was a little off. But I didn't care. I didn't care if I ever slept again.

I was paying no attention to cars going by, but I was vaguely aware that a car drove up, coming toward me, swung a U-turn, and then pulled up behind me. It was almost as though I noticed it retroactively. When I realized it had slowed to my speed and was pacing me, I remembered the earlier parts of the thing.

"Don't hurry off so fast there, son," I heard a voice say.

I stopped and turned to look, and the car stopped. That slim detective was hanging out the passenger-side window of a brand-new jet-black 1941 Chevy, his shouldered pistol visible in the morning twilight.

I wondered if they had been on their way to my house. I marveled over my good fortune—having left for school early enough that my mother hadn't needed to let these guys in the front door. Hadn't needed to know that one of my new friends was in trouble with the law. And that, by association, so was I.

"What?" I said, trying to pretend that my heart wasn't hammering and my mouth wasn't dry.

"Jump in, kid. We got a few more questions."

He reached back and somehow snagged the inside handle of the back door, swinging it open for me.

I took a deep breath and sat down in the back seat. And just waited, trying to breathe normally.

"Close the door," the slim man said.

I did, even though I had no idea why it mattered.

"Any thoughts on the whereabouts of your friend Nicolas?"

"No, sir."

"None whatsoever."

"I don't know where he is. No."

"You're saying you just have no idea what happened the night he disappeared."

I had to think fast. Part of me wanted to claim I knew nothing. But I had told Ollie and Suki that I'd seen Nick that night. And maybe the detectives knew that by now. I might not have been the first one they questioned. Besides, I decided, this was my chance to throw them off the scent. Nick was here. This was my chance to tell them he was out *there* somewhere.

And I remembered how Nick had told me that *no matter who asked*, I was to tell the same story.

"I didn't say that, sir."

I watched him exchange a glance with the driver, who was the same wide-waisted partner as before.

"You said you didn't know where he was."

"Right. I don't. But I have some idea what happened on the night he disappeared."

"Got it. Listen, son. If I was you I'd spend more time talking and less time parsing out our questions. Just go ahead and save yourself right now by spitting out every little thing you know."

The words "save yourself" froze in my belly, but I talked through the cold.

"He came to my house that night. Knocked on my window. Somebody tipped him that you were coming to arrest him, so he came to say goodbye. He told me he was going to run away. I asked him where he was going, but he said he didn't know. He said he was just going to pick a direction and see where he ended up."

"Who tipped him?"

"He wouldn't tell me. I asked him, but he said he promised not to say."

"And you didn't see fit to come tell us all this?"

I took a deep breath and got brave. I thought about the night before, telling Nick how I'd talked to Steadman for him. I remembered how bold and proud I'd felt, being able to tell him I'd done that. Tonight I would be able to tell him I'd stood up to the two detectives for him.

I was becoming a whole new Steven. It felt great.

"First of all," I said, "come where? You didn't leave me a card or tell me where I was supposed to find you if I knew something more. You didn't even tell me your names. Second, what was there to tell? I have no idea where he went."

A long silence fell. Or maybe it was a medium silence, and the fear made it seem long.

Then the thin cop twisted around to peer over the seat at me. He looked me right in the face, and I looked back. At the corner of my eye I could see the holstered pistol in front of his shoulder, and I wondered if that was purposeful. If he had turned around to be sure I would see it.

"Well, well," he said. "You're a confident little dope, aren't you?"

"I'm just telling you the truth."

"Well, let me tell you something, confident little dope. If you lie to us to cover up for your friend, that makes you an accessory after the fact to what could be a man's murder. He's not dead yet, but he's not out of the woods, either. You and your precious boyfriend Nick could end up being bunkmates at reform school."

I felt his words crawl through my belly. Scratchy and tickly, like insects.

"Why did you say that to me?" I asked the man.

"I'm telling you what the law would allow us to charge you with."

"No. Not that. Why did you call him my boyfriend?"

Had he seen something in my eyes? Heard something unsaid in the air around me? Or was he like my old group of friends, using it as the insult of choice for no real reason whatsoever?

Surprisingly, his partner spoke up in my defense.

"That was over the line, Ed," he said. "Don't you think?"

"Okay, fine, whatever," the thin man said. "I was just talking. But anyway, the part about throwing your behind in reform school still stands. If you're lying."

I looked him dead in the eye.

"I'm not lying," I said. I was confident. I was calm. If it all came crashing down, I would rather be in reform school with Nick than free out in the world without him. "Besides," I said, "I can't be an accessory to a crime that didn't happen. I mean, it happened, but it wasn't Nick. I told you. He was up at the lake with me and my other friends. He didn't do it."

"We got a witness says he did."

"And you didn't happen to notice that the witness just got himself a new truck out of nowhere? It's Nick's father's truck. He tells a lie to save Nick's father and then drives away in the man's truck. That didn't seem a little suspicious to you?"

I watched them exchange glances again. There were some genuine questions in those looks. The two detectives were something like Suki and me, in that they could talk a lot just with their eyes.

For a minute I thought I'd gotten through to them.

I expected them to ask me how I knew who the witness was. But it was a small town, and probably everybody and his brother knew by then.

"Maybe he bought the truck," the thin man said. "Mattaliano is doing ninety days for filing a false police report. He can't work during that time. He probably needed the money."

"But Steadman's boss told me he never has two nickels to rub together."

Silence. They seemed to be thinking.

Then the driver, the wide man, said, "A guy might have some money he didn't want his employer to know about."

This seemed to wake the thin man from his thoughts. He came up unreachable again.

"You leave the detective work to us, son. Here's my card." He held it over the seat. Shook it in my direction. I just stared at it for a time. "Take it. Put it someplace safe. Next time you know something, we don't want to hear this song and dance about not knowing where to find us."

"Yes, sir," I said.

I took the card.

"Now jump out and go to school."

"Yes, sir," I said.

But for a moment I didn't move.

"Jump out," he said again.

"That thing you said to my friend Suki . . ."

"Bad statement," he said.

"What's a bad statement?"

"'My friend Suki.' Don't be saying that. Don't let anybody hear you say a thing like that. We're at war, son. The Japs are the enemy. From now on, all your friends are white if you know what's good for you."

We all sat in silence for a moment. I could feel those words ricocheting around in the car. Rattling me on every trip through. I could feel that the detectives were done with me. I knew they wanted me to go away now.

Instead I pushed my luck.

"That thing you said to him. Is it true? Or were you just trying to scare him?"

"What did I say to him?"

"That all the Japanese are going to be . . . relocated."

"Both," he said.

"Both?"

"I wanted to scare him, and it's true. The government'll come out with something soon. Takes time to get those plans in order."

"Where will they have to go?"

"There'll be relocation centers. Plans will be made."

"Relocation centers?"

"Camps," the wide man behind the wheel said. He was losing patience with me. They both were.

"Jump out now, son," the thin man said.

This time I did.

———

I walked to school thinking how naïve I'd been. I had heard the word "relocation" and imagined Suki and his family being directed to a new town in a new place and told to start over there. I had not pictured "camps."

When I got to school, I saw Suki almost first thing.

He took one look at my face and said, "What's wrong? Are you sick or something? You look sick."

"No, I'm okay," I said.

I did not tell him what the two detectives had told me. Not then. In that moment I couldn't imagine how it could help him. It would only worry him half to death. And maybe it wouldn't turn out to be as bad as the detectives were thinking. And even if it did, Suki would find out soon enough.

What would an extra couple of months of anxiety accomplish?

I don't know to this day if it was the right choice or the wrong one. But it wasn't a selfish choice. I wasn't trying to save myself from being the messenger of truly horrible news. I was trying to do what I thought was the best thing for my friend Suki. Even if I was wrong.

Yes, my friend Suki. He was still my friend Suki, and I would still say that to anybody, anytime.

Clearly I did not know what was good for me.

Chapter Seven

Restless

The following Sunday I bounced along the road into the city with Ollie, who had borrowed his father's truck. The road was dirt, but pretty well graded. The truck looked good enough, but it didn't have much in the way of shock absorbers. Or maybe the ones it had were on their last legs.

I'd never had a friend who could drive before. I was beginning to think I could get used to it.

Suki had elected not to go. He'd stayed home because there had been three letters to the editor in one of the big California newspapers—I didn't know which one—demanding Japanese evacuation. He wanted to be with his family, and they were afraid to let him wander too far from home. It was a dangerous world, even compared to how dangerous it had always been.

"Nice of your dad to let us use the truck," I said.

Mostly I just wanted to make conversation. There hadn't been much in the way of conversation. But there was about to be. I didn't know it yet, but I had just blown the doors off our agreed-upon anti-sharing policy.

"I'm pretty lucky," he said. "My parents are nice. They don't have much money, but they give me what they can."

"Money isn't the most important part of the thing," I said.

He glanced over at me, then back at the road. I could see a handful of the tall brick buildings that marked downtown Fresno, but they were still a long way off.

"Suki is lucky, too," he said. "His folks are great. Nick, now Nick has problems at home. And they're nothing new. I mean, his dad never did anything *this* bad before, but it was always bad. I'm less surprised about all this than you probably are." That seemed to fall onto the floorboards of the truck cab and flop uncomfortably for a moment or two. Then he added, "You haven't told me much about your parents."

I'd thought that tight-lipped silence had been by design. But now the design was changing. I could feel the old deal slide into the past.

"Not so good," I said. "I mean . . . they don't lock me up or beat me or anything. It's just weird. It's like . . . I feel like I don't really know them. I'm around them all the time, but most of the time I feel like I'm on a movie set, and these are the actors who are supposed to be playing my parents. The whole thing just feels . . . I don't know. Fake, somehow. None of it feels real."

"Any brothers or sisters?"

"One brother. But he's kind of a jerk. You?"

"No," he said. "Only child. Do you love him anyway?"

"Who, my brother?"

"Yeah."

I sighed. Looked out the window at the dusty landscape. At the corner of my eye I could see a plume of dust rolling off the rear wheels of the truck and following us into Fresno.

"I suppose I do," I said after a time.

We rode in absolute silence for several minutes.

Then I said, "We never talked about this before."

"True," he said. "I just figured . . ." But then, for a minute or more, he didn't tell me what he just figured. "Pretty soon it's going to be just the two of us. Our circle of friends is going to be down to just us. Nick is gone, and Suki will have to go away soon. That just leaves us."

By now we had transitioned onto an actual paved boulevard, and I could see the county jail building in the distance at the end of the street.

I wondered if Suki and Ollie would ever forgive me if they found out what a big secret I'd been keeping from them. I still would have done what I was doing for Nick, either way. But thinking about losing them made me feel sad.

Well . . . sadder. I'd been feeling sad for as long as I could remember.

"And then . . . ," he began. Out of nowhere, and hesitantly. As if he was fighting with himself over whether to start the sentence at all. ". . . then it'll just be you."

"Wait. Why?"

"I'll be eighteen in a few months. I'll have to go join the war effort."

"Oh," I said.

Just for a moment I felt more alone than I ever had in my life. Even though none of those guys were actually gone yet. When Suki and Ollie were forced away from here, I knew I'd still have Nick. And Ollie didn't know. But, anyway, I had no idea how long I'd have him. I knew the risky and deeply unwise arrangement could be pulled out from under us at any time.

Ollie pulled up in front of the jail and parked at the not-too-crowded curb.

"Are you going in?" I asked him. "Or are you staying here?"

"I think I'm staying here," he said. "I think if I saw that man right now, I'd want to hurt him."

———

When I saw "that man," I was sitting at an old, banged-up picnic table in an outdoor exercise yard. It was placed on a patch of dirt and scrubby weeds. There were other tables, four of them, where inmates sat, mostly with women and children on the other side. Beyond them was a rough tarmac basketball court. Its hoop was just a metal ring with peeling orange paint and no net.

I watched an inmate reach across the table to take his wife's hand, and immediately saw a guard step in and bang his nightstick on their table. Everybody jumped. The hands came apart again, resting in the laps of their owners.

I looked up and saw Nick's father cross the tarmac court.

He was wearing blue dungarees and a faded short-sleeved blue work shirt. He had something bulky—probably a pack of cigarettes—rolled into the left sleeve.

A guard was walking him up to my table.

My body froze in fear, and I could feel a tingling in my guts, and at the base of my tongue. I wondered what I had ever thought I dared to say to him. I wondered why I had even come.

He was a mountain of a man, maybe six foot two or three, with huge hands and feet. His dark hair, which had always been unruly and long when I'd seen him before, was buzzed close to his head. He hadn't shaved any too recently, and his beard was about the same length as his hair.

He sat across from me, and the guard peeled away. For what felt like a bizarre length of time he said nothing, and did not meet my eyes. He unrolled his sleeve and took out the pack of cigarettes, which was more flat and depleted than its lump had seemed to indicate. He shook it, and two sad, half-squashed cigarettes popped partway out.

He held the pack in my direction.

"No thanks," I said.

Still silent, he took one for himself and lit it with a paper match from a plain white book, cupping his hands against the warm valley wind. Even in winter, that wind was warm.

When he had it drawing well, he spat a shred of tobacco off the end of his tongue and into the scrubby dirt. He looked straight into my face.

"Who are you?" he asked. His voice was booming and deep. More than a little intimidating.

"I'm a friend of your son. Nick."

Much to my surprise, his face relaxed and lit up. Just for a second. Before the whole thing caught up with him, he seemed to have a weird little moment during which he thought it was a good thing to get a visit from a friend of Nick's.

"You must be Steven," he said, his eyes still shiny. "I've met the other boys."

"Yeah," I said. "I'm Steven."

"He talks about you all the time."

Through the elation I felt at hearing this news, it struck me that Nick's father loved his son. It was right there. It came through in his voice and in his eyes. He was not a monster who couldn't have cared less who got hurt. He was a proud father. Which made what he had done a hundred times harder to understand.

Then it caught up with him. I could see it.

His eyes cut away again. He slid his left hand under his thigh, pinning it to the bench, and began bouncing his legs up and down, nervously. Restlessly. His right hand, the one with the cigarette high in the crook of two fingers, began drumming a rhythm on the battered wooden table, scattering a few ashes to the wind with each tap. He looked around as if we were in the midst of scenery he could not bring himself to ignore.

I watched his hand in silence for a long time. It was huge, but not brutish or beefy. He had long fingers with boxy, square knuckles. He had been biting his fingernails.

I glanced over at the nearest guard to be sure I wasn't on my own with this man.

"How could you do it to him?" I asked.

It was brave. I was brave. I was a whole new Steven.

"I don't know what you're talking about," he said.

But his voice had changed. It was smaller now, and more unsure. His shoulders seemed more stooped, making the whole man seem less imposing. Suddenly he looked like an enormous child.

"Sure you do," I said.

"I just said what happened."

"No you didn't."

"You don't know. You weren't there."

"I didn't have to be. I was up in the mountains with Nick. You can say anything you want to anybody you want, but I'll always know it's not true. You can never fool me or confuse me. The police don't believe me, so you'll probably get away with it . . ."

I actually added that last sentence for my own self-defense. I didn't want him coming after me because I knew his secret and he thought I was just about to tell it to someone who might believe me.

He glanced around himself, but not in the same way as before. Not as though there was something behind him worth seeing. Furtively, as though someone might be about to jump him and drag him away.

"He can do the time," he hissed under his breath. "He's young."

"But it's not his time to do."

"Four years," he said in a harsh, strained whisper. "Four easy years. Not even quite four. Three and a half. It's just reform school. Easy time. They have to let him out when he turns eighteen. Me, they'd send me to the state pen. You know what happens to guys in the state pen? You got any idea how vicious those places are?"

Just for a split second his gaze flickered across the table. I looked into his eyes and saw more shame and fear than I'd ever seen crammed into one pair of eyes before. I didn't say anything in reply to his explanation. What can a person possibly say to a thing like that?

"Why'd you come here?" he asked me, looking down at the dirt.

I started to say it was because I wanted to tell Nick the why of the thing. Help the world make more sense to him. I almost said that. Then

I remembered that I wasn't supposed to know where Nick was. I wasn't supposed to be able to tell him anything.

"I just wanted to understand," I said.

That sat unaddressed for a moment.

He dropped his cigarette in the dirt and ground it under the toe of his battered work boot. "And did you get what you came for?"

"Pretty much," I said. "Yeah."

I rose to go, but he stopped me with his words.

"Wait. Kid."

I paused, half up and half down, my thigh muscles holding me aloft over the bench seat. "What?"

"Tell Nick something for me."

"I can't tell Nick anything."

"Why the hell can't you?"

"He ran away."

"Well, what'd he go and do that for?"

My thigh muscles were beginning to tremble. But I didn't sit again. And I didn't stand fully. I just hovered there.

"Maybe because three and a half years in reform school isn't as easy as you make it sound."

"If you see him, then. If he comes back. Or gets in touch with you. Give him this message from me. Okay?"

"Depends on the message."

"Tell him his mother lives in Mesa, Arizona. Little town. Little patch of dirt outside Phoenix. In case he needs somebody might take him in."

"Think she would? Take him in?"

"Might. Now that he's grown and can do for himself. Worth a try."

"Okay," I said.

And I straightened up and walked away.

As I walked to the locked gate and waited for a guard to unlock it for me, I knew I'd have to give Nick the message. Right away. That night. And that, when I did, he might leave for real.

—

When I got back to the truck, Ollie had the engine running. He was listening to the radio, some big-band instrumental, nodding his head and tapping along to the beat with his knuckles on the driver's door.

"Done?" he said when he saw me standing at the open passenger's window.

"Yeah."

"Jump in."

I didn't exactly jump. But I got in.

He swung a U-turn in the street, and we headed back toward home.

We drove for a mile or two in silence. Back to the graded dirt of the road that headed toward those mountains.

"Understand anything you didn't understand before?" he asked. His voice startled me on the first word.

"Pretty much," I said.

Another mile rolled by, and then I added, "He's just incredibly scared."

"Some people could be scared and not make it anybody else's problem."

"True," I said. "But he's not one of those people."

—

I stood at the bathroom sink before bed, drinking water straight from the tap. Lots and lots of water. The poor man's alarm clock. Or, in my case, the secretive boy's alarm clock.

After a while of this my mom stuck her head in. I probably should have closed and locked the door, but I was only drinking water.

"What are you doing?" she asked, one eyebrow arched high to show disapproval and a lack of understanding.

I swallowed, and half straightened up. "What does it look like I'm doing?" I spoke into the mirror, and not to her. I never looked at her.

"It looks like you're drinking water straight from the tap."

"Then why even ask?"

"Can't you go to the kitchen and use a glass like a civilized person?"

"I could," I said. "But what difference does it make? It's the same water."

"You shouldn't drink so much water before bed."

"But I'm thirsty."

"But you'll be up all night going to the bathroom."

"So? I'll go right back to sleep. I'm thirsty."

"I might need to take you to the doctor."

I looked at her for the first time. Now I figured *my* face was the one full of disapproval. Now *I* was the one making it clear I was listening to nonsense.

"I'm not sick," I said.

"That can be a bad sign. Abnormal thirst. I had a cousin with diabetes, and that was the first sign that something was wrong. She was always standing at the kitchen sink drinking water. *From a glass,*" she added, her voice dripping with judgment.

"I'm fine," I said. "I just didn't drink enough water today. I'll go to the kitchen and get a big glass."

"Thank you," she said. "That's all I ask—that you behave like you weren't raised by wolves."

With that, she disappeared from the doorway.

I trotted to the kitchen and drank three big glasses.

I made a mental note to find another of those gallon glass jugs. I could keep it under my bed. I could fill it when I knew no one was around.

I practically sloshed going back to my room.

I tried to get to sleep, but I was worried about having to tell Nick the story of my meeting with his father. Worried that the truth might make it worse instead of better. And then I would have to tell him where his mother lived. After which he might disappear from my life. I wouldn't be the only one he had anymore.

It was after midnight before my eyes even closed.

———

My alarm clock bladder woke me at half past midnight. I had only slept for minutes. I hauled my book bag full of food and water from under my bed, slipped into my shoes, and burst as silently as possible out into the night.

It had been raining. The stars and moon were gone. Nonexistent. A dense fog lay close to the ground, and forced me to navigate by memory. I could feel the mist of all that moisture on my bare torso. I hadn't taken the time to put on a shirt or a jacket, but it didn't matter. It was a bizarrely warm night.

When I was sure I was far enough away from the house, I stopped and urinated against a wooden fence that I knew the workers used for the same purpose. The smell alone would tell you. I stood there for the longest time, waiting to be done. But it just went on and on and on.

Then I trotted in the direction of the remote outbuilding again.

When I found it in the fog and darkness, I looked around behind it. No Nick. The past couple of nights I had found him outside, his back up against the east wall of the structure, stargazing. But there were no visible stars that night, so I told myself I shouldn't have been surprised.

I opened the door and stepped into the dank darkness inside. The trapdoor in the floor was standing wide open. I was hit with an odor. It wasn't urine or feces, but it was definitely unpleasant. It wasn't sweat, or any other smell one tends to associate with a human body in a small space. It was sour and sharp and disturbing.

"Nick?"

"Don't come down here," he said.

His voice sounded horrible. Listless. Deep. Discouraged.

"Why not?"

"I don't want you to get sick."

"You're sick?"

"Oh yeah."

I went down anyway.

"You shouldn't get near me," he said. "You don't want this. It's terrible."

He was sitting on his rubber pad, his back up close to the far wall, but not quite touching it. I could just barely see that he had his arms wrapped around his knees.

As my eyes adjusted to the darkness, I saw that he was rocking back and forth. And shivering. And shivering. And shivering. That seemed like a bad sign in a cellar that was so warm and humid that I could feel myself sweat.

I started to lower myself down against the far wall, but as I reached to steady myself, I could feel that the walls were wet. They were weeping moisture from the rain we had just gotten. And the packed dirt floor was wet.

I crouched on my haunches. Squatted without touching anything. I didn't want to have to explain to my mom how my pajama bottoms got muddy dirt on their seat between the time I went to bed and the time I got up in the morning.

"Is it influenza?" I asked, hoping he would say no. People died of influenza. The influenza pandemic of 1918 had been in our parents' lifetimes. Nobody took it lightly back then.

"Probably," he said, his teeth chattering. "I've been throwing up."

I understood the bad smell in that moment.

We sat in silence for a time. Well, I squatted in silence.

Then I said, "I'll bring you some pallets from the barn. We have to get you up off this wet floor. And I'll see if I can find you something to use as extra blankets. Maybe some empty feed sacks or something."

"Thank you," he said through chattering teeth.

I sat a moment and watched and listened. There wasn't much to see in that complete lack of light, but I was aware of his trembling. He was reminding me of myself after jumping into that mountain lake. We had traded roles.

Now *I* might have to save *his* life.

"I brought you some food and water," I said.

"Thanks. But I can't hold anything down. Not even water."

"Uh-oh." Then I stopped myself from going any further down that verbal path. But I knew if he couldn't hold down water and he was throwing up, he could get dangerously dehydrated, and fast. "Try," I said. "Try to take just a few sips of water. I'll go back to the house and get some sugar and salt."

"What for?" he asked in his shaky voice.

"For the water. When I was a kid and I was really sick, my mom always gave me water with sugar and salt in it. She said it puts back what your body is losing."

"Thanks," he said. "I'll try."

I rose to my feet in all that damp darkness.

"Steven?" he said, before I could go.

"Yeah, Nick?"

"I'm scared."

"I'll take care of you, though."

"Promise?"

"Yeah. I promise. But if it gets really bad, I might have to get a doctor."

"No!" he said. Shouted, really. "No, you can't do that. That's what I'm afraid of. I'm more afraid of that than dying."

"How can you be more afraid of that than dying?"

"I don't want to go to reform school, Steven. If I'd really done something wrong, then maybe. Then I would just buck up and take it. But I don't want to be humiliated by my dad like that. I'd rather die."

"Please don't talk like that. I'm not going to let you die."

"Good," he said in that frighteningly trembling voice. "Thank you."

I moved toward the stairs, but he stopped me with words. Cutting, amazing, welcome, frightening words.

"Steven, wait. You love me. Right?"

I just stood at the ladderlike steps for a moment, one hand on a damp rung. Trying to convince my heart to start beating again. Trying to remind my lungs how to draw air.

"Yes," I said. "I love you."

The words seemed to come out of some kind of reverberating hollow drum. Not out of me at all.

I waited to see if he would say it to me in return.

Instead he just said, "Good. Thank you. Somebody has to love me."

As I absorbed the sting of his not saying it, I wanted to tell him I thought his father loved him, too. But it might be a difficult pill to swallow. The moment I'd realized his father loved him—when I felt I'd seen that with my own eyes—the whole situation had felt considerably more tragic, and even harder to bear. If such a thing were possible.

I decided it might be best to wait and talk about his father when he wasn't in fear for his life. And it would do no good to tell him where his mother lived, because he was far too sick to travel there.

"I'll go get everything you need," I said.

I ran up the steps and out into the night. It was raining again, a warm rain that soaked my hair and turned my pajama bottoms into wet, clinging film.

I made two trips in the rain with pallets. I found packing blankets he could use to get warm. I snuck into the kitchen for sugar and salt. I brought Nick the oil-burning lantern my father used when we went camping at the lake.

I got him set up with all that, then stayed until he fell asleep.

I ran home and snuck back into my room and changed my wet pajama bottoms for dry ones, hanging the wet ones at the very back of my closet to dry.

I snuck back down the hall to the bathroom, urinated again, washed my hands, and toweled off my hair as best I could.

Then, finally, I crawled back into bed. I glanced at the clock. It was after three. And I had to get up at six. But some things simply needed to be done.

Chapter Eight

Secretive Boy

I fell asleep in math class in the morning. Twice. The teacher did not seem inclined to let it go by.

He wrote a note that he handed me after the bell rang, as Suki and I walked out of class.

"What's this?" I asked, staring at it as though it might be poisonous.

"You will give this to your parents," he said. "And don't think I won't check."

I took it without further comment, shoving it into my book bag as Suki and I walked out into the hall together. I was fortunate to have two book bags. The other one would have to dry for a while, and then have as much mud brushed off it as possible.

I was always thinking two or three logistical moves ahead, overwhelmed by the thought that I could make a mistake that would give the whole thing away. It would be so easy to screw up and leave some kind of clue or trail.

"Why so tired?" Suki asked me as we walked down the crowded hall together.

"I don't know," I said. "I just couldn't sleep."

"I know why *I'm* having trouble sleeping . . . ," he began. Then he trailed off, as if leaving the sentence for me to finish.

"I'm worried about Nick. How he's getting by, wherever he is. I'm worried about you and your family having to go away. I'm worried about Ollie having to go fight. And probably my brother, too. I know it's worse for your family than mine, and maybe I have no right to be scared, with what you're facing and all. But there's a war on, and I don't know what's going to happen, and it's just been keeping me awake."

"You have a right to be scared," he said. "Everybody has a right to be scared."

Then, just as I was thinking what a good friend he was—just as I opened my mouth to say so—he peeled away toward the gym. He had gym next, and I had chemistry lab.

I stood still in the hall for a minute or so, watching him walk away.

A group of four girls walked by, shooting daggers at me from their dark eyes. And I knew why, too. I had made no secret of the fact that I was still good friends with Suki. Among the white youth of this town, that was an unforgivable sin. I honestly think they hated me more than they hated Suki. I guess they figured he had no choice but to be Japanese, while I, on the other hand, should have known better.

At least, that seemed to be the way they looked at the thing. It's not like anybody talked to me about it. It's not like anybody talked to me at all.

———

When I got home that afternoon, after a bit of back-and-forth with myself, I left the teacher's note on the kitchen table. I didn't read it, because I couldn't. It was sealed. I didn't dare throw it away, because the teacher had made it clear he would check.

I went straight to my room, flopped down on my bed, and immediately fell asleep.

My mother woke me with a massive shout.

"Steven!"

I sat upright, my face tingling and cold. I thought, *This is it. I'm really going to get it.* I rose, crossed to the door, and stuck my head out into the hall.

"What?" I shouted back. With a bit less enthusiasm and volume.

"Dinner!"

Of course, that had not been at all what I'd expected.

I combed my hair into place as best I could with my fingers and trotted out to join them at the table, cutting through the kitchen to check on the note.

It was gone.

I sat down for dinner and looked around. Nobody looked back at me. Nobody. It was all four of us in our own little worlds, just like always.

I glanced down at my plate. Dinner was a mixture of ground meat and what appeared to be canned baked beans. I glanced over at my mom, trying not to be obvious. I knew she must have read the note. But she seemed to have nothing to say.

I pushed the unappetizing-looking stuff around with my fork. I took one bite. But, as was common with my mom's cooking, it didn't taste like much of anything.

A minute or two later she startled me by speaking up. It was loud and sudden.

"I made that to eat. Not to play with."

"Yes, ma'am."

She did that thing with her eyebrow. Arching it up. "Since when do you call me 'ma'am'?"

I shrugged. "Since now, I guess."

I knew I was in trouble, and she knew I knew it. I could tell.

I shoveled in a couple of big bites of dinner, watching her at the corner of my eye. She never took her attention off me.

She lit a cigarette. Right there at the dinner table. Not that it was new or anything, but usually she at least finished eating first. I watched her plant her elbow on the table and lean on the heel of her hand, blowing a stream of smoke in my general direction. I tried not to cough.

"Why so tired, Steven?" she asked. Her voice was so loud that my father looked up from his plate.

"Just having a little trouble sleeping."

"First excessive thirst, now trouble sleeping. I really do think it wouldn't hurt to get you in for a checkup."

"I don't need a checkup," I said.

My father chimed in immediately. "Absolutely right he doesn't. He had one a few months ago. I don't make money just so you can throw it away, woman."

"I think we should know why he's having trouble sleeping."

"I know why I'm having trouble sleeping," I said.

Bizarrely, everyone ignored me. Or, at least, in any other household it would have seemed bizarre.

"Who *wouldn't*?" my father bellowed. "There's a damn war on!"

"I'll thank you to watch your language at the dinner table, Marv."

They were raising their voices at each other now. Fighting. About me. And yet somehow I felt I could walk away without their even noticing. I may have been the subject of the fight, but I didn't seem to matter to it at all.

"Everybody's a little jumpy right now, Beth. Leave the boy be."

"I think I should take him into Fresno to see that . . . you know . . . doctor."

"What doctor?"

"The one we used for Terrence that time."

"The *head doctor*? He's not crazy, Beth. He's just having trouble sleeping."

Terrence's head jerked up. "Hey!" he shouted. "I'm not crazy, either!"

They ignored him, too.

"But a . . . you know . . . doctor . . . he can prescribe medication."

"He doesn't need any stinking medication, Beth. There's nothing wrong with him."

He bumped my elbow, startling me. Knocking it off the table. I had a raised forkful of beans in that hand, and they landed on the cloth napkin on my lap. One rolled onto the rug.

"Boy. Why d'you think you're having trouble sleeping?"

"Because . . . ," I began, ". . . there's a war on?"

"See? Now what'd I tell you, Beth? He's not defective. And that head doctor costs a fortune. Leave the boy alone and let him grow up."

She sat back in her chair and took a long draw on her cigarette. "Sure, Marv," she said. "Anything you say."

But there was something off about the way she said it. Something wry and sarcastic. At least, it seemed so to me. My father, on the other hand, appeared perfectly satisfied with it. He pitched back into his dinner, and not another word was spoken at the table that evening.

———

When I arrived inside the outbuilding in the middle of the night, the trapdoor was standing wide open again. *Probably for the best,* I thought. *Everybody needs to breathe.*

A comforting spill of glowing lantern light came up through the open square in the floor.

"Nick?" I asked. I could feel something trying to come up through my throat. A lump that felt like my heart, but I knew it couldn't be.

"Yeah," he said quietly.

I breathed. And breathed. And breathed.

"I brought you more food and water. Did you manage to hold anything down?"

"No."

"Oh."

I started down the steep steps, but he stopped me with words.

"No, don't, Steven. Really. I don't want you coming down here. You'll get sick, and then I'd never forgive myself. Sit and talk to me from up there. I'll still know you're here with me."

I sat at the edge of the open trapdoor, where I could see him in the glow from the lantern. He was stretched out on his side on the bed of pallets, covered with two packing blankets, his backpack pulled up onto the bed with him to keep it dry.

My heart flew down to him. My body stayed upstairs. It was a wrenching experience. It felt like being torn apart.

"I'm here," I said.

"I know you are."

A long silence.

Then, his voice frighteningly weak, he asked, "What's new up there in the world?"

"Well. Everybody in school hates me because I'm still friends with Suki and I won't pretend I'm not. And my mother wanted to take me to a doctor who . . . you know. Works with mental problems."

"What for?"

"She's worried because I'm not sleeping enough."

"Then you should go back and sleep."

"Later I will."

"No. You really should, Steven. You were up so long with me last night. Of course you're tired. Get one good night's sleep. I'll see you again tomorrow."

I sat without answering for a minute or so. My heart felt as though it was being crushed in a vise. My stolen nighttime visits with Nick were all I really cared about. All I waited for. All that was holding me up anymore. Having one snatched away felt unbearable.

"You sure you'll be okay?"

"Yeah."

"I brought you a fever thermometer. It's in my book bag with the jug and the food. Want me to bring it down?"

"No, leave it up there. I'll come up for it later, after you're gone. I'd never forgive myself if you got this."

"Okay," I said.

I pulled to my feet, nursing the raw, empty chasm that had formed inside my chest. But a second later he spoke again, and the canyon closed. And warmed. And filled. As though nothing had ever been missing inside me. Not one day of my life.

"I love you, too, Steven."

I said nothing in return because I couldn't. My voice didn't work. Nothing worked.

I ran all the way back to the house and snuck in through my unlocked window. I slept like the dead all night long.

———

The principal stepped into my history class about 10:30 the following morning, scanned the faces briefly, then looked straight into my eyes and barked a single name.

Mine.

"Steven Katz!"

I jolted up straight. I knew he wanted me to stand, but I was utterly immobile. My limbs had been filled with concrete, and it had already begun to set. I was too afraid to function.

My first thought was that they'd found Nick. Somebody had found him. And now he was on a bus to reform school, and I had a seat waiting for me on the next bus out. Then I wondered if they had even found him alive. And, if not, whether my decision not to call a doctor made me responsible for his death—legally, and in my own heart for the rest of my life.

At the corners of my eyes I saw the other students staring at me. Waiting for me to move.

"Come along, Steven."

My ears had taken to buzzing, filled with hundreds of bees that I figured only I could hear. I looked down at the desk and saw that I was standing. But it was only my spatial relationship to the desk that tipped me off. I swear I couldn't feel my body move at all. I hadn't felt myself do it.

I watched the scenery change as I followed him down the hall and into his office.

I stepped inside, still trapped in that weird dream sensation, and almost ran smack into my mom. She looked at me with wide eyes, and I think I looked back. It was hard to tell for sure.

"You look like you've just seen a ghost," she said.

"What is it, Mom? What's wrong? What happened?"

I vaguely registered that, in or around that moment, she might realize why I was so afraid. She might understand that being dragged out of class was something like a phone call at three o'clock in the morning. It induced panic because it seemed to have disaster attached.

She did no such thing. She simply brushed my reaction aside the way she might relocate a ladybug that had landed on her blouse.

"Nothing's wrong. We just have an appointment is all."

She moved to the door as if expecting me to follow. I did not follow. I saw the principal standing there, observing. But I didn't really focus on him.

"What appointment? Where?"

"It's in Fresno," she said, straining to keep her voice light. "Come along."

"Dad said no."

"I don't—" she began in a sharp, loud voice. Then she stopped. Glanced past me to the principal. Altered her outward attitude. "It's a long drive and we have plenty of time to talk on the way. Come along."

Those last two words were spoken fairly softly, but they were laden with an ominous meaning that I could not fail to hear or heed. Still I stood, my feet planted on the floor of the principal's office as if rooted there like an old tree.

The principal spoke up, jolting me. "You'd best do as your mother says, son."

My feet unstuck themselves and I followed her out into the hall. She paused briefly to let me pull level with her. Then she slapped me hard on the upper arm.

"Ow," I said.

"You don't *ever* do that to me again! Humiliating me in front of the principal like that!"

"But Dad said no."

"I don't care what your father says. You're my son, too. He doesn't get to decide everything."

I stopped dead in the hall, and when she realized I was no longer with her, she stopped, too. She turned to face me and our gazes drilled into each other. I felt defiant. I'm sure it showed.

"I'll tell him," I said.

Then I waited. To see how much of a bill I would be forced to pay.

I watched the thing swirl around behind her eyes for a moment. She was mad. I knew she would either lash out hard at me or put it away, like she always did when she was mad at my father. You couldn't out-angry my father. It didn't pay to try.

A second later I saw her put it away.

"Fine," she said. "Tell him. It'll be over by then, and there won't be a single thing he can do about it."

She turned and walked again, pushing open the front door of the school and stepping out into the light. The hallway had been dank and cool without my even realizing it, and when I followed her out into the sun, the light felt like daggers in my eyes.

I walked with her to the car and got in.

She was right that it was a good, long drive. She was wrong to think we would get any talking done on the way.

———

Dr. Speier was a man in his late fifties, or maybe even early sixties, with a receding jet-black hairline, and a slight widow's peak. It wasn't until I sat across from him in his plush, quiet office that I flashed on how much Terrence had hated him. How bitterly he had complained about having to see him. But it had fallen on deaf ears. Terrence had burned down the old barn—accidentally, I'd assumed, until Dr. Speier entered the picture—and my parents weren't interested in his view of things.

I glanced briefly at Dr. Speier's face, then quickly looked down at his deep-burgundy Persian rug. He had intense, piercing brown eyes that seemed to be trying to get inside my head and drag something out into the light. I had nothing I was willing to let go of that day.

"Your mother is concerned about you," he said. His voice was steady and deep. More than a little bit intimidating.

I was in no mood to be pushed around.

"I know she is. But that doesn't mean she's right to be."

I watched him take notes on a pad with a narrow silver pen.

"Anything troubling you?"

"Of course there is. We just got pulled into a war. The whole world is blowing up. My brother might have to go fight. My friend Ollie might have to go fight. It's looking like all the Japanese are going to be rounded up and put in some kind of camps. Maybe even the citizens. The US citizens."

I was careful not to mention Suki, or let on how closely affected I would be by such a decision, because I didn't want it getting back to my mom.

He seized on this immediately.

"And what is that to you?"

"What is what to me?" But I knew.

"Why are you concerned about Japanese relocation?"

"Because it's wrong," I said.

"Interesting," he said. And scribbled on his pad again.

"What's so interesting about it?"

"I just can't help noticing that you seem to be very sure that you're right and all the responsible adults are wrong."

"You don't need to be an adult," I said. "You just need to have a conscience."

He set the pad and pen down, and bored right into my eyes again with his own. I looked away. Again. The chair I was sitting in was a buttery soft leather wing chair, and it made slight squeaking noises as I shifted my weight around.

"May I make an observation?" he asked.

I felt defiant. I was not playing his game. My mother could drag me here, but she could not make me play along.

"If I say no, are you going to do it anyway?"

"Probably. Yes."

"Then why even ask?"

This time *he* shifted *his* weight around in *his* chair. His leather also squeaked.

"You speak of having a conscience. I believe you do have a conscience. It's our conscience that allows us to feel shame. We are only as sick as our secrets, Steven."

I felt it as a punch in the stomach. I thought, *So that's what he was seeing.*

I said, "I'm not keeping secrets, and I don't feel ashamed."

It was true, and it was untrue. Of course I was keeping secrets. Plenty of them. And I know I said earlier that shame was my default setting at that age. But I meant shame about saying the wrong thing. About *being* the wrong thing. Just your garden-variety teenage anxiety. I was not ashamed that I loved Nick, or that Suki was my friend. I knew I was supposed to be, but I had begun to internally refuse that burden.

"Your eyes say otherwise. You're trying to keep your eyes away from me, as if there's something you're afraid I'll see. You really have no idea how obvious it is."

I pulled a curtain behind my eyes. I can't explain it any better than that. I steeled myself, and made sure everything that showed on my face was blank. A shuttered window. I protected myself from his prying.

I looked him right in the eye. "I'm not ashamed," I said again.

"Then why not get everything out on the table? I promise you anything you say here today will be held in confidence."

"Just because you think people won't understand something doesn't mean it's anything to be ashamed of."

"There you go again," he said, and picked up his pad. And scribbled. "That's the third time you've told me you know better than anyone. Well, never mind. For now. It's our first session, and I don't expect you to trust me right off the bat. I just want you to know that your burden shows. There's a lot going on in there that you seem to be determined to carry alone. That's a lot for a lad your age. But . . . we'll speak of easier subjects for now."

For most of the balance of the session we engaged in something more like small talk. How I liked school. If I played any sports. What I liked to do for fun. If my home life was all right. Part of me felt it was useless, and I wondered how much my mother was paying for us to talk about nothing much. Another part of me feared that everything I said, no matter how mundane, revealed me to him.

I made sure to tread carefully with every word.

———

Just as the clock ticked down to the hour, he leaned over to his desk, slid open the top drawer, and pulled out a prescription pad.

"I'm going to prescribe some mild sleeping tablets," he said.

"Okay."

But I didn't figure I would take them. I might ask Nick if he was getting enough sleep, and give him the pills if the answer was no. But then I had a frightening thought. What if Nick's influenza went into his lungs? Turned into pneumonia? A sleeping pill might keep him down and unaware as he stopped breathing.

"What would you prescribe for someone who has pneumonia?" I asked.

He looked at me strangely, which wasn't surprising. "But you don't. Do you?"

"No. But one of the men on my dad's farm is really sick. He doesn't have the money to go to a doctor. I'm afraid he'll die. My father doesn't pay him enough money for food and rent and then anything unexpected after that, like a doctor. Why do we do that? Leave people on their own to die because they can't afford to see a doctor? It doesn't seem right."

He narrowed his eyes at me for a time. He looked as though he was trying to judge if I was for real.

"But I haven't seen this patient. I don't know his condition. I don't even know his height and weight. It's not safe to prescribe without knowing the patient's size."

"You don't have to worry about giving him too much. He's a big guy. Over six feet tall. I weigh one thirty. He must be at least fifty pounds heavier than me."

I braved his piercing stare for what felt like a long time, my heart pounding.

"It's irregular," he said, "but I might consider making a deal with you. I'll write a prescription for this gentleman you feel so concerned about if you promise to come back for another session. And to be more forthcoming with me next time."

"It's a deal," I said.

But it was a deal I knew I might break. Without shame.

He scribbled on his pad again and then tore off the two sheets and handed them to me. I glanced quickly at the one for Nick. I was worried he had prescribed penicillin. Because my mother would know what that was. She would question it. I wouldn't be able to get it filled on this trip. I would have to get Ollie to drive me all the way back here to Fresno again. I would have to waste more time. I would have to tell more lies.

It was for a drug called sulfathiazole.

I breathed deeply. I didn't figure anyone but a doctor would know what that was. I was certainly ready to take the chance.

I rose, and walked out into the waiting room, where my mother sat reading a women's magazine.

"We have to stop at a pharmacy," I said, "before we leave town."

"Happy to," she said. "Glad to hear you're willing to accept some help for a change."

———

I waited in the car while she stepped inside the pharmacy, listening to the blood roaring in my ears. I was taking a huge chance, and I knew it. She might ask the pharmacist about the drugs, or he might offer an education about them as he filled the prescriptions.

She might march out any minute, demanding an explanation.

All I could think to do was to tell her the same story I'd told Dr. Speier. That one of Dad's workers was sick. Except my father would know if that was true or not. Maybe I should make it one of Joe Wilson's workers. Maybe the parent of one of my new friends.

I had to take the chance. What if I left Fresno without those pills and something happened to Nick that night?

I waited in low-grade panic for what felt like an hour. My watch said it was more like six minutes.

She came out with a small white paper bag. She walked to the car, opened the driver's door, and flung the bag in the general direction of my lap. Then she got in and started the engine.

I breathed. The blood roared a bit more softly inside my ears.

"I know one of those is a sleeping pill," she said, shifting into first gear and pulling away from the curb. "Because I had the same one prescribed for me the year we were having that trouble with your brother. But what's the other one? That . . . sulfa . . . something something."

"It's to help you relax," I said.

"Oh. Well, good. Good for you. I'm surprised you're going along with all this, but I think it's wonderful. You're just a young boy. You shouldn't have to be so worried all the time. You shouldn't have so much weight on your shoulders."

I could have told her that a great deal of the weight on my shoulders had been stacked there by her and Dad.

I didn't.

I was busy being relieved that I had successfully skated through something. That it was over now, and I had won, because I hadn't gotten caught. I was happy just breathing naturally for the first time in as long as I could remember.

Then I saw the sign for the bookstore at the end of the block, and I knew I was going to have to put myself out there again. For Nick.

Chapter Nine

Parts Unknown

I showed up at the top of the cellar stairs at a little after midnight, my school book bag heavy on my shoulder and my heart hammering so hard I thought it might kill me. The book I'd gotten for Nick was clenched under my arm so no leakage of food or water in the bag could damage its precious cover or pages. The bottle of pills was an uncomfortable lump in my pants pocket.

I took a deep breath and spoke his name, knowing there was a small chance he would never answer me. Never answer anybody again.

"Nick?"

"I'm here," he said quietly. His voice sounded shaky and small.

All the air flew out of me in a sort of desperate sigh. I felt so relieved that it made my head swim, and the room—such as it was—seemed to sway around me.

I carefully made my way down the stairs.

"Good news and bad news," he said in that miniature voice.

He was sitting with his back up against the cool, damp dirt wall. Which couldn't have been too comfortable. Then again, sometimes you need your back up against something.

I sat a respectful distance away, the things I'd brought him crowded onto my lap.

"I could use some good news," I said.

"I can hold down water now, and I even had a few bites of apple."

"That's great. What's the bad news?"

"It feels like it's going into my chest."

"Oh," I said, ecstatically relieved to have a good answer for him. "I have something for that!"

I took the bottle of pills out of my pocket, and stretched it out to him, and he examined it in the glow of the lantern. I made a mental note to bring him more lamp oil to keep the thing going.

"Where did you get these?" he asked, his voice full of what sounded like awe.

"It's a long story. I'll tell you when you're feeling better."

He unscrewed the cap from the little glass bottle and carefully rolled one pill out onto his palm. He tossed it into his mouth in one smooth movement and swallowed it without the benefit of water.

"That's a lifesaver," he said. "Maybe literally." His voice had gotten bigger and stronger. As though that pill had helped him as it touched his throat. But of course that was impossible. If anything had helped him, it was likely the promise of aid. A sense of helplessness lifting.

He leaned back against the wall and sighed.

"Thank you," he said. "Maybe I'll get through this after all."

"Of course you will. Don't even talk like you won't."

We sat for a time, nursing that moment in silence.

"I brought you something else," I said, suddenly remembering it.

I pulled the book out from under my school bag and held it in his direction. In the glow of lamplight I saw his eyes go wide.

"This is for *me*?"

I nodded, though I was unsure whether it was light enough for him to see.

It was a big, solid hardcover with illustrations of the planets on the cover.

"Does it have a picture of that nebula in Orion?"

"I was afraid to look. It was the only astronomy book they had."

It was pathetic, but it was true. I had literally been afraid to look, because it would have been such a disappointment if Orion was not there. I knew Nick would like the book regardless. But the pursuit of that nebula he'd tried to describe to me had blotted out everything else in my world. Everything surrounding Nick had taken on an inordinate importance, and I couldn't have changed that even if I'd been willing to try.

He flipped a few pages, and ran his finger down the table of contents.

"Here's something about the Orion Nebula," he said.

A few seconds later he held the wide-open book out for me to see. I took hold of the lantern and pulled it closer to illuminate its pages.

I sucked in a deep breath.

"That's amazing!" I breathed.

The image was in black and white, as book images tended to be in those days. It filled both facing pages. It looked like a ball of flame in the sky, pointing downward at an angle. Four bright stars nested in the base of it, making that area especially bright, and the nebula seemed to bloom around that like some kind of celestial flower. Clouds and streams of whatever nebulae are made of—now I know it's gas and dust, but I had no words for it at the time—created swirls and patterns unlike anything I'd ever seen.

"It's beautiful," I said.

"Imagine what it would look like in color."

"There's color out there?"

"Of course there's color out there. There's color everywhere. You don't think space is all black and white just because the books about it are, do you?"

"I guess not. I guess I just never thought about it before."

"Help me get up the stairs and outside. Please. I've only been going out to empty that pot, and it's hard. I've been kind of weak. But I want to go sit under the stars." I was already gathering myself to stand when he added two more stunning words. Literally stunning. They hit me like a stun gun. "With you."

I was too overwhelmed to say anything in return, but I braced my shoulder behind him as he pulled himself up the stairs, to avoid any tumbles.

We stepped out into the night.

I sat with my back against the eastern wall of the shed while Nick tottered slowly over to a nearby fence and relieved himself against it, his back to me. Then he ambled unsteadily back and sat down beside me. Not as close as I might have liked.

He seemed to sense my disappointment.

"I still don't want you to catch this from me," he said.

"Right. Thanks."

We sat in silence for a time, gazing at Orion hovering over the mountains. It may seem that I could only know where *I* was gazing, but after looking at that image in the book, I figured it would be impossible not to stare at Orion's sword and imagine being able to see that nebula hovering up there.

I made a mental note to quietly borrow my father's big binoculars.

"Sure feels good to be out," he said.

"Are you cold?"

"No, it feels nice. Thanks for that book. How did you get it? Where did it come from?"

"My mom and I were in Fresno."

"Oh."

More silence.

Then he said something I had not expected. It hit me in a bad and wrong place, ending that welcome sense that all was briefly well in my world.

"It's just weird," he said.

"What is?"

"Well . . . I sort of . . . owe you . . . *everything* at this point. Like I might not even survive without you."

"Is that bad, though?"

"It's just weird."

"You trust me, though. Right?"

"Oh, yeah. Absolutely I do. I'm just not used to leaning on anybody. I don't even lean on my parents."

I looked over at the side of his face, only barely visible in the starlight, searching for some kind of clue to his emotional state. But I couldn't see much.

He coughed violently for several seconds before trying to speak again. It sounded as though the spasms would turn his lungs inside out. It hurt to listen.

"Don't get me wrong," he said, his voice husky with congestion. "You've been great. And it's not that I don't appreciate it. I do. I really do. It's just that when one person gets to be your whole world like this . . . I don't know. I guess I just feel like it leaves you with a lot to lose."

"You're not going to lose me," I said, still staring at the side of his face as he stared at the night sky.

"No, I know. It's just weird."

A silence fell. I looked back at Orion, but it was quite nearly obliterated. A misty fog had assembled almost from nowhere and was now obscuring all but the one star that formed his bright orange shoulder.

"Oh, it's going to be cloudy now," Nick said. "Too bad. I should go inside and try to get some sleep."

"Okay," I said, but I was crushed.

I helped him to his feet.

"You need sleep, too," he said.

"I guess."

"You do. I know you do."

"You need help getting down the stairs?"

"Nope. Down is easy. Gravity on my side."

I turned toward home, but he spoke, stopping me.

"Steven."

I turned back to the dim figure of him, standing under the foggy night sky.

"Yeah?"

"Thanks. For everything."

Then he walked into the shed, coughing.

I walked home and put myself back to bed. But I got precious little sleep.

—

We sat outside at our usual picnic table adjacent to the school playground. Suki, Ollie, and me. Suki was eating real food—soup straight out of a bowl from the cafeteria—so I figured everything was reasonably solid in his world. All things considered.

For a long time I ignored my sandwich and stared up into the shifting leaves of the stand of trees at the edge of the playground's tarmac. The sun was hovering behind them, causing occasional flashes of light as the warm wind rustled them around. My exhaustion was making me feel less than real. I was disconnected from my own life, as though my head had been stuffed with warm cotton.

I looked down again to see them both staring at me.

"You look terrible," Suki said.

"Gee, thanks."

"I didn't mean it like that. I just meant . . ."

"No, I know what you meant. I'm sorry. I don't even know why I said that."

We all ate in silence for two beats. Maybe three.

"You just look tired," Ollie said.

"I guess I am."

"Having trouble sleeping?"

"Yeah. Pretty much."

"Something I need to tell you," Ollie added suddenly, looking decidedly uncomfortable. As if he'd needed to spit the sentence out all at once. "Something I need to tell both of you."

"I already heard," Suki said. "And I'd be surprised if Steven didn't know it, too. It's all over town."

Ollie wrinkled his brow. It was a slightly exaggerated gesture. "I don't think we're talking about the same thing. Because I'm the only one who knows this."

"Oh," Suki said. "Sorry. I was talking about that guy."

"What guy?" I asked. My ears had perked up, thinking this was important. And it was. But, looking back, I'm not sure what tipped me.

"That guy who was in a coma," Suki said. "You know. From fighting with Nick's dad."

I felt my back go rigidly straight. I tried to hide my reaction. I'm not sure why. It wasn't a secret from them that I would care. My belly felt icy. I was sure he was about to tell me the guy had died.

"What about him? *Was* in a coma? You mean . . . not anymore?"

"No, not anymore. I'm surprised you didn't hear. It's all over town."

"It's where we live," Ollie said. "Where Steven lives, it's different. We're so close together. All the houses are so close when you live right here in town. People talk without even stepping off their own front stoops. One front door to the next. But Steven is way out there—"

"Wait a minute," I said, interrupting. "Go back. Did he die? Or did he wake up?"

"Oh, I'm sorry," Suki said. "I forgot you didn't know that part. He woke up."

"Did he tell them who really did it?"

They both shrugged at exactly the same time.

"Don't know," Suki said. "That part I didn't hear. But I don't see why he wouldn't."

We sat in silence for a moment, not eating. I was absorbing this sudden news. Feeling as though my whole world had just shifted. Like a tectonic plate under the soil, moving over into new territory just when I was sure everything was solid beneath my feet. I was wondering if I could sit still through the rest of the school day without learning more—I was absolutely squirming inside to know more—when Suki interrupted my thoughts by speaking.

"What were *you* going to say?" he asked Ollie.

"Oh, that," Ollie said. "Right."

We waited. An awkward space of time crawled by. It struck me that Ollie had spit out the fact that he had news the way people do when they're purposely trying to fix it so they can't back out again.

He blinked his eyes closed. Either he left them closed just a split second too long, or time skipped a beat. "I'm enlisting," he said.

That sat on the table for a moment. Nobody seemed to want to touch it.

"You're what?" Suki asked.

"Did you really not hear?"

"How can you enlist?" I asked Ollie. "You're not eighteen."

"You can enlist at seventeen. You can even enlist at sixteen. Your parents just have to sign off on it if you're not eighteen."

"Will they?" Suki asked.

"I think so."

"But you haven't asked them yet," I said. I wasn't sure if it was even a question.

"No, I wanted to talk to you guys first."

I took a deep breath and said, "Why would you want to go sooner than you have to?"

"Because I know I have to. It's hanging over my head. And I hate that. When something is sitting out there waiting for me like that . . .

I don't know. I'd rather just jump in. Get it over with. That way I can stop thinking about it. Don't you ever do that?"

He seemed to be talking to me. Not to both of us. I think that's why I was the one to take it on.

"No. I don't think I do. I put bad things off as long as I possibly can."

"Well, you're braver than I am," Ollie said.

It seemed like a strange thing to say. I think I made a snorting sound through my nose.

"It's not brave," I said. "It's me being a chicken."

"No, it's braver your way," he said. "Because it's harder your way."

I remember thinking that I needed to mull that over a bit. See what I felt about it deep down inside. But I don't think I ever did. Because the man who could exonerate Nick was up and talking. And that, quite simply, was destined to steal the show.

———

I stuck my head into the principal's office, my brain swirling with cover stories. To use their phone, I would have to make it sound as though I had important new information to give the detective. Not the other way around. I couldn't be sure from looking at the phone number on the card, but I thought it indicated that his office was in Fresno. Which might have made it an expensive call. Which was plenty of reason for the principal and his staff to refuse me.

I was surprised to see the office utterly empty. The outer office, where the assistant principal and the attendance monitor worked, was unmanned. The door was open to the principal's inner sanctum. Nobody there. Everybody must have been out at lunch.

My head swirling with the excuses I would give if caught, I trotted into the principal's office and picked up his phone.

If we had been in Los Angeles, or even in Fresno, I'm sure the school would have had one of the modern rotary-dial phones. But this was the sticks, and it was one of those older models that forced you to lift an actual metal horn-shaped piece off a hook and ask the operator to get you the number.

I read her the detective's number off the card and then waited, obsessively watching the door, sure I was about to be caught. When the line rang, it made me jump.

"Engel," said a sharp, no-nonsense voice on the line.

I recognized it as the tall, thin cop who always seemed to want me to note that he carried a gun.

"Oh," I said, already messing up. "Um . . ."

"Who've I got on the line?"

"Steven Katz."

"You're gonna have to give me more than that, son."

"You were questioning me a couple of times about that . . . crime. That Nick Mattaliano's father committed. But you thought it was Nick."

"Right," he said. "Right, right, right. But I still think it's Nick. Why wouldn't I think that?"

"Because . . . well, I heard the guy woke up."

I waited for what was surely no more than two seconds. But it felt like an hour. A painful, never-ending hour.

"You heard right, son. Edward Mulligan regained consciousness at the hospital at seven ten yesterday evening, according to the nurses."

"So he told you Nick didn't do it."

"No. He did not."

I felt a panic rising up through my chest. The world was not behaving properly. I wanted to seize it by the throat. Force it to do the right thing.

"Why not? Did you talk to him?"

"We have not had a chance to question him, no."

I lost my ability to stay calm. I could actually feel it go. It felt like a cherry bomb detonating. I watched myself as if from the outside of me. I remember wondering how I had kept from losing it as long as I did.

"You didn't take the time to go talk to him? I can't believe you're saying that! How can you say that to me? Do you not get that a guy's life is on the line here? How would you like it if you were accused of something you didn't do, and the police had the chance to find out the truth, but they just couldn't be bothered?"

I stopped. Breathed. Stared out the window as I waited for his reaction, watching the swaying leaves. I vividly remembered sitting in this same office, watching the same trees out the window, while he questioned me in person. I would never have spoken to him that way. Then again, it's hard to be intimidated by a gun that's miles away on the other end of a telephone line.

"Hey there, buckaroo," he said, his voice heavy with sarcasm and intimidation, "I think you lost track of that respect-your-elders thing, and I'd get it back right quick if I were you. We took the time and we managed to bother. We showed up at the hospital at eight o'clock this morning to hear what he had to say, but he was gone."

The word "gone" rattled around in my gut, causing numbness in every spot it touched.

"What do you mean, 'gone'?"

"You don't know what the word 'gone' means? And here I pegged you for a halfway smart kid. Smart enough to get by, anyway. I mean sometime in the night he left the hospital against medical advice and headed for parts unknown."

At the corner of my eye I saw the assistant principal walk into the outer office and take a seat at her desk by the window. She didn't seem to notice me.

My lips felt numb, but I used them anyway.

"Why would he do that?"

She looked up then, at the sound of my voice. But she didn't rush in and take the phone away from me. She just watched me. As if an explanation for my behavior would come soon enough, and she only had to be patient.

"Sonny boy," the detective said into my ear, "I've spent my whole professional career trying to understand why men do what they do, and guess what? I'm still not there yet. Now if you'll excuse me, I got another man in handcuffs sitting here at my desk whose behavior I have to try to understand, likely to no avail. I'll just be going now."

"Okay," I said.

He hung up without saying goodbye.

I replaced the horn of the phone on its hook and walked out into the outer office, where the assistant principal still had me in her sights like a hawk watching a mouse from the trees. Laser focus. Except we didn't have lasers back then as far as I know.

"Sorry," I said. "There was no one here, and I had to call home. It was urgent."

I figured no matter what she said in return, it wouldn't matter. Even if she said, "You're in big trouble," or "You're suspended," it wouldn't matter. I had made my call, and she couldn't take it away after the fact.

"As long as it was local," she said.

I walked out without further comment.

I knew the call might come up on the phone bill at the end of the month, and that I might be in trouble then. But I had bigger problems, and I couldn't bring myself to care.

———

Dinner was a pale piece of chicken, a thigh, with the skin on but not very well cooked. It was wrinkled, and looked sickening to me. There was a dab of canned spinach beside it, looking vaguely gray, and some wax beans that might actually have been fresh.

I looked up from my plate, at each member of my family. One at a time. Nobody was speaking. Nobody was looking at anybody else.

Something burst out of me that I hadn't realized was in there, seeking its freedom.

I directed it straight at my brother, Terrence.

"You could enlist, you know."

All eyes came up to my face. Then I wondered why I had poked the bear that was my family. Why I hadn't just left well enough alone.

"He can't enlist," my mother said, sounding deeply defensive. "He's not eighteen."

"He can," I said. "He just needs you and Dad to sign off on it."

"That's not true," my mother said. "Where did you get such an idea?"

My father set down a chicken drumstick and spoke with his mouth disgustingly full. "It *is* true, Beth. He could enlist now if we let him."

"Well, we're not going to let him," she said.

My father opened his full mouth to speak again, but he never got that far. He ran into the brick wall of my mother's maternal instincts. And, believe me, there was no getting over that wall.

"No, Marv," she said, half standing. Her cloth napkin slid off her lap and onto the floor, unnoticed. "No, don't say another word. I will not allow it. I'm putting my foot down. You put your foot down all the time, over every little thing, and I never do, but I'm putting my foot down now. I will *not* have this. He's just a boy."

She hovered there a moment, looking vaguely embarrassed. Then she sank back down into her chair. She reached for her napkin, which was not surprising, as she had a bit of grease on her chin. Not finding it, she had to bend down and fish around on the floor.

"Makes no difference," my father said. "It's only four months anyway."

Those were the last words anyone spoke on the subject. The last words anyone spoke at that dinner. I tried to keep my eyes on my unappealing food, but I could see both my mother and Terrence shooting daggers at me with their eyes.

I wasn't sure what I'd thought I might accomplish by bringing it up. So of course I had no idea if I'd accomplished it. I guess I figured if someone good and kind like Ollie had to go, it didn't feel right for someone selfish and irritating like Terrence to stay home, waiting it out in safety. And maybe I was poking around to see if Ollie's theory was correct—that it's less painful to just get a thing like that over with—and if other people shared his thinking. But the whole exchange had gained me nothing. Which, in my family, was so typical that I couldn't remember why I'd even bothered to try.

———

I crouched in a corner of that damp cellar, across from Nick.

"Feeling better?" I asked.

"So much better," he said. "Those pills are really doing the trick. Well . . . not really so much better. Just a little better. But it's such a relief because now it's going in the right direction, and the worst is over. I was scared I was going to die. Get pneumonia and die."

"I was scared you were going to die, too," I said.

It was only in that moment, when I heard myself say it out loud, that I realized just how terribly afraid I had been.

"Well, I'm not. Now I know I'm not. So I feel happy tonight."

I opened my mouth, knowing I was about to slam the lid on his happiness. But I had information that I couldn't in good conscience keep from him any longer.

"I have a bunch of things to tell you," I said.

I waited there for his reply. He must have known by the way I said it that it wasn't happy news, and I felt as though I needed his consent to keep talking.

"Okay," he said.

"I would have told you sooner, but you were so sick. I figured you had enough on your mind, just getting through it."

"Go ahead and tell me," he said. "Because this is making me nervous."

"I know where your mom lives."

Silence. Stunning silence.

"How? How do you know that if I don't even know?"

"Your dad told me. I went to see your dad in jail because I wanted to get an answer for you. You asked me why he would do a thing like that, and I wanted to get you an answer. He told me your mom lives in Mesa, Arizona. And that there's a chance she might take you in, now that you're old enough to do for yourself."

In the silence that followed, I wondered if I had really put off telling him because he'd been sick. Or if I hadn't wanted to tell him because, once he knew, he might go.

"What if she wouldn't, though?" His voice had grown small again. It sounded the way it had when he was sick as a dog and afraid of dying. Like a small, scared boy.

"I think there's a bigger problem than that. I think the police would look for you there."

"Oh," he said. "Right."

"And there's another thing I have to tell you. Kind of good news and bad news. It's about that guy. The one your father put in a coma. The good news is, he didn't die. He woke up. The bad news is, he took off before anybody could ask him what happened."

We sat in silence for a bizarre length of time. It could literally have been five or ten minutes. I could practically hear his brain turning, trying to process all this new information. I figured the least I could do was leave him alone to try.

"Wow," he said, and his voice startled me. "I had no idea there was so much going on up above. It seemed so quiet underground where I was. That's more stuff than usually happens in a year around here. I figured you were just bored like we always were."

"Actually, there's more."

"Whoa."

"Can you manage more?"

"I guess. Go ahead and tell me."

"Ollie's enlisting."

"Now?"

"Pretty much now."

"Not when he's eighteen?"

"No. Pretty much now."

He fell quiet for a few seconds. I felt as though he was chewing over what I'd just told him. It was hard to hear a thing like that without putting yourself in Ollie's shoes. Trying to imagine if you'd make the same decision.

"We're lucky we're fourteen," he said.

"I know."

"Think the war'll be over by the time we turn eighteen?"

"No idea. I guess we just have to hope so."

He coughed for a time instead of talking. It still sounded like the cough was trying to turn him inside out.

Then he said, "Did you at least find out why?"

But by then I had lost track of which part of the thing he would have been focused on.

"Why which?"

"Why my dad did that to me."

"Oh. That. Well, he didn't say straight-out. But I got the sense that he really does care about you, but he's scared. It's like he woke up after a hard night of drinking and realized he'd gotten himself into more trouble than he was prepared to face."

"So he decided to make me face it for him."

"I know it's not fair."

Another long silence.

Then Nick said, "Well, I guess I'm here for the long haul, then."

"It's not much to have for the long haul. Just a damp root cellar."

"Better than what I'd have without it. Besides. After a few months they'll give up looking for me. And then maybe I can sneak off to my mom's."

The words cut like a jagged saw blade, but I buried my reaction away again. At least he wasn't leaving *now*.

I opened my mouth to speak, but just then we heard a noise. Like a thumping against the outside wall of the shed. Like someone had taken their fist and pounded once on the door or the siding. I heard Nick suck in a sharp breath, maybe too loudly.

"Blow out the lantern," I hissed.

He did, and we sat trembling in the dark. For how long, it would be impossible to say. Seconds? Hours? There was someone out there. Maybe even several someones. We could hear it. We could feel the vibrations of their footsteps on the ground where we sat.

I could barely keep my heart swallowed down. I swear I could hear its panicky hammering. It pulsed in my ears.

I wanted to tell Nick I wasn't sorry. Even though someone would come down in a second and drag us out of here. Even though I would now end up in reform school just as surely as he would. I was scared, sure, but if I had it to do over, I would help him again. But I didn't say it, because I didn't dare say a word. I just sat there, wanting him to know.

A ridiculous amount of time passed. It felt like the universe was playing with us. Tormenting us, the way a cat tortures a bird or a mouse before he ends its life.

No one opened the door. No one came down.

Nick leaned over until I could feel the brush of his warm breath against my ear. "Should we go look?" he asked, with almost no volume at all.

My first thought was *No. We shouldn't. Someone's out there, and we shouldn't do anything at all.* Maybe they were unaware of a basement under the shed. Maybe their presence had nothing to do with us.

Maybe we could wait it out.

But if the sun came up while we were waiting . . . that was a whole other form of getting caught.

"I'll go," I breathed.

I made my way up the ladder steps in almost perfect silence. Crept to the door. I could hear some brushing sounds outside, but nothing more. The door had been left just barely ajar when I came in, which was lucky. I pressed the pads of my fingers against it. Pushed it open maybe half an inch.

A steer looked up at me with blank eyes, his jaw working.

I pushed the door open a little farther, and saw about twenty head of cattle milling around outside the shed.

"Nick," I called, breathing freely for the first time in what felt like forever. "You have to come see this."

He met me at the door, and together we stepped out into the night. It was a blindingly clear night, with every square inch of sky cluttered with the faint pinpoints of thousands of stars I could only barely see. It looked like a rough texture of light on darkness.

"I didn't know your father ran cattle," he said.

"He doesn't. Must be a fence down somewhere."

"Whoa," he said. "I thought that was it for us. I thought we were cooked."

Meanwhile the cattle had begun to give us grudging looks and move farther away to graze.

We sat down behind the east side of the shed, our backs up against the wall, enjoying the view of the mountains and the stars. Enjoying our lives not being effectively over. I never answered his comment about thinking we were cooked. But I knew the feeling wasn't about to leave us. Just because it turned out this wasn't our moment, that didn't make it all better. We knew now how it felt to be cooked. The real moment may have been postponed, but it felt inevitable.

I didn't address any of that. It was too awful.

"Maybe I could find the guy," I said, but it was a stupid thing to say. Also completely out of context.

"What guy?"

"The guy who woke up from his coma and took off."

"That would be good, but I have no idea how you could do that."

"No. Neither do I."

I was wondering if, with his father in jail for years and no legal pressure on his own head, Nick would still go off to his mom's. Or if he'd stay around here. With me.

"If there's a fence down," he said, jumping topics again, "you should go tell somebody. Won't they start eating the crops?"

"Yeah. I'm sure they will. But I can't tell anybody. How can I? How am I supposed to say I found out? I'm supposed to be in bed asleep."

"Oh. That's right."

I looked around the side of the shed and watched the cattle lazily move off in the direction of the almond orchard, which was anything but good news.

"Don't worry about that guy," Nick said. "If he doesn't turn up . . . if I have to stay here for months, I just will. You'll make sure I don't starve."

There was a lot packed into those two sentences. A kind of desperate reaching. A request for assurance that I would take care of him. And, at the same time, a whiff of resistance to being taken care of, as he'd expressed the previous night when he'd admitted it was "weird."

"Of course I will," I said. "But it still seems like a hard place to live for months."

"No better choices." Then a tentative silence. Then, "Hey. You're a good guy to risk all this for me."

"I'd risk anything for you," I said.

I was hoping it would trigger a deeper discussion of our feelings. It didn't.

That was the last we spoke of his options—such as they were—for a strangely long time.

Part Two

Early 1942

Chapter Ten

The Other Side of the Mountains

Suki's dad drove us up into the Sierras. At least, as far as a truck can go into those mountains. We were not headed to the same trailhead as before. We were not cruising up to a mountain lake for pleasure. There was a pass in the Sierras that would allow us to crest, and get a good look down into the Owens Valley below. The eastern side of the mountains. This was a serious exploration, a fact-finding trip of some importance.

I could feel the difference in the mood. There was gravity everywhere. The literal kind, of course. But also the other, more intimidating kind.

We bounced up that dirt road in the pitch dark, in the wee hours of the morning. Suki and I rode up front in the cab with his dad, our big packs behind us in the truck's bed.

It was just the two of us going. Ollie was finishing up basic training and about to head overseas. Nick was still hiding in my root cellar, that weekend with an extra-large supply of water and food. He had been growing pale and losing weight and muscle mass, and I was worried about him. I hated going away and leaving him, even for a couple of days. But that weekend my friend Suki needed me, too.

Suki was sitting in the middle, between his father and me. I had my elbow resting on the edge of the window pocket. The metal felt cold through the sleeve of my shirt.

"Your truck looks great, Mr. Yamamoto," I said, to break the figurative ice of the moment.

His face twitched into the closest thing to a smile I had seen that morning. "Thank you, Steven!" he said.

He didn't talk often, so I was absurdly flattered.

In January he had painted his pickup, or had it professionally painted. I wasn't sure which. No more two-tone. It was now a beautiful deep maroon all over. It was a top-notch paint job. I couldn't see much of it now, in the dark, but when they had first picked me up, under one of the only two streetlights in town, I had marveled at its beauty.

I peered ahead in the dark, wishing I could see farther than the beam of the headlights. I had no idea how much of that road was passable before the winter snows melted off. But I was heavily invested in finding out. This would be a strenuous hike, no matter where he dropped us. I wanted the drive to go on forever.

But in time the snow built up under the tires on the rutted dirt. The first time we felt the truck skid in the deep powder, I knew we were walking from there.

"Ki o tsukete," Mr. Yamamoto said.

I knew what it meant. I really hadn't learned much Japanese, if any. But that one phrase I had learned, and had not forgotten. I couldn't have forgotten it if I'd tried. It was burned into my brain, as if by one of those leather branding tools.

Be careful.

The only difference between his statement and the months-earlier warning from Mr. Ito is that he did not tack on the name Itsuki at the end of the sentence. In other words, he seemed to be concerned for both of us.

—

I hiked behind Suki up the snowy trail, my load heavy on my back. When you have four guys hiking and camping, the load is not four times heavier. There's still just one tent. One flashlight. One cook pot. Plus we had to bring snowshoes, which were currently on our backs, and my father's big binoculars. As a result, we were each carrying far more, and climbing far higher.

I followed him without complaint.

In my jacket pocket was a letter from Ollie. I had gotten a letter, and Suki had gotten one, on the same day. The day before we were to leave for this hike. We had agreed to bring them along. And we had agreed that later, by our campfire, I would read him my letter. He would read me his.

"We're lucky," he said. I was guessing it was an hour into the hike. It was the first he had spoken as we climbed. "There wasn't too much snow this year."

We had both known, going in, that too much snow could turn us back before we reached the pass.

"Plus we had those really warm days," I said, raising my voice because I was several steps behind him. "That might have melted it off some."

"I doubt it," he said. "I doubt it got very warm *up here.*"

We came around a bend in the trail, and he stopped. And I caught up to him, and stopped just behind his left shoulder.

He pointed up.

"There it is," he said.

"That's the pass?"

"Yeah. And it looks pretty clear."

I swallowed hard. That little keyhole between the imposing peaks was miles away, and thousands of feet above where we stood. It seemed unimaginable to have to carry our loads all the way up there. But Suki needed me to do it, and I would do it.

"I don't know if there's a place to camp up there at the pass," he said. "I can't remember."

He turned his body sideways on the narrow trail and leaned back on a snowy boulder in such a way that it supported his heavy pack. I did the same.

"What if there isn't?"

"It's probably best if we don't camp where we can be seen from the valley anyway. Not that anybody would see us that far away unless they were scanning the mountains with really strong binoculars. But if we made a campfire, that would be seen. That would draw attention. I figure we'll cross over and get a good look, and then we'll backtrack and camp on the western side for the night."

We leaned a while longer, for no reason I could identify, other than the fact that a rest was nice now and then. Except . . . I had the sense that maybe his mind was busy, and that he would rather wait and move his feet after it quieted down some.

"Looks like we won't have to use the snowshoes," he said, "or won't have to use them much. That's a relief. I wasn't looking forward to your finding out how it feels to walk on snowshoes on such a steep trail. If you step just wrong, it's a little bit like trying to get up the side of the mountain on skis."

We leaned for another minute or so. I could feel his words jangling around in my belly.

"Well," he said. "Let's go."

I set off hiking behind him. Not thirty seconds later I ran into his back. He had his left arm out to stop me, but I missed it and plowed into his pack, nearly bowling him over.

"Wait," he said.

"What?"

"There's somebody hiking down the pass."

I looked over his shoulder, and at first I saw nothing. Then I saw a flash of two bright-red vests pop out from behind a string of boulders. At the distance they looked like two bouncing red dots.

"Hunters?" I asked.

"Probably."

"What do we do?"

"Let's just wait and see where they go. There's a trail junction a few hundred feet underneath them. Heads south, toward Visalia. If we're lucky, they'll take it. If not, we'll go off trail and stay quiet till they're gone."

We stood, hearts pounding, waiting to see which way they would go. At least, my heart was pounding. I couldn't imagine his was calm. He was the one with the most to lose.

It's not that we had no right to be where we were. Anybody could trek around in the Sierras if they had the skill and the guts to do it. But Suki was a Japanese boy. And I was a white boy consorting with a Japanese boy. The farther we got from civilization, and the more there was no one around to witness, the more likely we were to pay for our perceived transgressions at the hands of strangers.

Suki spoke, knocking me out of my fearful imaginings.

"They took the cutoff," he said.

I could hear us both release deep sighs of air not previously exhaled.

We took off walking again. Immediately I felt my lungs and my heart strain in the thin mountain air.

I was looking for a return to relaxed normalcy, I think. So I small-talked. Just to clear the air of our recent fright.

"Your dad must be really proud of that truck," I said.

"Oh, he is. It's his most prized possession." A few steps. Then he added, "Other than his family, I mean. Not that we're possessions, I just meant—"

"I knew what you meant."

We puffed up the trail for a time. I was thinking we would say no more about it.

Then he volunteered more.

"Before he left Japan, he had a lot. I mean, his family had a lot. He was used to having nice things. But since then it's been harder. He's had to struggle for every little thing he gets."

"Why did he come?" I asked.

It hit my ears wrong, like a dumb thing to say. I was hoping it hadn't sounded as bad to him.

"He didn't have much choice," Suki said. "He was seven."

I was tempted to ask why his grandparents had pulled up stakes and left so much behind. But it didn't feel like my business, and I didn't want to pry. I felt like one of those typical white boys who didn't understand a thing. Who didn't even know, until a Japanese boy told me, that his family was not allowed citizenship. Maybe he wouldn't have minded my trying to learn. But I felt intimidated by my own ignorance, sure that every word out of my mouth would be a mistake.

I followed him in silence, all the way up to that mountain pass.

———

"There it is," Suki said.

We hunkered down into a squat, resting on our heels. We slipped off our packs and let them sink onto the snowy trail.

Below us, in the far distance, a tiny patch on the long, flat Owens Valley, we could clearly see something major being built. Strings of long buildings. Row upon row of them. Blocks of rows, like Morse code in the desert soil, but with all dashes.

"It's true," I said. "I was hoping it wasn't true."

That was not entirely accurate, what I said. I knew there was a camp under construction. I would have been surprised to hear it was nothing but a cruel joke. I guess what I had been trying to say is that hearing about something feels entirely different from seeing it with your own eyes.

I dug out my father's binoculars and handed them over to Suki without looking through them myself. I wanted to look. But I felt he had the right to look first. To me it was just a dark curiosity. Nobody was about to force me to live there.

He looked through them for a long time in silence. Not that I would expect him to be chatty at a time like that.

In time I asked, "Who's building it? The army?"

I used "army" as an inexact term, because in that moment I could not remember the phrase "War Relocation Authority." There hadn't been a War Relocation Authority until after FDR signed that damned order for Japanese exclusion. Maybe I kept forgetting what to call it because I didn't want there to be one now.

"No, a bunch of Issei and Nisei volunteered to go over and do the construction."

The Issei were people like Suki's parents. Japanese-born immigrants who were not citizens because nobody gave them the chance to try. Nisei was the name for Suki's generation. American-born citizens. As if that mattered to the government now.

"*Why?*" I asked, shifting my weight around on my sore legs.

"Why did they volunteer to build it?"

"Right. That."

He let the binoculars drift down from his eyes. Allowed them to hang at the end of his hand, between his heels. "Not sure. Maybe they thought they'd get points for being helpful. Or maybe they're like Ollie. Maybe when they know something is out there, hanging over their heads, they'd rather just jump in and get it over with."

He was still not using the binoculars, so I reached my hand out toward them.

"Can I see?"

He reached them out to me without answering.

I held them up to my eyes and watched the tiny ant-sized figures at work. With the help of that magnification, I could see several more lots leveled, but not yet built upon, and I knew that the blocks of barracks I was seeing were only the beginning.

I scanned around a bit. Saw power poles going up, and posts at the margins of the property that I figured would be strung with wire to form a fence. I could think of no other way for evenly spaced poles to become a fence. They were too far apart to place boards in between. I imagined wire with vicious barbs, even though there was nothing there yet.

"If you have to go, are you sure you'll be sent *there*?"

"No. Not sure. They don't tell you. And they don't always send you to the closest ones, either. Our next-door neighbors left with the volunteer order, and they got put in Santa Anita."

"The racetrack? Maybe that's better."

"It's a bunch of horse stalls. Used horse stalls."

"Oh," I said.

I scanned around some more with the binoculars, feeling slightly queasy. My eyes came to rest on two wooden towers at the front edge of the property, closest to the road that snaked through the valley. There was a third under construction. Board bases filled with *x* shapes of wood, and a railed platform at the top, where it seemed a gunner would be stationed.

My belly went cold with the sight of them.

"Are those *guard towers*?"

"Seem to be," he said. His voice had grown lifeless and dull.

"Why do they need guard towers? None of you did anything wrong."

"That might not actually be too bad," he said. "They're saying one of the reasons to send us there is so there won't be violence against us. Maybe the guard towers are for us. You know. With the guns pointed out. To keep us safe, not to keep everybody safe from us."

"I sure hope so," I said.

He reached for the binoculars, and I gave them back. For ten or fifteen minutes I just watched him watch. Neither one of us said a word. Really, what more could a person say at a moment like that?

———

We hunkered in front of the campfire, on the western side of the pass, warming our hands. We had found a spot far enough off the trail to be invisible to any passersby, though there had been none. We had cleared it of snow as much as we could, using the snowshoes as shovels. They were not very good shovels.

We sat on our rubber pads for warmth, and to keep the moisture from soaking through our pants.

Suki took out his letter from Ollie, carefully unfolding its pages.

"'Dear Suki,'" he began out loud, the firelight flickering on his face.

"'We just finished basic training, and tomorrow we get on a supply ship carrying troops and equipment to the Pacific theater of the war. First stop they say is New Guinea. I've heard some pretty scary stories about the place, but I guess every place is scary during a war.

"'I think I figured out the purpose of basic training. I mean, other than the obvious—being able to shoot the gun they give you and such. I think the point is to make your life so hard that, after you're done, even combat feels like a step in the right direction.

"'It feels really strange to think about going off to fight the Japanese. I know it needs to be done, and I know the Imperial Army is not the same as you and the other folks I know from California. But I think the way they get us to go over there and be ready to kill somebody is to convince us that the enemy is not really human like us. But that's not working on me. I think of looking down the barrel of my gun at an enemy soldier, and I'm not sure what makes them so very different from you and your family. Or from me, for that matter. I know they have guns and will try to kill us, but we have guns and we'll try to kill them, so that's not really helping me tell us apart.

"'I'm a little bit ashamed to admit that I haven't told anybody about these doubts. And it's not because I'm ashamed to feel that way, or that I think I'm wrong. More that it's their job to convince me, so the more I say I'm not buying it yet, the more they'll scream at me and whomp on me to get me there. It's just one of those things you tend to keep to yourself just for mostly practical reasons.

"'I miss you and Steven, and of course I miss Nick, but I'd miss him even if I was home. Damn, I wish I was home, not on my way to New Guinea. How long can a war last, do you think? That's not a real question. When you write back, you don't have to answer it. There's a word for that kind of question, but I can't remember it, and when I asked some of the other guys if they knew what I meant, they just stared at me like I was speaking in tongues.

"'Maybe go by if you get a chance and see how my parents are doing. Or, I don't know. Maybe your family has enough going on without my problems, and then maybe Steven can. But just if you can manage.

"'Pray for me, if you pray. Funny, but in all the time I knew you, I never thought to ask.

"'Your friend, Ollie.'"

It was so different from mine, that letter. It felt good to hear words that seemed to carry Ollie's voice. It made me feel less alone.

Granted I was there with Suki, but Suki was about to be gone. I had Nick waiting for me at home, but Nick was about to be gone, too. I knew any day could be the day he announced that he had waited long enough. That they had likely stopped looking for him, and it would be safe to run to Mesa, Arizona, to look for his mother.

It made me a little sick to think about that brand of aloneness, so I pushed the thought deeply into hiding again. But it bothered me even from there.

"Rhetorical," I said.

"Right," Suki said. "That's what I was thinking, too. He meant a rhetorical question. Read me yours now."

I had been so lost in thought that I'd forgotten he was waiting.

"'Dear Steven,'" I began.

"'I finished basic training. I complained about it in my letter to Suki, but maybe too much. Yeah, it's hard. That's no joke. But there was this part of me that got along with it okay. The things they want you to do, like keeping your boots shined and your bed made just so, they made sense to me. It felt like something that I was better off knowing than not. Maybe because my dad taught me stuff like that, just in a much nicer tone of voice.

"'Tomorrow I get on a ship. It's going to take us a few days to get where we're going, which they say is New Guinea, and I still haven't decided whether I should tell them I get very, very seasick. Part of me thinks I should, because maybe they have some kind of medicine to hand out, but another part of me thinks their idea of seasick medicine is pointing you over to the rail so you miss the deck and nobody has to mop after you. It probably sounds like it can't hurt to ask, but in my short experience so far, it seems like it can. I've gone a long way just by thinking things I never say out loud.

"'If you get a chance, maybe go by and see my folks and check if they're doing okay. I asked Suki that just now in my letter to him, but then right away I felt bad, like I wish I hadn't asked. Maybe his family has enough problems of their own.

"'And if you see Nick, ask him if he's thought about enlisting. I'm not saying you'll see him, but just if you do. I wonder if he's thought about joining up, wherever he is, because if you're alive and willing to jump in there, I don't think they ask a lot of questions. I know he's only fourteen, but he looks older, being so big and all. I've met a lot of guys so far who lied about their age and nobody called them on it.

"'Pray for me, Steven, if you pray. Funny how you never think to ask your friends questions like that. I'm not sure if I ever even thought to ask myself. And then suddenly there's a war, and you're headed right for it, and then it seems to matter a whole lot.

"'Write back when you can.

"'Your friend, Ollie.'"

We sat in silence for a time. I could feel the muscles in my legs begin to stiffen up. The fire had died down some, and there were no more fairly dry limbs to feed it to keep it going. I knew we would have to retire into the tent soon, and use the sleeping bags for warmth.

"I'm going to say something," Suki said. "I've been wanting to say it for a long time. Don't say anything back. I mean, you can. But you don't have to. I'm not judging you. It's just right there, and it's been right there for so long, and now I feel like I have to say it."

A very brief silence fell. I wanted to urge him to go ahead and blurt it out, because the waiting was killing me. But I was too frozen in fear. I opened my mouth but no words came out.

"I know you know where Nick is," he said.

For a minute, a full minute, I just absorbed the blow—the way a person who's been punched in the stomach will need some time to straighten up and breathe again. I thought of Ollie, in his letter, writing, "I'm not saying you'll see him, but just if you do." Did he know, too?

"How do you know that? I mean . . . why would you say that?"

"Don't take this the wrong way, Steven, but you're a very bad liar. That's actually a compliment. You don't want to be a good liar, right? Being bad at it just means you're not really a liar at the heart of things, so when you try to do it, it's obvious you haven't had enough practice. Whenever you talk like you don't know where he is, you always look uncomfortable. You always look away. I'm not going to tell anybody. I just had to tell you that I know. It hurt my feelings at first. I've known him so much longer than you, and he told you things he didn't tell me. That stung for a while. But then I decided . . . I figured he didn't really dare tell anybody, but he had no choice but to tell you. I haven't forgotten what you said to us that day. That you could hide us. Either one of us. Anyway, I know you probably promised to keep his secret. Don't even tell him I said all this. I just had to spit it out. We're friends, and it feels weird not to talk about that with you."

"We *are* friends," I said. "I never wanted to lie to you. I'm sorry."

"It's okay," he said.

"Is it really?"

"Well, it is and it isn't. But you've been a good friend, and I know you're trying your best."

"Thank you."

We sat in silence for a time, leaning closer and closer to the dying fire. Then Suki said, "I'm cold. I'm going inside."

We put ourselves to bed, wrapped tightly and shivering, in our individual sleeping bags.

I thought our conversation, and my look at that half-constructed camp, would keep me up until dawn. But I was exhausted from the exertion of the hiking, and sleep took me almost immediately, and held me down all night.

Chapter Eleven

Fool's Paradise Lost

There were a few similarities between my two trips to the mountains, but many more differences. I hiked up. Suki was there. It was the Sierras. That's about it for similarities. The differences seemed to be just about everything else imaginable.

But when we got back down, I was smacked with that same sense that the world had utterly fallen apart in our absence, and that we had been living in a fool's paradise for a day or two longer than everybody else. It was almost enough to make you never want to go into the mountains again.

Suki's dad was waiting for us on the road, a little higher up than he had managed to make it on the first trip. We settled our heavy packs into the truck's bed and climbed into the cab, Suki going first to sit next to his father.

We headed downhill toward the sparse lights of town with only the headlights to guide us. It was probably barely seven in the evening, but it was dark.

Suki and his father had a long, subdued conversation, but not a word of it was in English. Maybe it's wrong to call it a conversation, because the only person who spoke was Suki. His father listened, offering only an occasional noise in his throat, a kind of resigned grunt, as a reaction to what he was hearing.

It didn't take a genius to figure out that Suki was reporting to his father everything we had seen through the binoculars. Every detail of the camp that might soon hold them behind barbed wire.

We eventually pulled out onto the flat, wide dirt road heading into town, and rode in absolute silence toward home. And when I say absolute silence . . . well, it's hard to explain. It might sound strange to say it this way, but it was more silent than any silence I'd heard in my life, even growing up with my family. Which was pretty damned silent.

Town seemed fairly deserted as we rumbled along the main drag.

Then Suki shot an arm out across his father's chest, as if to prevent all forward motion, and he spoke quick, shocked words. "Otōsan. Yamete! Bakku suru!"

Mr. Yamamoto pressed hard on the brake pedal, then shifted into reverse. I could hear the transmission groan and grind slightly as the gears meshed. The truck rumbled in reverse for a hundred feet or so, then stopped.

We sat there in the middle of the road, doing nothing. Saying nothing. I glanced over at Suki, and his face was a solid block of stone. He was staring at something, transfixed. But I had no idea what he was seeing. All I saw was a grouping of the small houses that crowded onto the huge dirt lots behind the business section of town. There was a long gap between the general store and the tavern, and we were staring through it at a clump of small homes.

"What are we looking at?" I asked Suki.

For a moment he sat in stony silence. Then he seemed to rouse himself to speak. "That's Ollie's house," he said.

"Which one?"

I should have known. I had been there twice, both times after dark. I had met his father briefly. Frankly, all of those little shack-like homes looked alike to me. I had followed Ollie to his house, but I had never had to identify it on my own.

Suki pointed.

The little house had a light glowing in the window, behind drawn curtains. In front of the curtains, secured to the inside of the glass, I saw a gold star.

"No," I said.

"Get out," he said. "We have to get out."

We stepped out into the cool night. We walked toward the house as if in a dream.

"It can't be," I said. "It's impossible. He just got there. He hadn't even seen any combat yet."

"I think those letters take a long time to get to us."

"Oh. I hadn't thought of that."

Weirdly, I hadn't. I felt as though I had talked to Ollie as recently as the night before, by the campfire. How old was the news he had written down for us?

"Maybe he has a brother," I said.

It was a desperate last chance. The minute it was out of my mouth I knew he didn't have a brother. On that ride into Fresno to see Nick's father in jail, he had asked about my brother. If I loved him. He had told me he was an only child.

And when I thought about that drive, it reminded me what a good guy Ollie was. Which was unfortunate timing.

"He doesn't," Suki said.

And then, suddenly, through some unexplained trick of time, we were standing on the door stoop. I heard Suki rap on the door, and the sound rattled in my gut as if he were knocking directly on my intestines.

The door opened, and Ollie's father stood in the open doorway. He looked at Suki, then at me. Then he sobbed openly.

He embraced Suki. "Suki," he said. "Dear Suki." He stepped side-ways away from Suki and embraced me, where I stood stunned and stupid on the tiny porch. "Steven," he said into my ear.

"What happened?"

"Torpedo," he said.

I didn't quite know what he meant, but I was afraid to ask for more explanation. As it turned out, I didn't need to ask. He volunteered it.

"He was on a supply ship headed for the South Pacific, and the ship was hit."

He stepped back into the doorway, and I stood frozen, feeling my brain and gut tingling. I believe it was just dawning on me in that moment that all of this was happening. Genuinely happening. That it would never unhappen.

I vaguely heard Suki and Mr. Franklin speaking to each other, but it seemed far away and impossible to follow. I know he asked about Mrs. Franklin. Mr. Franklin said the doctor had come by and given her a sedative, and she was sleeping it off in bed. I think Suki asked how long they had known, because Ollie's father told the story of the soldiers coming to their door. It had been just that morning. Ollie's mother had fainted dead away at the sight of them. Before they could even open their mouths to speak.

Meanwhile my brain was running through all the reasons it could not possibly be true, and upgrading my opinion of the dangers of war. We had just spoken to him, in a manner of speaking. He hadn't even arrived at the actual war yet. We were sitting eating lunch with him not two months ago.

I had known that war could kill you. What kind of idiot doesn't know that? But I'd imagined it more as a place where you arrive, fight several battles, and maybe—if you're unlucky—you could be hurt or killed in one of them. The fifth, maybe, or the sixth. But how can a war kill you when you hadn't even managed to arrive at it yet?

I came back to the moment, standing helplessly on the stoop. There was a lull in the conversation, so I asked, "When was his birthday?"

"June," his father said.

In that exact moment I changed a great deal of my views about the world. I changed the way I would navigate through the world for all of time.

If Ollie had waited for his birthday, my brain told me, he would have avoided that torpedo. Granted, it was simplistic thinking, because that was no guarantee he would have come home anyway. But brains are what they are, and they take what it's their nature to take from any given situation, and at a very deep level. I guess it's the caveman part of us, some deep reactionary section of our brain stem telling us where we'll be eaten by a dinosaur and where we'll be safe.

From that moment forward, it would be my solid habit to put off any unwanted task until the very last moment. Until I felt my toes up against the deadline, and I had not one more second to postpone the inevitable. And no amount of logic could ever shake that habit. It was a part of me, beginning in that instant, with the one-word answer to that question.

June.

It's a part of me to this day.

—

We climbed back into the truck, and Mr. Yamamoto set off toward my family's farm. He asked no questions. He must have seen the gold star in the window. He must have known.

He patted Suki's knee affectionately, but said not a word.

Now, if they had been going straight to their own house, rather than going on to take me home, they would have turned off a block earlier. I mention this as a way of explaining how Mr. Yamamoto had joined us in our fool's paradise until the moment I'm about to describe.

That is, why he hadn't seen the crowd and the posted notice on the way to pick us up.

We drove past the post office. Around the corner, on the dirt side street, we saw a crowd. Maybe thirty people. They were all Japanese—every single one as far as I could tell. They were crowded around the bulletin board on the side of the post office building, jostling and pushing to get close enough to read a notice posted there, under a flickering light.

Mr. Yamamoto swung an unexpected turn and stopped the truck on the other side of the road from the gathering.

"Kokoni ite," he said firmly to Suki, and maybe to me as well.

Even though I spoke no Japanese, I knew enough to sit still while he got out, leaving the engine running, and crossed the street. His tone of voice was a universal language.

Suki and I waited in absolute stunned silence.

The posted notice had a large headline, designed to grab attention, and then several paragraphs of very small print below. The headline was big enough to read from where we sat.

INSTRUCTIONS TO ALL PERSONS OF
JAPANESE ANCESTRY

The word "Japanese" was huge. I felt as though I could read it looking down from the window of a low-flying plane.

I wanted to say something to Suki. Something comforting. The kind of thing a friend will say to his good friend in such a moment, to offer support. But I might as well have been mute. My whole body felt immobile, and no words came.

In time Mr. Yamamoto walked back to the truck and climbed in. He did not immediately shift the truck into gear and drive. He did not immediately speak.

After that brief pause he spoke for about thirty seconds in Japanese. I couldn't understand what was being said, so I watched Suki's face to see how the news was being received. I watched him squeeze his eyes shut.

His father ran out of words and shifted into gear, driving toward my home.

"We have a week," Suki said on a long sigh. For my benefit, of course. "One week. We can only take what we can carry. No pets of any kind."

I knew Suki's grandmother had an older, beloved little terrier bitch. It might sound strange or harsh to use that word, but that's what you called a female dog back then. I didn't know what would happen to her. I thought about Mr. Yamamoto's beautiful, freshly painted truck. Would it be safely waiting for him when the family was allowed to come home?

Would the family be allowed to come home?

Much to my shame, I never managed to utter a word. We drove to my house in perfect silence.

———

My mother was sitting up waiting for me when I stepped through the door. She was on the couch, drink in hand, cigarette burning in the ashtray, waiting to blast me. I could see it on her face.

"What's this I hear about you palling around with some Jap boy?"

I stood for a second or two, blinking. My initial thought, quite frankly, was not to be surprised that she had heard about it. It was to be surprised she had not heard sooner. The people of this little town had been seeing me with Suki for months. Most of them must have thought better of reporting me to my mother. It seemed strange to have waited so many months to run afoul of the good graces of our neighbors.

"Don't call him that," I said.

I didn't raise my voice. I spoke softly but firmly. I probably sounded calm, but I wasn't calm. I was just too physically and emotionally exhausted to raise a bigger fuss.

"Call him what?"

"You know."

"Jap? That's what he is. What else would I call a Jap?"

"Try *Japanese*," I said. "It's only two more syllables. Won't take too much time out of your busy schedule."

She rose to her feet and loomed in front of me, whiskey glass in one hand, cigarette in the other. "Are you sassing me?" she asked in her don't-mess-with-me voice.

"I don't know," I said. "I don't care. I just don't want to hear any disrespect for my friends. One of them just died in the war. One of them is being locked up in a camp In a week. What difference does it make what you thought about them—if you thought they were the right sort of friends or not? They're gone."

"The stain on our family's reputation is not gone."

"You told me you wouldn't stop me from being friends with who-ever I wanted."

"And you told me they were all American."

"He *is* an American. He was born here. He's a citizen."

She leaned closer to my face, her breath smelling of tobacco and booze. "He's a Jap," she said.

"If you say that one more time . . ." But the sentence had no proper ending. I couldn't physically threaten my own mother.

"What? If I say it again, you'll do what?"

"Nothing. I don't know. I don't know what you want from me. You want me to go back and change the past? Well, I've got news for you. If I could, I'd be friends with him all over again."

"You. Are. Grounded," she said, each word its own terse sentence.

"Fine," I said. "Who cares? I have no friends to go around with anyway."

I walked to my room and left her standing there, fuming.

I stopped in the bathroom and drank quarts of water from the tap on the bathroom sink. Because I wanted to wake up in a few hours, and because I was thirsty.

As I was going to sleep, I thought about all the disasters that had been waiting for me every time I hiked down from those mountains. I wasn't really deluded enough to blame the mountains. But, in a strange form of magical thinking, I remember feeling that the world needed me to stay close to home and keep a good eye on it at all times. The minute I turned my back, terrible things happened.

I would simply have to be more vigilant.

———

I found Nick sitting out behind the shed at a little after two.

"Nicky," I said.

I had never called him that before. I was feeling desperate. I expected him to hear that in my voice, but it didn't seem like he did.

"Glad you're back," he said. "I missed you."

"I missed you, too."

I didn't sit with him. I stood leaning my shoulder on the wooden trim at the corner of the outbuilding, staring off at those mountains. Wishing I didn't have to tell him all the things I had to tell him.

"You're awful quiet," he said. "Was it really terrible?"

For one brief, uneasy moment, I thought he was reading my mind.

"Was what really terrible?"

"Did you see that camp they say they're building?"

"Oh. Yeah. We saw it. It's pretty bad. It has guard towers."

"Like with guns?"

"Well, there were no guns that we could see. But it's not finished yet. It looked like it was set up for big guns. Suki says maybe the guns will be to protect *them*. Not to protect everybody *from* them. Like maybe they'll be pointed out at the world, so nobody can get any big ideas about going after Japanese families. But I don't know. He has a week, Nick. Suki and his family have a week. One week. They can only take what they can carry."

"What happens to everything else they own?"

"No idea."

We stood and sat, respectively, watching Orion hover over our world. The hunter had moved quite a bit in the intervening months. He was no longer low in the east, over the mountains. Now he was much farther west, depending on the lateness of the hour, and angled more downward, toward the western horizon. I watched the way the constellation's shoulders seemed to align with his starry bow, pointing downward. I had a strange thought. Maybe *we* were the hunted. Maybe he looked down over the world, singled out Ollie, drew back his bow . . . I knew what I was thinking wasn't literally true, but the world felt unfriendly in that moment, and the great starry hunter looked like an unfriendly part of it. Fate seemed to hover above us, waiting to take one of us out.

"Nicky," I said again.

This time he seemed to catch the desperation.

"What? What's wrong, Steven?"

"Ollie's gone."

To my surprise, I heard a sound come from his chest that sounded like a short bark of a laugh.

"Well, of course Ollie's gone. He's been in basic training for weeks."

I didn't answer right away.

Looking back, I think he halfway knew. I don't think he entirely thought I meant "Ollie is gone from our neighborhood." I think he knew it was something worse, but he wanted—just for another few precious seconds—to live in a world where it wasn't. I could be wrong. It's hard to know about the insides of other people.

He seemed to read my silence. He jumped to his feet and stood with his face a few inches from mine, and, even so, we could still only barely see each other in the faint starlight.

I shook my head, opened my mouth to speak . . . and cried. I hadn't seen it coming, either. I just surrendered myself to whatever was about to emerge, and it was tears—the first tears I could remember crying since I was a much younger child. At any time prior to that moment I would have been horrified by the idea of anyone seeing me cry. In that moment, it couldn't have mattered less.

I felt his chest bang roughly into mine. He threw his arms around me.

"Steven, no," he said near my ear.

I held him in return and didn't try to answer.

"How? Why? He wasn't even over there yet. Was he?"

"He was on a ship, headed there, and it got hit by a torpedo."

We stood there wrapped in each other's arms for a time, saying nothing more. I could feel his ribs. He was wasting away from not enough food or sunlight, combined with too much worry.

He let go of me suddenly and backed up a step.

"I won't leave, then," he said.

"Were you about to leave?"

"I was thinking about it while you were gone, yeah. I'd rather be here with you. I don't even really know my mom. I just need to walk around in the daylight."

"I know you do."

"But I won't leave until . . . you know."

"No, I don't think I *do* know."

"Till we get over this."

"Do people ever get over this?"

"I don't know."

He reached out and took my hand, and pulled gently on it, and we sat side by side with our backs up against one side of the shed, watching Orion hunt his next victim. Nick didn't let go of my hand.

We had never held hands before. We had never embraced. The closest thing to physical contact we'd ever had was that casual arm draped over my shoulder up at the mountain lake, and the way he and Suki had sandwiched me in the tent to help me warm up. It was exhilarating, yet at the same time that high, lofty feeling mixed poorly with the grief. It felt exhausting to be so all over the map emotionally.

I took a deep breath and said something that was difficult to say, to phrase it mildly. "If you really need to go, I'll understand."

"No, it's okay," he said. "Not yet. I've been doing push-ups and sit-ups, and running in place in the cellar. I'll manage." A long silence. "It's just weird," he added.

"I know. You need some daylight. A real bed."

"No, not even that. It just seems weird about Ollie. It seems impossible. Like something I can't really believe. How do you get killed in a war when you haven't even gotten to where they're fighting it yet?"

"I know," I said. "I was wondering the same thing."

"I hope we don't have to go fight."

I thought about Ollie's letter. His advice to Nick, "if I saw him." I wasn't going to give Nick that advice. I chose to believe that Ollie would have withdrawn that suggestion now, if such a thing had been possible.

"Maybe it'll be over by then," I said.

"Sure hope so. I'd like to go up there."

"Up where?"

"Up to that pass, where you went with Suki this weekend. I'd like to see that place with my own eyes."

"Think it's safe?"

"There's hardly ever anyone up there except in the summer. Did you see anybody?"

"We saw two hunters. But not from very close."

"Maybe we could think of some kind of disguise for me or something."

"Yeah. Maybe."

"If I could get out into the world for a few days, and get some sun on my face, then maybe I could come back and be okay in the root cellar for a while longer."

"Then we will," I said. "We'll find a way."

We sat in silence for a long time. Long enough that I fell asleep without meaning to.

He woke me with a firm kiss on the forehead.

"Go home and sleep," he said. "We'll talk some more tomorrow."

I staggered home as if in a dream, feeling as though there was a "me and Nick" in a way there never had been before.

It was still a very strange mix with the sorrow.

———

When I finally drifted off for a few minutes, I had the most disturbing dream. I dreamed I was plunged into cold water and sinking like a stone. But it wasn't that clear, beautiful mountain lake. There was something steely and harsh about it. And I was not the only one drifting down through those miserable waters. Other young men were drowning all around me. Sinking. No one was thrashing. Just drifting. It was already over. Everybody knew better than to argue.

And there was debris. Big pieces of metal and plank, and wooden crates. And we were all dying. And the humans seemed no more concerned about it than did the debris.

My eyes shot open and I stared at the ceiling for a time.

Then I got up, got dressed, and walked out to see Nick a second time.

———

Nick immediately shifted gears from my dream of drowning to my experience with it in real life.

"Like you almost drowned in that lake the first time we went camping?" he asked me.

We were sitting back to back on his pallet bed, our backs tightly pressed together. Why we were faced away from each other, I can't say. I only remember that we were.

"No. More like the way Ollie drowned."

"How do we know how Ollie drowned?"

"We pretty much know what happened."

"But we don't know what he saw or felt."

"I guess this was just the way my brain imagined it."

He didn't speak for a time, but I remember he pressed his back up even harder against mine. I remember the way his shoulder blades felt above my own.

"It just seems like the most horrible way to die," I said.

"What did it feel like to you right before I pulled you out of that mountain lake that time? Was it horrible?"

"Not exactly. It's hard to explain. It's like I'd just . . . accepted it. But that's different. I jumped into that lake. It wasn't somebody shooting me out of existence because they hated me."

For a minute nobody moved or spoke. Then he turned around and wrapped his arms around my shoulders and set his chin down near the crook of my neck. When he spoke, I could feel the warmth and brush of his breath across my ear.

"Maybe he didn't know he was drowning," he said.

"How can you not know you're drowning?"

"Because maybe the torpedo just knocked everybody out and they never knew what hit them."

"That's a good thought," I said. "I'm going to just keep hoping that's true. Can I stay awhile longer?"

"Stay as long as you like," he said.

We sat there in silence as long as I could manage without getting caught out in the light at sunrise.

Chapter Twelve

Bright and Dark

I think it was five nights later when a noise at the window launched me out of a sound sleep. It might have been six nights.

Of course the light rapping sound startled me—the slightest thing does when you're sleeping deeply. But the minute I opened my eyes and came up out of a dream, I felt with a comfortable certainty that it was only Nick.

Granted, he never came to the house. Not once, in all the weeks I'd been hiding him. As I pulled back the covers, I got an icy little dart in my belly, thinking he might have a serious problem. Still, I never once doubted that it was Nick.

I walked to the window in the darkened room.

Standing outside, looking surprisingly bright and well lit in a spill of moonlight, was Suki. Clutched in his arms was his grandmother's little dog.

I opened out the two sections of my window.

"What time is it?" I asked him, rubbing my eyes.

"Not even nine. I figured you'd be up."

"We go to bed early around here," I said.

An awkward silence fell, and I looked at the dog in his arms.

She was maybe fifteen pounds, if that. She looked to be a rat terrier, though I couldn't tell if she was a full one. She had big ears that stood straight up from her head, and a smooth, flat white coat. Her head was marked with two colors, a light honey and a dark brown. Both colors arched up over her eyes in layers, making her look as though she had two sets of wide, cartoonish eyebrows. One ear was dark brown, the other white. The fur on her small, tapered muzzle was shot through with gray, giving her a wizened, wise-old-soul appearance. Her eyes seemed alive with worry.

I looked into her eyes, and she looked back into mine, and I knew she was one very intelligent dog. There was no mistaking it. She knew a great deal of what was going on. She knew nothing of Pearl Harbor, or FDR's Executive Order 9066. She did not understand the War Relocation Authority, or that a camp called Manzanar was currently under construction not far away. But she knew her future was uncertain. And she knew that this trip to my house, and the boy she was watching inside the window, were all tied into that uncertainty.

I looked away from her, and into Suki's face. His eyes were puffy and red. He had been crying a lot, and for a long time.

"I have to ask you a really huge favor," he said.

———

We sat side by side in the dirt, our feet over the edge of an irrigation ditch. We had gone just far enough from the house that we could talk without waking anyone.

He'd set the little dog down between us. She had come to my side, strangely aware that it was time to make her peace with me. She sat placidly, close to my hip, and I stroked her back. Her small, dark eyes half closed, as if hypnotized by my hand on her.

"I would if it was just me," I said. "I would in a minute. But I really don't think my parents would let me keep her."

"I thought of that," Suki said. "But it's time for some pretty desperate measures. My father was going to take her to the vet in Fresno today and have her put to sleep. Not in a mean way. He adores her. He was crying the whole time we talked about it. The whole family has just been sitting around her, crying, almost the whole day today. He doesn't want her life to end on suffering. We can't just turn her loose. She's had people to take care of her always, her whole life. She's old. She needs shelter. She might not need it for much longer. I mean, she's healthy enough. She's not hanging by a thread or anything. She'll still play with you. She'll fetch a ball and do tricks. She can still take walks with you. She has some life left, but I'm not quite sure how to fix things so she can have it. I knew your parents might say no. But then I thought . . . I remembered that time you said you could hide me. I didn't ask you to, of course, but then I thought, if you could hide me, maybe you could hide a little dog. She's quiet. She doesn't eat much. She can just have a little bit of whatever you're having. She can't be all alone in a hiding place all the time, though. I'm not sure that would be much better than what my dad had in mind. But if there was already somebody hiding in the hiding place, well . . . maybe they'd keep each other company."

My hand stopped on the little dog's back. I could feel the heat rise in my face, and I figured that meant it was reddening.

"But even if there *was* a person," I said, "there might not be a person there for all that much longer."

"Sure. Right. Well, here's what I think about that. If you could keep her happy for a little while, and then you couldn't anymore, and she had to take that last trip to the vet, at least she would've gotten a little more life out of it. I figure it's still better than if she had to go today. But, look, I get it. It's a big thing to ask a guy to do. It's hard. But I was out of ideas. I just had to try. I really didn't know what else to do. We all love her."

I heard a slight catch in his voice on the last sentence, and knew I was hearing his tears angling to get out again.

"If I say I'll do the best I possibly can for this dog, is that good enough?"

"Definitely good enough."

She turned her head and looked up into my face, as if she understood the emotional meat of the agreement I'd just made. I looked into her eyes in the moonlight and felt a little shiver when I saw how much she knew.

"What's her name?" I asked Suki.

"Akira."

"Akira," I repeated, and her back curved into the beginning of full-body wag. "She seems like a really bright dog."

"That's how she got her name," Suki said. "That's what it means."

We sat for an awkward length of time, and then he said, "I don't know for sure if I'll get to come back and say goodbye. I'll try. I'm just not sure what all will be going on and . . . you know . . ." I didn't know, or I would have stepped in and rescued him from having to say. "I'm not sure I'll even be . . . free to."

"Oh," I said. I really had nothing better to offer.

"I'll say goodbye to you now, just in case."

He leaned over and gave me a hug with only our shoulders touching. The dog looked up at us from in between, but didn't move.

"I appreciate it so much," he said near my ear, "that you'll at least try to take care of her. When the war's over, and we get to come back, I'll owe you a huge favor. I won't forget this. And tell Nick I said goodbye too, okay? I mean, just if you should happen to see him."

"Right," I said. "If I should happen to see him, I will."

He let me go and sat up straight again.

"Now do me a favor and pick her up and carry her back into your room with you, and don't let her look back if you can. If she tried to follow me away I think it would be more than I could take."

I stood, dusted off the seat of my pajama bottoms, and picked up the dog. She didn't resist me. I think she was half expecting it.

"Take care of yourself," I said. I wanted to add "in that place." I almost said it. But it just seemed so dark. "And take care of your family."

I walked back to the house without looking back. Without letting the dog look back. I think she knew better than to try.

That was the last time I saw Suki until we were both grown men. Young men, but grown.

—

I huddled with her in the corner of my room until I knew Suki had walked most of the way home.

At first I'd tried to lie down on the bed again, but she kept inviting herself up. I didn't mind, but I didn't want to have to explain dog hair on my bedding to my mom on laundry day.

After a suitable time I opened my windows, and we stepped out into the night.

I set her down and began walking in the moonlight, but immediately I wondered if I'd made a mistake. What if she dashed in the direction of home? What if I couldn't catch her? If she got lost or fell prey to some native wildlife, I would regret it for all of time.

Instead she just stopped and stood looking in the direction Suki had gone. I'm not even sure how she knew the direction, because she was in my room while he walked away. Maybe there was a scent, or maybe she knew he would have retraced the same steps he'd taken to come onto our family's property. I know I've mentioned that she was a very bright dog.

"Akira," I said quietly. Nearly a whisper. I didn't want to wake anyone in the house.

She had good ears for an old girl. She turned her face up to me as if to say, "What?"

"I'm sorry," I said. "I know this is hard on you. But he's gone. You're with me now."

She heaved a deep sigh and then returned to my heels and followed me all the way out to the distant shed. The moon cast shadows of the two of us, walking side by side.

I stepped inside the old outbuilding and held the door for her, and she followed me in without a fuss.

"Nicky," I said from the top of the stairs.

"You're early." His voice sounded upbeat and eager. He sounded as though it meant the world to him that I had arrived.

"I brought someone to see you."

His tone—his apparent mood—did a lightning-fast U-turn. "Steven, no!"

"It's okay. Really."

"I don't want anyone to—"

"Nick, it's okay. It's not a person."

"What do you mean it's not a person?"

I heard the scratching of a match as it flamed. He lit the lantern and held it up toward the edge of the open trapdoor, where the dog and I crouched on all fours—both of us—looking in.

"Oh, you have Akira!" he said, making a sudden turn back to delighted. "Why do you have Akira?" Before I could even open my mouth to answer, he said, "Oh. Never mind. I get it. They can't take her, can they?"

"No. They can't take her. No pets of any kind."

"How can they do that to people?"

"I have no idea," I said.

"Well, hand her down to me. And then come on down."

———

"Don't even tell your parents you have her," Nick said.

It might have been half an hour later. The dog was up on Nick's pallet bed with him, curled with her back up against his belly. She had her head down on her paws as if to sleep, but her eyes were open. She had clearly chosen Nick over me, but that was okay. She had known him longer.

"Just leave her down here with me," he said. "I could use the company."

I opened my mouth to speak, but he had more to say on the subject.

"No, maybe not. Maybe I shouldn't say that. It's not fair to her. It would mean a lot to me to have somebody down here with me. Sometimes I feel like I'm going half-crazy in here all by myself. But she's probably better off living in a real house."

"They're going to say no anyway," I said. "Besides, I'd be at school all day, and she'd have to be alone with my mom, and my mom hates dogs. She might be better off down here with somebody who at least likes her."

"Well . . . go ahead and ask them, I guess. And then we'll do what's best for her."

"There's just one thing," I said. "Let's figure they won't let me keep her. Because they won't. Then she lives down here with you. But if you leave to go find your mom . . . what will she do? That would be the end for her."

"I won't leave, then," he said.

I looked into the little dog's eyes in the lantern light, and she looked back. She always seemed to know when someone was looking at her. For a minute I thought she might have been a very small angel, sent into my life to get Nick to stay.

"Unless my mom would let me bring her," he said.

I sat in silence as my world, so very recently stitched together, fell to pieces again.

"I guess it would be kind of hard to know, though," he added. "Until I got there."

"I'm tired," I said. "I'm going back to the house to get some sleep."

It was a rare statement from me. I was never the one to cut short my precious time with Nick. But my world kept falling apart and coming back together. Falling apart and coming back together. It was exhausting. I couldn't take much more.

I think he heard some of that in my voice, but he asked me no questions about it.

As I was climbing up the ladder stairs, he stopped me with a strange statement. Something I never in a million years expected him to say.

"I know you were a little sweet on Suki first. Before you really noticed me much. But it's okay."

I hung still on the ladder, nursing my shock.

"Is it?"

"Sure it is. Suki's a great guy. It's pretty easy to understand."

"I think I might have seen the last of Suki for a long time. He told me he might not even be free to come say goodbye. He asked me to say goodbye to you if I happened to see you."

"You think he knows?"

"I think he suspects. But I don't guess it matters now."

"No," Nick said. "I guess not."

I moved my feet again and made my way home, his words still whirling through my deeply exhausted brain.

———

I sat at the breakfast table with my parents, trying not to yawn. My brother was already gone. I'm not sure why. He might've had track practice before school. My dad had likely been up since four thirty, doing chores, but he had come in for breakfast, as was his usual routine.

Breakfast that day consisted of two massive sausages each, and a pile of potatoes that were supposed to be fried, but had ended up weirdly soft and pale. And I do mean a pile. How my mother thought anybody could eat that many potatoes was a mystery to me.

I looked up, first at one of them, then the other. They didn't seem to notice.

"I'm wondering if you would let me keep a dog."

"Absolutely not," my mother said. No hesitation.

"This dog wouldn't be much trouble. She's an older dog. Very quiet and well behaved."

Amazingly, this knocked my father out of his trance. "Why would you want an older dog? Wouldn't you want a puppy?"

"He can't have a puppy, Marv," my mother said. "Don't even talk to him like he can."

"I just happen to know this dog who needs somebody to take care of her." As I spoke, I stood outside myself, shaking my head as to why I even bothered to try.

"If her owners don't want to keep her," my mother said, "then she's a problem. These are the things you don't see when you're fourteen. This is why you have parents."

"No, it's not like that at all," I said. "They would love to keep her, but they can't."

I was aware of the fact that she was drawing me down a bad road, but I wasn't sure how to stop or turn around.

"Why can't they? They have a commitment to her, right?"

"They have to go away."

"Why can't they take her?"

"They just can't. Do you always have to give me the third degree?"

But even before I had risen up and snapped at her, I could see the truth of the situation dawning in her eyes.

"Just go ahead and explain it to me, then, Steven. Under what circumstances does a family have to go away, and they don't even have a say in whether they get to take their own pet? Why don't you tell me how that goes?"

"Never mind," I said. "I'm sorry I even brought it up."

My father looked up from his plate again. It made me wonder if he was always listening but mostly didn't care. He had eaten every bite of his mountain of half-fried potatoes. I guess that was the answer to the question of who could eat that much.

"Why're you so hard on the boy, Beth? You're always talking to him like he's an idiot or a felon or both."

That was a mistake. We could feel my mother's rage flare, like a small fire hit with a big handful of grease.

"Make up your mind, Marv. Do I make a mama's boy out of him, or do I hurt his little feelings too much? Can't have it both ways."

"Never mind," my father said. "I'm sorry I even brought it up."

———

I was walking through town on my way to school when I saw Mr. Yamamoto's beautiful maroon pickup truck. It was parked on a slant in the dirt in front of the post office.

I felt suddenly ecstatic, thinking I would have a chance to talk to him. To find out exactly when they had to leave. To say goodbye.

I walked into the post office and looked around, but he wasn't anywhere to be seen.

I stepped out onto the board sidewalk again, squinting my eyes against the morning sun.

A man I had seen around town but did not actually know was walking in the direction of the truck, as if he were about to climb right in. He was maybe in his forties, wiry thin, with a thick shock of blond hair just starting to go to gray.

As his hand touched the door handle on the driver's side, I spoke to him. I couldn't help myself.

"Wait a minute," I said.

He shielded his vision against the slanted morning light, took me in, then narrowed his eyes at me. "What am I waiting for?" he asked. He sounded wary.

"That's Mr. Yamamoto's truck."

His expression morphed into a sneer as he began to understand where I was headed with this. "Well now," he said. "She might've belonged to that Yamamoto man yesterday, but today she's all mine."

I walked closer to him, feeling my heart pound. I was headed into a confrontation, and I knew it. I didn't really want one, and I had no reason to think I would prevail in this one. But I was running on auto-pilot, and there was no way to change the course of events. At least, not that I could find.

"Did you steal it?" I asked him.

It occurred to me that the townspeople might've known that as soon as the Japanese families were forced to leave, they would be unable to defend their belongings.

He seemed to consider me for a moment. He could answer my question, or he could refuse to speak of it anymore. Or he could knock me flat in the dirt. I could see him trying to decide.

"I bought it legal," he said. "Here. I'll show you." As he walked around to the passenger side he added, "Not that it's any of your concern."

He opened the passenger door and then the glove box. He produced a paper, which he proceeded to hold in my face. In fact, he pressed it so close to my face that I had to pull my head back to read it.

It was a bill of sale, and it was signed by Mr. Yamamoto. Not that I knew his signature, but anyway, that was the name at the bottom. If the document was real, then Suki's father had sold his beloved truck for the less-than-princely sum of ten dollars.

It made my stomach roil.

"So you did steal it," I said, my voice measured and artificially calm.

"Can't you read, sonny? I bought it off the man."

"For ten dollars."

"That's right."

"It's worth at least twenty times that, and you know it."

A pause, as he—again—tried to decide whether to answer me or flatten me.

"If the man wants to let it go for that . . ."

"He didn't *want* to let it go for that. You know he didn't. You took advantage of him."

The paper disappeared from in front of my face. The man behind it looked peeved.

"Now, I've had just about enough of you, sonny. They can only take what they can carry on their backs. Not my fault if he thought this truck was a few pounds too heavy for that."

I looked at his face for a split second. He thought he was funny. He thought this whole situation was funny. I think that's why I lost it.

I swung on him. I hadn't ever done that before, with anybody. I hadn't known I was about to do it this time. But that's what happened.

I threw my whole body into the swing, but he bobbed at the last minute and I mostly missed him. I could feel the slightest brush of his stubbly beard as my fist flew by his chin, but that was all I got of him. My momentum carried me forward, and I fell onto my chest in the dirt road. As I rolled over to try to rise, he kicked me viciously hard in the belly. It doubled me up and knocked the wind out of my lungs. Then he climbed into his new ten-dollar truck and drove away. I didn't see it, but I heard it.

I lay there in the road for a minute or two, until I could get myself together. And the strange thing is, nobody offered to help me. I could hear footsteps on the board sidewalk as people walked into and out of the post office. A couple of cars went by, and one even had to swerve around me. But nobody came to help me up or ask me if I was okay.

On a different day, in a different week, I think somebody would have. On that day, in that week, there were going to be tempers flaring. There were going to be fights. Nobody seemed to want any part of anybody else's troubles. It was every man for himself.

———

When I got to school, Suki wasn't there.

In fact, about fifteen percent of the students I had studied alongside for so many years weren't there. They had been subtracted from our world, leaving a void of silence.

I moved from class to class, occasionally feeling around on my torso to try to see if my ribs were cracked or only bruised. Each room was pockmarked with empty desks.

I kept waiting for one of our teachers to say something about those who were missing. Anything. It seemed impossible to ignore. No one could have failed to notice.

I expected someone to talk to us about how we were to look at the thing, or how best to get through it. Not having a storehouse of faith in the adults around me, I wouldn't have been surprised if one had told us what we were expected to think on the subject, even if their views were totally, boneheadedly wrong.

The only thing I had not been prepared for was nothing. A complete vacuum of words. It was as if those boys and girls had never existed.

I guess what they said about it was exactly what they wanted us to think. Nothing. We were being asked to think nothing of it. We were being asked to rewrite history and act as if we had never known them.

I didn't do that, of course, but I also didn't say anything about it out loud. Maybe I should have. Then again, what good would it have done? My views were a drop of water in a very big, uncaring ocean. They were destined to have no impact at all. There was only one of me, and that was not nearly enough.

By the time I got home and used the bathroom, there was blood in my urine, but I didn't say or do anything about it. I was learning my lesson well. Whatever is obviously wrong, just pretend it isn't there at all.

What could possibly go wrong?

—

The world was a great ocean of moonlight as I walked out to see Nick that night. The moon was so big and bright that the sky wasn't even dark. Only a few very bright stars could survive all that moonlight.

Nick and Akira were not there. Not in the root cellar, and not behind the shed.

I stood looking off toward the mountains for a minute or two, gingerly touching my bruised belly, wondering if he had taken her and gone. Part of me was always prepared for that loss. Nick was the only thing I had that was worth having, and I knew he could be subtracted at any minute, much the way Suki had been. Much the way Ollie had been. The feeling never entirely left me.

Then I heard a small noise that almost sounded like the bark of a human laugh.

I started walking east, toward the mountains. Toward Manzanar. It was now burned into my consciousness that it existed, even though there was a mountain range blocking my access and my view.

A few hundred yards east of the shed, the ground dipped away. Then a few hundred yards beyond that it rose again. Maybe water had come flowing down from the mountains in much wetter eras, carving out the trough. Maybe a glacier had even come through.

I stopped at the lip of that rise and looked down.

Nick and Akira were playing in the bright moonlight.

Nick would run in a half circle, then stop and crouch suddenly, as if challenging the dog to react. Akira would run in an opposing half circle, then stop when Nick stopped. Her front half would then go down until the backs of her front legs lay flat on the dirt. Her back end would stay high in the air in a classic doggy play bow, her tail whipping joyously.

I watched them for a long time.

It was the only truly pleasing thing I had witnessed in just about as long as I could remember. It was pure. It was a thing immune to prejudice and war. Nothing in this rapidly deteriorating world could touch it. It would always be the wonderful moment it was, no matter how much society fell to pieces around it.

In time Nick looked up and saw me there.

At first he did a double take, and I thought he would run away. He almost began to run. It dawned on me that he had purposely gone down into that wide gully because it was a brightly moonlit night, and he knew better than to chance being seen. A half second later he paused, looked again, then waved broadly at me.

I waved back.

I walked down to where they stood waiting. Akira wagged her tail at me, and I reached down and patted her head.

"What did they say?" Nick asked.

"Pretty much what I thought they would."

"She can stay with me."

"You're about all she's got," I said.

"Good."

He didn't mention taking her with him to his mother's house in Mesa, so I chose to believe that both of them would stay.

And, for quite an extended time, I got my wish.

Part Three

Early Summer 1942

Chapter Thirteen

Life While You're Doing It

The sun was above the horizon but still below the peaks as I stepped onto the trail leading up to that mountain pass. It was the nervous start of the hike I'd promised Nick we would take. Just the two of us, and nobody else. There *was* nobody else. We were all we had.

We had purposely waited until school let out for the summer, so I could be away longer than a two-day weekend.

Nick had hiked all the way up to the trailhead in the dark the previous night, following that cut in the land and staying far from the road.

Now, at seven in the morning, after I'd paid one of my dad's farmhands twenty-five cents for the lift and hit the trail, Nick was hiding in a thicket of pine trees high above me, signaling to me with a bird call I knew to be his. He couldn't have gotten much more than a quick nap after that long night of hiking, but he seemed chipper enough.

I think he was just ecstatic to be out in the world.

He came trotting down to the trail with his huge pack on his back and Akira in his arms. Instead of a disguise, I had loaned him a huge wide-brimmed hat, and a dark hood of mosquito netting that was designed to be worn over the head. It pulled snug with a drawstring at his disturbingly white throat.

We figured if we ran into anybody, we could claim he was desperately allergic to mosquitos or bees. I would do the talking. But there was still plenty of snow up in the mountains in late May, and so far we had the trail to ourselves.

Akira wagged her whole body when she saw me. She wiggled so hard that she looked as though she were trying to jump from Nick's arms into my own. But she just wanted to say hello to me. I leaned in to greet her, and she licked me on the nose. I was so flattered by her affection it was downright silly.

"How do you feel?" I asked as we began the steep climb.

"Tired," he said.

I said no more for the moment. Asked no more questions. Nick had shrunk to a shell of his former self, and was plagued with a cough he could never seem to shake. I had been careful to bring him extra food so Akira could eat, too, but I strongly suspected he was giving her too much and keeping too little for himself. She looked nicely plump, and he was wasting away.

We'd both had questions as to how he would do with his first extended strenuous exercise in months. Now we had our answer.

We climbed in silence for a long time, though much more slowly than I had imagined we would. Akira was perched with her front paws over Nick's left shoulder, facing back toward me. Now and then I looked at her face, and she always noticed. She always drilled her gaze right back into mine. It was a gaze that said she knew there were dangers in the plan, but she was prepared to live with them. She'd seen worse—or at least knew worse was out there to be seen.

For all of her sensitivity and her small size, she was not an easily intimidated girl.

The sun came up over the pass before us, shining and glaring into our line of sight. I squinted, wondering how it must feel to Nick. He raised one arm and leveled it in front of his face like a vampire, shielding his eyes.

"Damn," he said. But nothing more.

We walked until the sun rose over our heads, making its light easier to bear. The sky turned the deepest, richest navy blue I could ever remember seeing.

When we reached a series of twisty, hidden switchbacks with steep boulder sides, he stopped, and we stood very still, listening. Akira was listening, too. I could see it.

"Here, hold her," he said, and handed the dog to me.

She felt warm in my arms, and I could feel her little heart beating.

Nick took off his hat and then pulled away the mosquito netting. He pressed his eyes tightly shut, as if the sun hurt right through their lids, and turned his face up to the sky.

For a long while I stood there, holding the dog and watching him take that sunlight right in the face.

"I sure missed this," he said.

Then he sighed, dropped the netting back over his head, and snugged the hat back on top of it.

We climbed—slowly—for about an hour more.

———

When Nick stopped in the middle of the trail and said, "I can't go another step," I was not the least bit surprised. I was more surprised that he'd gone as many steps as he had.

We found a camping spot well off the trail, up a hill, looking down over the only route through that territory. It was wooded, and shielded, and made us feel safe.

Nick lay on his back—Akira sleeping curled on his belly—while I pitched the tent. They looked so sweet that way. For a second I almost wished I had a camera. Then I realized what an insane thought that had been. The last thing I needed was any kind of evidence that all this had taken place. I had a mental flash of the fictional photograph being offered up as evidence in court while I was sentenced to reform school for harboring a fugitive.

I shook the thought away again and lay down in the dirt beside them.

"I'm sorry," Nick said without opening his eyes. "I'm just not in the same shape I used to be."

"You don't have to be sorry," I said.

He never answered.

For a time I just lay there, watching the leaves and pine needles sway in the wind over our heads.

Then I asked, "Are you sure this is worth the risk?"

"Oh yeah."

"Just to see that camp?"

"Not really. Maybe not just for that. I mean, I want to see it. But it's worth it to get out in the sun. If I couldn't have gotten out in the sun soon, I think I'd've turned myself in. At least the place they put me in would probably have a yard. At least a basketball court or something."

I had no idea what to say to the idea that reform school was sounding good to him in comparison, so I said nothing at all.

"You know what's weird?" he asked.

I expected him to tell me. Just tell me. But he seemed to be waiting for me to answer the question.

"I don't guess I do, no."

"It's weird how you can only do life while you're doing it."

I was hoping he'd say more—something to help me make sense of that cryptic sentence. He didn't. Not just on his own like that.

"I don't think I follow."

"Well. Life is really hard," he said. He still had not opened his eyes.

"I won't argue with that."

"But we do it every day. We don't even think about it. We just do it. But then if you get out of life for too long . . . if you get sick, or you have to go into hiding like I did . . . then you think about doing life every day, and it just seems impossible. It's just too scary. It's like you look at a simple thing like going to school, and you think, 'How did I ever do that?' Life is so hard that you can't stop practicing for a minute or you'll forget how you used to do something so hard. Do you understand what I mean?"

"I actually think I do," I said. "Because I had scarlet fever when I was nine."

"Oh!" he said suddenly, and the dog's head shot up. "I have to show you something."

He sat up, holding Akira to his chest with both hands. "Here, take her for a minute. It's in my pack. Don't let her get away from you for a second. There are coyotes and bears up here."

"Mostly at night, though," I said. Nervously. As if I was trying to make it more true by saying it.

"Yeah. Mostly. But let's not take any chances."

I took her and held her tightly in my arms, and we both watched Nick plowing through his pack.

"I've been working on this for weeks," he said, still plowing.

"I didn't know you'd been working on anything for weeks."

"I know. I wanted it to be a surprise."

I got a flutter in my belly, thinking he meant something for me. That he had made me some kind of gift. But a moment later he pulled it out into the light, and I swear it was even better than that.

He held it out for me to see.

It was a carefully constructed wooden cross, carved smooth with some kind of small knife, its two sections lashed together with what looked like hand-cut leather cords. On the crossbeam of wood he had carved the name **OLLIE**.

The middle *L* was right at the intersection, between the leather lashings, with two letters on either side. Above the name, right in the middle of the upright piece, he had carved a surprisingly intricate angel. She was detailed right down to the individual feathers in her wings.

The whole thing was small, not much more than a foot high. But it was beautiful.

"I thought we'd put it all the way up at the top of the mountain," he said. "He loved it up here. He would like that."

"He *would* like that," I said. "Are you sure you can get up there?"

"I just will. I just need a night's sleep first."

I handed him back the dog when he reached for her, and we lay on our backs in the dirt again. I knew I should get up and start a fire to cook some food for us, but it felt too good just to lie by his side in the sun.

I wanted to reach out and take his hand, but I never did. We hadn't held hands since the night I told him about Ollie's death. Still, there was precedent for it. It was a possible thing. And yet, to me, in that moment, it felt impossible to initiate. Maybe because it was broad daylight. Maybe just because I was me.

He spoke, startling me out of those thoughts.

"What's my life going to be now, Steven?"

"I don't know what you mean."

"I mean . . . what have I *got*? I'm not going to graduate high school. I can't get a job, because they're looking for me. I forgot how to do that living thing. I'm just not sure where I go from here."

"I guess you wait till they're not looking for you and then get a job, or go back to school or something. You may get your life going a little later than some other guys, but you'll still have one."

"I guess," he said. "I just feel like I've lost everything." Then his tone changed. I could almost hear him pulling himself together. "I didn't mean to sound like I'm feeling sorry for myself."

"You didn't."

That wasn't entirely accurate, what I said. In truth, he sounded like he was feeling sorry for himself, but with good reason.

"I'll make a fire," he said. "Here. Hold the dog."

—

We retired to the tent that night fully clothed, right down to thick socks and jackets, with one sleeping bag underneath us to shield us from the cold ground, the other thrown over us like a blanket. I lay very still on my side, my back to Nick. I had no idea what would happen, and I was far too petrified to initiate anything—even simple affection.

Akira pressed her head under the sleeping bag blanket near my chest, and I lifted it for her. She slithered under and curled up with her back against my belly.

In time Nick rolled over and moved just close enough so that part of his jacketed chest touched my back. I might have stopped breathing, at least for a time. Then he threw one arm over me. But it was more or less around my neck, like a loose yoke. It was impossible to interpret the gesture, other than the fact that he was expressing some sort of affection for me. What sort, I wasn't sure. It was maddeningly ambiguous.

We lay still for a long time, and I gradually accepted the fact that this was as far as things would go. It was actually helpful, in a weird sort of a way. I was able to breathe again.

I felt his chin rest against the back of my shoulder.

"I'm sorry about what I said before," he whispered. I could feel the movements of his chin as he spoke.

"You didn't say anything to be sorry for."

"When I said I felt like I lost everything. I haven't lost *you*. And I don't want you to think that's nothing to me."

"No, I don't," I said. "I knew what you meant. And you're not going to lose me."

He said nothing in reply. And I said nothing more. In that vacuum, that absence of words, I could hear how untrue my last sentence had been. Nick would have to move on, and, in doing so, he would lose me. And I would lose him. Maybe not permanently. Hopefully not. But it was out there, waiting for us. Neither one of us cared to talk about it in that moment.

I might have dozed for half an hour, or maybe half sleep was the best I ever managed. Still, it's fair to say I didn't sleep much that night, if at all.

———

In the morning we trudged slowly and painfully up to the pass, which was still covered with deep patches of partially melted snow.

"Find a good hiding spot off the trail," I told Nick. "I'll look and make sure there's nobody coming up the other side. Here, I'll hold the dog."

He dropped his pack onto the trail, and I watched as he scrambled over boulders to find a secure hiding place. I felt pain on his behalf as I watched. I could see from his movements how much his body hurt. How much his muscles ached with the unfamiliar exertion.

I dropped my pack next to Nick's, and Akira and I crested the pass and looked over the Owens Valley on the eastern side. I was wishing I had thought to bring the big binoculars from my pack.

I could see two hikers on the eastern side of the trail, but they were headed away, walking downhill toward the valley. They must have passed us the previous night as we huddled in our camp. They didn't wear bright vests, but they might have been hunters. It was hard to know. Or maybe Nick and I weren't the only people on the western side of the mountains who wanted to see what was happening in the far valley.

I looked down at the camp. Manzanar. But I couldn't see much without the binoculars. Just that it was colorless, and sprawling, and even from a distance you could see it was not someplace anyone would ever choose to go.

I watched the two hikers until they fell out of sight. Then I back-tracked to the western side and summoned Nick with our signature bird call. He scrambled back down to the trail looking painfully stiff. It hurt to watch him.

He had probably lost thirty pounds. He looked like one of those pictures you'd see in a newsreel about captives in a prisoner of war camp. For a moment I felt a visceral flash of regret for what I had done by hiding him. Suddenly it didn't seem like much of a favor to him at all.

Wordlessly, we climbed the few yards back up to the pass, our heavy packs dangling from one hand. He took Akira from me so I could plow through my pack and find my father's huge binoculars.

He took them from me, holding them with one hand and her with the other, and stared down at Manzanar for a long time. Then he handed them to me, and I looked for a while. The place had changed since I first saw it. There were guns on the guard towers now.

They were not pointing out at the surrounding world.

Nick never said a word about it and neither did I. Not in the daylight that day.

Then again, I'm not sure what I expected us to say.

Res ipsa loquitur. It was a Latin phrase I didn't know at the time, but later learned in law school.

The thing speaks for itself.

———

When I woke in the tent in the middle of the night, Nick and Akira were not there with me.

I climbed out into the cold night and looked around.

The moon was full again. Very few stars were visible, but it felt easy to navigate in all that light. Still, I had no idea which way to go.

I whistled my little bird call into the night, and he answered me immediately. We spoke back and forth that way as I scrambled up boulders, following the sound of that little bird I knew to be Nick.

I found him at the very top of the mountain but high up above the trail, looking down across the moonlit valley. He was looking through the binoculars. As I climbed closer, I saw that he had Akira buttoned into his coat, with just her head protruding. She looked contented and warm, and seemed happy enough to see me.

I sat cross-legged in the dirt between boulders, my knee bumping up against Nick's.

"You have to see this," he said.

He handed me the binoculars.

I looked down at the camp through those strong lenses. It was hard to see much in the dark, but it was clear what Nick felt I should see. There was really only one thing he could mean. Inside the camp, near the fence, on the side nearest the road, I saw a massive spill of light. It was a spotlight coming from one of the watchtowers. The gun towers, I guess I should call them. No need to sanitize the thing.

In that glaring cone of light, I saw a person walking.

I can't tell you much about the person, because, even with binoculars, this was all taking place a long way away. The person looked about the size of an ant. Detail was impossible. The very fact that I saw a person moving at all was a testament to the brightness of the spotlight and the strength of my father's binoculars.

It was tempting to think maybe I was watching Suki. Because a sighting of him, however distant, would be welcome. So welcome, in fact, that I got a lump in my throat just thinking about it. And it would make a better story that way. But, realistically, the chances were thousands to one. Furthermore, I got a vague impression that the figure moved more like a young woman, but I really can't recall what I saw that made me think so.

The figure was moving across the dirt of the camp. The spotlight was following.

I saw no more action than that, so I did not get the sense that anyone was about to be apprehended. More that the person's movements were being carefully monitored.

She—I'm guessing she—moved slowly and carefully back to one of the long barracks and disappeared inside. The light remained trained on the door for a minute or two. Then it cut out. Disappeared, leaving only a dark field through the binoculars.

I let them sink down into my lap.

"I don't suppose there are bathrooms inside the barracks," he said.

"No," I said. "I don't suppose."

It may sound like a leap, but indoor bathrooms were quite the luxury in highly rural areas in 1942.

I silently pieced together that if a person interned in that camp had to get up and use the latrine in the middle of the night, it was a long, cold walk, made dozens of times worse by an armed guard following their movements the whole time.

"The guns aren't pointed out," Nick said, knocking me out of that thought.

"No," I said.

"What they told them . . . how they were sending them away for their own protection . . . that was a lie."

"Seems that way," I said.

We sat in silence for what might have been ten minutes or more. I was cold, and feeling trembly inside, but it was peaceful—albeit sad—on top of that mountain with Nick, and I didn't want to go back to the tent and spoil that moment of togetherness.

He was the one to finally break the silence.

"I thought this would be a good place to leave Ollie's marker. Right on top of the mountain but not really where anyone'll see it."

"I think he would like this spot," I said.

I held Akira while Nick used his pocketknife to carve out a little hole in the frozen dirt, and he set the base of the cross inside it. He tried to pack the dirt around it as best he could with fingers I knew must also be frozen. But it didn't really stand up straight.

"It droops," he said. "Does it matter if it droops?"

"I don't think Ollie would care. I think he would just care that we remember him."

"I think so, too," Nick said. "Now we should just think of all the things we remember about him."

I was strangely relieved not to have to find presentable words and say them out loud.

Chapter Fourteen

And Then There's Real

As we walked down from the pass the following day, I have to admit
the mountain curse weighed heavily on my mind. I fully expected to
climb down and arrive back in civilization and find that the world had
fallen to ruin in my absence.

As it turned out, it would be quite different this time. Almost as
though the world fell back together instead. But I shouldn't get ahead
of myself.

I was walking behind Nick on the trail, following rocky switchbacks, my calf muscles tight and burning. I want to say I was watching
the back of Nick's head, but it was so well covered that I was really just
watching the hat and the mosquito net. And Akira. She was riding on
his shoulder, facing rear, as she had been on the climb up, her front
paws draped in my direction. She seemed to be keeping me in her sights
the same way I was with Nick. She seemed content as long as she could
see me. If Nick rounded a boulder and passed briefly out of sight, when
I caught up I would see Akira with an alarmed look on her face. Then
when she saw me, her eyes would soften and half close.

I was deeply braced for Nick to tell me he couldn't go back into the root cellar, having been out in the light. That he would take his chances running to his mom's. When he spoke suddenly, it alarmed me.

"I never ask you how you're doing," he said. "Every time we talk it's always about me and my problems. I feel bad about that."

"I'm doing okay," I said.

My heart began calming, because he hadn't made the dreaded announcement.

"No," he said. "I meant a real talk."

"Oh." I felt a lance of shame, because I had "I'm fined" the most beloved person in my world. I dug a little deeper. "Well. Let's see. School was weird because nobody would talk about the Japanese kids. It was like this unwritten law. Nobody ever said you can't talk about them, but everybody knew it. How did everybody know it? It's like somebody sent out an instruction sheet on how to behave and everybody got it but me. I don't know. I don't know if I can explain it. It felt like this big dark hole. This pit. No light, no sound. And it weighed on me. And I can't figure out if it only weighed on *me* or if everybody else was just faking. Or maybe it's because I was on the outside of them and the inside of me. And I kept wondering what the Chinese kids were thinking. Every time I was in class or in the hall with them, I felt like I was trying to catch their eye, just to see how it was for them. But they mostly looked away because they're extra scared right now. They don't even dare make eye contact."

Nick stopped briefly in the middle of the trail. I almost slammed into his pack. He cocked his head in a funny way.

"That must be strange," he said.

"It *is* strange."

He set off hiking again. Akira sighed and looked relieved. I watched her eyes soften.

"And things at home are really bad," I added, "because my mom has been absolutely crazy with worry ever since Terrence shipped overseas."

He stopped suddenly again. This time I anticipated it.

"He's overseas already?"

"Yeah, he's in Guam. I thought I told you."

"I remember you telling me he was in basic training. I didn't know he shipped out already."

"Yeah, last week."

"I'm sorry," Nick said. As though he had some genuine guilt regarding the situation.

"What about?"

"Because I should have asked how you were doing sooner."

We trudged down the trail again. For three or four switchbacks we hiked in silence.

Then he asked, "How do you feel about him being over there?"

Oddly, it was a question that nobody else had thought to ask me. I hadn't even asked myself. The only person who had ever inquired about my feelings for my brother was Ollie. I felt a pang of loss, remembering. He had asked me if I loved Terrence. And I had admitted that I probably did . . . in there somewhere.

"We're not really all that close," I said.

"I know. But he's still your brother."

"Right. I was just about to say something like that. I guess . . . I think I wouldn't have worried too much about it if Ollie hadn't died. I would've figured he'd go over there and fire his gun and see some terrible things, and then the war would be over and he'd come home. I know that sounds stupid. I mean, I'm not such an idiot that I don't know people die in wars."

"I understand," he said.

"Do you?"

"Yeah. I do. It's like . . . there's real and then there's real."

"Right," I said. "It's exactly like that."

We hiked in silence for close to an hour. I'm guessing, of course. Then he asked me a question he asked once a week or so.

"Seen my dad around town?"

"Nope. Still no."

"He must be out by now."

"Oh, yeah. I think he's been out for a while. They only gave him ninety days."

"He must've left town."

"That's what I think."

He stopped. Turned around to face me on the trail. I could see and hear him sigh.

"I shouldn't go any farther than this," he said. "You go on without me. I'll wait till it's dark and then come back."

It was dusk by then. But not dark.

For a few seconds I breathed as though I hadn't breathed in years. Because I'd been pretty sure he was about to announce he wasn't coming back.

"Okay," I said. "Be careful."

"I will. But Steven. Look." In the pause, I think my heart stopped. For two beats, anyway. "I'm just not sure how much longer I can do it."

"I know. I get it. I knew that already."

"I worry when I say that. I worry you'll think I don't appreciate everything you're doing for me."

"No, don't worry about that. I get it. It's a root cellar. It's not as much as a person needs to be okay. But, anyway, maybe just a little longer. The longer you stay, the safer it'll be to go. Because the case just keeps getting colder."

"That's true," he said.

Then he embraced me. I can't really say in what way, because I didn't really know. It was half a guy hug, mostly shoulders, clapping each other on the back. Or on the backpacks, in this case. It was half a show of actual caring.

"Go on without me," he said.

I started to. Then I stopped, and called back to him.

"Wait," I said.

"What?"

"But not forever, right?"

"What's not forever?"

"When you go away, it's not forever. Right?"

"No, of course not. How can you think that? I'll be back when I can. When it's safe. We're a team, you and me. We belong together."

I said nothing in reply because my words had stopped working.

———

When I'd hiked down to the road, I walked about a mile along it, then hitched a ride the rest of the way.

The guy who stopped for me drove an actual car. An early model Ford coupe. You didn't see too many cars in those parts. Almost everybody drove pickups. I knew he was one of Joe Wilson's farmhands. I thought his name was Phil, but I wasn't sure if I was remembering correctly, and I didn't ask.

"Anything interesting happen while I was gone?" I asked him.

He furrowed his brow, as though that would help him think better. He was smoking a cigarette in his left hand, which he dangled out the window in between puffs. I watched a shower of sparks stream from its lit tip in that dusky light. He had a big, long mustache that curled down over his upper lip, and I kept thinking he was going to light it on fire.

"Interesting how?"

"I don't know. Just . . . did anything unusual happen?"

He still seemed confused by me. Then again, why wouldn't he be? What did he know about the curse of mountain camping?

"Nah, it's been pretty dull," he said.

I let out a long breath and leaned back against the seat, settling my mind and heart. Nothing had happened.

Except it turned out plenty had happened, but Phil hadn't heard about it.

—

We were sitting at the breakfast table in the morning when the knock came at the door, and I just knew. I didn't know what exactly had happened, or what I was about to find out, or who was at the door, but I knew the curse had struck again.

My dad didn't even look up from his bacon and eggs, so my mom got up to answer the door. I wanted to stop her. To tell her I would get it. But I had frozen.

She stuck her head back into the kitchen a few seconds later, and her face looked alarmed. I wondered if we were about to be given a gold star for our window.

She looked straight at me, her eyes drilling into mine.

"There's a man with a *gun* at the door, and he wants to talk to *you*."

Through the icy little tingles in my gut, I watched my father react. He jumped up, hitting the edge of the table with his big thighs, spilling coffee and orange juice.

"What? He has a gun?"

"Relax, Marv," my mom said. "It's just in a shoulder holster. He showed me some kind of badge. He swears Steven's not in any trouble, but why would a law officer be coming to our door?"

I think she kept talking. I was vaguely aware of her voice. But my numb, hollow body was walking from the kitchen into the living room in a dreamlike way. I had no idea what else she said.

Tall, thin Detective Engel was waiting for me in the open doorway. He was wearing a gray fedora, and a suit and tie, but with the coat over his arm. It underscored my theory that he let people see that gun on purpose.

"What now?" I asked him. It sounded disrespectful. I hadn't meant it to. It was just what came out.

"You'll be happy to know you were right," he said.

My brain wasn't putting two and two together well. To put it mildly.

"What was I right about?"

"Edward Mulligan was arrested in Nevada this weekend. Shoplifting. The police there questioned him at our request. He says it was definitely *Daniel* Mattaliano who assaulted him. It was definitely not the son. You were right."

"I don't need to know I was right about that," I said. "I've known it all along."

He seemed inclined to let that bit of rudeness go by.

"Now we just have to pick up the elder Mattaliano. Which might be tricky, because right at the moment we don't know where he is. Do *you* know where he is?"

"No, sir."

"You know where the son is?"

"I've told you over and over I don't."

"Time has gone by," he said, with no heat whatsoever. Just matter-of-fact. "I thought he might've gotten in touch."

"Well, he hasn't."

I caught myself looking away as I said it. I had a flash of memory from my camping trip in the mountains with Suki. Sitting by the fire. He told me I was a terrible liar because I always looked away and looked uncomfortable when I was lying about Nick. I forced myself to look right into his face, hoping that wouldn't be worse. But he wasn't even paying attention to me. He was looking over my shoulder at something behind me.

I turned to look and saw that my parents were standing in the middle of the room, listening to everything. Of course they were. If I had stopped to think about it, I would have known that of course they would listen. I just hadn't stopped to think about it.

"Well, if he should happen to get in touch," Engel said, seeming to address my parents, "you tell him there's no longer a warrant out for his arrest. It's been vacated."

"Okay."

"And listen. If we get the father, he might plead guilty, or we might have to take it to trial. And if it goes to trial, you'll need to testify."

"That's fine," I said.

"He's not going to testify," my mother said in her most strident voice.

"There'll be a subpoena issued," Engel said. "He'll need to."

"He won't," my mother said.

She was sounding increasingly agitated. I could hear it in her voice. I looked over my shoulder and gave her rant my full attention.

"He's just a child, and he didn't do anything wrong. You said so yourself. I won't let you drag him into court."

"Beth!" my father said. It was a voice somewhere between a bark and full-on yelling. "Stop talking now." A silence fell. I would have bet you money that wouldn't work on my mom. But she stopped. "This man is an officer of the law. You don't tell him how it's going to be. He tells us."

I waited a second, but nothing more was said.

I looked back to Engel.

"I'll testify," I said.

"I'll be in touch."

He tipped his hat, more to my parents than to me, and walked back to his car.

———

It would be understating the case to say that my mom did not calm down. My father and I had gone back to eating our breakfasts, but she paced the kitchen in jerky movements, and wouldn't stop talking.

It was interrupting my thinking, but there was nothing I could do about that. I was trying to figure out if Nick would leave town or not. He wouldn't have to hide anymore. He could just come out and go back to his house. Or could he? Would the authorities let him live alone at barely fifteen? Or would he have to go to his mother's to have some kind of guardian?

Meanwhile, as I mentioned, my mother was talking nonstop.

"See, this is what I'm always trying to tell you, Steven. You don't choose your friends wisely enough. You think it doesn't matter until the day the police show up at the door. And then all of a sudden there's a subpoena for you to appear in court. That's what happens with low-class friends. We never had problems like this with your old friends. I'll never understand why you dropped them."

"They're not low class," I said. It was the first I had spoken to her that morning.

"There was a warrant out for one's arrest!"

"But for something he didn't do."

"But his father's in trouble with the law. You have to have friends from good families. You bring shame on this house when you pal around with boys from bad families."

"You can't choose your family," I said.

I almost went on to say that if you could, I would've chosen better. I wanted to say it. But it would have sounded cruel, so I didn't.

I thought the one sentence I did say was pretty mild. But my mom lost it in that moment. Lost her cool. Lost any ability she might have had to handle her stress. Looking back, it probably didn't have anything to do with what I said. Maybe she just held up her problems until she couldn't anymore.

She lunged at me, and grabbed me by both shoulders. Her face was just inches from mine, and the whole world was her mouth moving. I couldn't see anything else. I could feel flecks of spittle landing on my forehead. It was weirdly alarming.

She was going on about how I never listen to her and I don't take her advice and the world is a dangerous place and she knows that and I don't and I never accept her guidance. But the words seemed to tumble over each other and make less and less sense.

Suddenly her face retreated and I saw light again. The kitchen reappeared.

"Beth!" my father shouted.

He was holding her back with one arm around her waist.

I looked into his eyes and he looked back.

"Go on to your room now, son," he called to me. "I'll take care of this."

I ran outside and walked toward town, wishing school were still in session, so I could be away all day. I wondered if my mom would return to her normal self—such as it was—or if she had lost something that she would never be able to find again.

—

"Unless it's a trap," Nick said.

We were lying together on his pallet bed in the root cellar, close but not touching. Spending nights together in the tent had broken through that much of our inhibitions. We at least had a precedent for lying in bed. Akira was wedged in between us, sleeping on her back with all four paws in the air. I felt that as I moved to pet her. She was snoring.

The lantern was off, and the world was black. We couldn't see each other at all.

"A trap?" I said.

"Sure. They can't find me, so they tell you to tell me I'm not in trouble anymore. And then I come out. And then they arrest me."

"Oh," I said. "I never thought of that."

"Besides. Even if it's true, and there's no more warrant for my arrest, I can't come out right away. Because it would get you in trouble. You've been telling them you don't know where I am. And if I suddenly come out because I know I'm not in trouble, then they'll know you were lying."

"Oh," I said again. "I never thought of that, either."

In the silence that followed, I was pleased that *he* had thought of it. Because it showed he was thinking of my welfare over his own. And, though it may sound selfish to say it, I was happy because our nighttime visits were not quite over.

"Maybe soon, though," he said. "If they find my father and arrest him, then we'll know they're telling the truth. And maybe by then a little time will've gone by. And we can say I wrote you a letter or something. But I can't leave now."

"But you're so unhappy here," I said.

"Not really. Not entirely. I'm unhappy with being in a root cellar. But I'm happy with you."

My stomach buzzed with pleasure. I wondered if the blackness helped him speak more freely. There's nothing like speaking the truth into darkness.

"Besides," he added. "Now that I know it's just a little while longer, it's not so bad."

We lay silent after that. I was feeling contented with everything that had been said. I think we both were. And, in that contentment, we made a mistake we had not made in all the months Nick had been here with me.

We both fell asleep.

—

I woke in the morning with Nick shaking my shoulder.

"Steven," he said. "Steven. Wake up. We fell asleep."

I bolted into an upright position, scaring Akira. She jumped.

"Oh no! What time is it?"

It was a stupid question. He had no watch or clock down in that cellar. I didn't wear my watch when I went to visit him because I didn't wear it in bed.

"I don't know," he said. "But I climbed up the ladder, and it's light out. I could see light under the door."

I said nothing, because my gut was too full of iced fear and my brain was too much of a jumble of panic.

The only good thing to report about the situation is that I was reasonably dressed. I no longer walked out to see Nick in pajama bottoms and bare feet. I wore loose linen drawstring pants and an undershirt to bed because I knew I'd be out in the world a few hours later.

I swung my legs off the bed and slipped into my shoes.

"What'll you say if you run into somebody?"

"No idea," I said. "I guess I'll just have to say I woke up early and couldn't get back to sleep, so I was taking a walk."

I trotted up the ladder stairs and over to the door. I held the door open about an inch, and looked and listened.

It was highly unlikely that anyone would be anywhere near the shed. The land around it was unplanted and unused, a field that had long ago gone fallow, and it could not be seen from any road. That's why I'd chosen it. Still, I wasn't taking any chances.

I heard and saw nothing, so I opened the door by a foot or so and looked around. It wasn't fully light—more like civil twilight—but it was lighter than I wanted it to be.

I saw no one, so I ran. I ran like I'd never run in my life. I sprinted like a track star. Like my brother, before my brother had to ship overseas.

I still didn't know what time it was, but I didn't figure it could be six. It would have been lighter if it were six. And the hired men didn't show up till six. The only person likely to be up and around in the morning twilight was my father. But my father was also exactly the person I couldn't afford to bump into.

When I had run completely out of sight of the shed, I slowed to a walk. Not just so I could rest and breathe, although that, too. Because I was out of view of the shed, and because running would only make me seem more guilty. Taking a walk would seem a lot less suspicious than sprinting like a bank robber trying to evade a police chase.

I walked beside the irrigation ditches, gradually getting my breath back. I walked in the borders between crop rows, past the barn, between the parked tractors and threshers and combines and seeders.

And then, just as I was turning the last corner for home, I ran smack into my father. Literally. Ran into him.

"What the hell?" he said.

He put his hands on my shoulders and moved me back a step. He did not let me go. He held me there, as if for further examination. I looked down at the soil and said nothing.

After what felt like a very long minute, he dropped his hands to his sides.

"I'm not a stupid man," he said.

"Never said you were," I mumbled, still looking at the dirt.

"I know what's going on here."

"You do?"

I braved a look at his face for less than a second. He didn't look as upset as I expected. He looked almost . . . amused. If such a thing were possible.

"You're a normal, healthy, growing boy. It was bound to happen sooner or later."

Which, from my perspective, made precious little sense.

"What was?"

"You got yourself a little girlfriend."

I stood frozen for a few seconds more, looking down. As if the earth were doing something genuinely entertaining beneath my shoes. It was beginning to dawn on me that I was surviving this moment.

"Am I right or am I wrong?" he asked, his voice jocular.

"Well. Like you say. You're not stupid."

"I'm actually kinda relieved. Seemed like you were taking a little bit too long to get interested in the fairer sex. But anyway, better late than never."

"You're not mad?"

I looked up at his face as I asked it. His hair was a wild tangle, seeming to rise straight up from his head. He hadn't shaved yet. He was clearly not mad.

"You're forgetting I was a young blade myself once upon a time. But one thing, though, boy. Under no circumstances is your mother to know about this."

"No, sir. I agree. That would not be good."

"She's been even edgier than her usual self lately. But I don't guess I have to tell you that. Seeing as you live here, too."

"Yes, sir. I've noticed. She's worried about Terrence."

He didn't answer for a strangely long time, so I braved another look at his face. He was looking straight into me, as if seeing something he'd never known was there.

"That's a thoughtful observation," he said, scratching his stubbly chin as he spoke.

"Is it? Not sure why. It's obvious. I mean, what mother wouldn't be?"

"No, it's more thoughtful than you think. Most boys your age, they only think about how their parents affect *them*. They don't think about why things are the way they are. Most boys your age would just hate their mother for being so difficult and not bother to look all the way through into the reasons why. You're a good boy."

I did not look up from the dirt as those unexpected words vibrated through me.

"I am?"

"Yeah you are, and I know your mother won't tell you, so that's why I'm telling you now. But you knew anyway. Right?"

I looked into his eyes and said something blazingly honest. I said, "No, sir."

"You didn't? Really?"

"No, sir."

We were having a rare moment, and somehow I thought my honesty would tear us open even further. He opened his mouth to speak, and I expected him to express regret over the fact that I hadn't known. Maybe even take responsibility for it.

Instead he punched me on the shoulder. Hard enough to make me say "ouch," but I didn't say it. "Well, you are," he said.

Then he turned and walked into the barn.

I stood watching him go for a minute, feeling that window of communication close. It was okay. Surprisingly okay, really. Because it was at least something I understood. It was a return to something bad but familiar. The devil I knew.

I crept into the house and climbed back into bed before my mother woke up.

To the best of my knowledge, she never knew the whole thing had happened.

Chapter Fifteen

Over

It was about ten days later, and I was standing in a patch of shade behind the barn, lubricating a bunch of grease fittings on the combine. I could explain that at greater length, but it's painfully boring, and only important if you're about to use a 1930s-vintage combine for the first time in a long while. In other words, who cares?

It was early June, no school, and the more work I did around the farm, the more my allowance went up.

My dad came up behind me, but I was so lost in thought I didn't hear him. When he clapped me on the shoulder, I nearly leapt into the next county.

"Jumpy," he said.

"Whatever you say."

I pulled a rag out of my coveralls pocket and mopped sweat off my forehead.

He stared at my forehead for a minute. Then he said, "Now you got a big old smear of grease on you."

"Okay," I said. "What did you want?"

It was unlike him to disturb me when I was doing chores.

"I just thought you might want to know they arrested that man."

"What man?"

"The one they want you to testify against. I forget his name. Matty-something."

"Daniel Mattaliano," I said. My heart started to pound, because I wasn't sure how to know absolutely and for a fact that it was true before I told Nick. "How do you know?"

"Well, it's been all over town this morning. People talk because they knew him. Well, let's face it—people talk for every damn reason." He was still staring at my forehead as he spoke. He paused. Pulled out his own handkerchief and handed it to me. "Here, wipe that off proper," he said.

"With your good white linen hankie? Mom'll have a fit."

"Wouldn't be the first time."

I didn't know quite what he meant by that. Not the first time a greasy hankie came back into the house? Not the first time she had a fit?

I took it from him and wiped off my forehead. Then I handed it back in a very un-Mom-like condition.

"They hauled him into Fresno and charged him with attempted murder," he said.

"That's a pretty serious charge for a bar fight."

"I guess it was more than just a bar fight. Seems he was banging this guy's head against the cement foundation of the tavern." He pronounced "cement" in that weird way with emphasis on the first syllable and a long *e*: *cee*ment. "Pretty remarkable the guy even lived to tell the tale. But anyway, you saw it, right? Why am I telling *you*?"

"I didn't see it. I was up in the mountains with my friends."

"Well, then what do they want you to testify to?"

"He—the father, Daniel—lied and said his son did it. I was up in the mountains with the son at the time. You know."

"Oh, I get it. You're not so much the witness as the alibi."

"I guess."

"Damn. He did a thing like that and then tried to put it off on his own son? That's *low*. I mean, that's lower than dirt. Who *does* that?"

I turned my palms up and spread my arms wide. It was more than just a shrug. It was more than a gesture of "I don't know." It was more of a gesture that said, "No one on the face of the planet could answer a question like that one." I would've bet money that even Daniel Mattaliano couldn't have done justice to the question. Maybe not even to save his life. And I should know. I'd given him a chance to try.

My father shook his head and left that great mystery in the dust. "Anyway, that detective called this morning and told us about the arrest. Told us what I already knew. He was just checking in to make sure you're still willing to testify."

My heart drummed again, because I felt like I'd gotten my answer. It wasn't that somebody had just started a rumor that Nick's dad had been arrested. People knew it around town *and* the officer was double-checking my willingness to appear in court. It didn't seem like a trap anymore. It seemed like it was over.

I had never been so thrilled and so disappointed all at the same time.

"Who answered the phone?" I asked him. I could hear the wariness in my own voice.

"Your mother did."

"Is she even going to let me testify?"

"She isn't about to get a say in the matter."

"Good."

He looked past me to my work for a few seconds. Examined the V-belts and the grease fittings.

"That looks just fine," he said. He turned to leave, which felt like a relief. But only seconds later he stopped, turned around. Considered me again. "Whatever happened to that group of friends of yours? You were so keen on them."

"Well. One had to go on the run because he got accused by his own father of something he didn't do. One enlisted in the army early and got killed straightaway. And the other . . ." I paused. I had no idea if my mother had told him I'd been keeping company with a Japanese boy. I had no idea how he would react. "The other one, his family moved."

"Oh. That's too bad. Doesn't give you much to do in a long summer, now does it?"

"No, sir."

"Oh well. More work I'll get out of you. More money you'll get to sock away."

"Yes, sir."

But I wasn't going to sock the money away. I was going to give it to Nick. He had a long journey in front of him, and the time had come.

He walked away in the hot sun, sending up trails of dust from the heels of his work boots.

I waited until he was entirely out of sight. Then I quickly finished my job on the combine. I walked around the farm for ten minutes or so, memorizing where everybody seemed to be stationed.

Then I did something I had never done, and never thought I would do. I snuck out to see Nick in broad daylight.

———

"Nick," I said from the top of the stairs. "It's only me."

I knew it would scare him to hear somebody come into the shed in the middle of the day. He had every reason to assume I would never do such a thing.

I heard him blow out a breath he must have been holding since the shed door opened. I actually heard it from my perch at the top of the stairs. That's how hard it burst out of him.

"Jeez, Steven, what're you doing here? You scared me three-quarters to death."

"It's over," I said.

"What did you say?"

I think he'd heard me. I think the whole situation just took a few seconds to process.

I made my way down the steps.

Nick was in the corner in the dark with his back pressed up against the cool dirt wall, holding Akira tightly to his chest. I could tell he had not yet shaken the scare I'd given him.

"It's over," I said. "You're free."

I said it like I was very happy for him. Because, at least in that moment, I *was* very happy for him. In most of the moments that followed I would be happy for him but sad for me, and I mostly guessed that would have to do.

"How do you know?"

He broke his statue-like pose. Set the dog on her paws on the dirt. She trotted over to greet me, and I scratched behind her ears.

"They arrested your dad. They charged him with attempted murder. Everybody in town is talking about it. And then that detective called again to make sure I was willing to testify."

"I thought they were going to issue you one of those . . ."

"Subpoenas?"

"Right. That. And you wouldn't have any choice."

"Yeah. That's how it'll be. I guess he was just checking to see if my mom would make any trouble. Anyway, it doesn't seem like a trap. It seems like you're free to come out."

For a few beats, he said nothing. He still seemed to be processing the information.

Then he said, "That's good news. Isn't it?" He asked as if he really wasn't sure.

"It *is* good news," I said. "It's really good news. Only thing is . . ."

"You wish I didn't have to go."

"Yeah."

He moved the three or four steps to where I stood half ready to cry in the middle of that dirt dungeon. To my surprise, he took me into his arms. Tenderly. Not a guy hug at all.

"Part of me wishes I didn't have to go, too," he said quietly, more or less directly into my ear.

"Maybe you could just go back to your house. Then we could still see each other."

"I don't think that'll work. Everybody knows how old I am. They'll send me to some kind of orphanage or something. Or just send me to my mother's. But I have to go there on my own, otherwise I won't be able to take Akira."

I won't say it hadn't occurred to me that I would probably lose both of them at the same time. But, as was pointed out to me earlier, there's real and then there's real.

We still had our arms around each other. Speaking of real.

"What if your mom won't let you keep her?"

"Then I won't live with my mom. Nobody knows me there. I'll tell everybody I'm eighteen. I can pass. I'll find some work or something and live where I can keep her."

I breathed quietly in his arms for a few seconds, then asked the question I could no longer keep locked away. He had answered it once already. But I needed reassurance.

"You'll come back, though. Right?"

For a moment he held me even more tightly. Then he let go and stepped away. He dropped to one knee on the hard dirt floor and looked up into my eyes. Grabbed one of my hands. As if he were about to propose marriage.

"I, Nick Mattaliano, promise I will not leave you for good, Steven Katz. As soon as I'm old enough to live on my own . . . hell, even when I'm old enough to pass for old enough to live on my own, I'll be back for you. If you'd leave home and run away with me . . ."

"In a minute," I said. "Without even thinking twice."

I was so happy with the state of that moment that I didn't feel torn apart that he was leaving. I felt like we were hammering out a whole new us, and it would be enough to sustain me in his absence.

I was wrong, of course. But in that moment, I was happy.

"Where will we go?" I added.

He towed me by the hand over to his bed. My heart jumped up into my throat, thinking something was about to happen for real. But instead we just lay on our backs, side by side, hands laced behind our heads. Elbows bumping. Akira climbed up onto my belly and walked around and around in a circle before curling up there to sleep. I absent-mindedly petted her with one hand, leaving my elbow pressed against Nick's, thinking how much I would miss her. She was the closest I had ever come to having a dog, even though she was clearly more Nick's than mine. I wondered if he would make it back before the natural end of her life, so we could own her together.

"I was thinking Los Angeles," he said. "Because we could see that telescope they built on the hill in Griffith Park. And there's farmwork there. Orange and lemon orchards in the valley. And we know farmwork."

"That sounds good."

"San Francisco's supposed to be nice. But I don't know about farmwork there. We might have to learn to do something new. Or maybe even New York City."

I didn't have to ask why he was suggesting only the biggest cities in the whole country. I knew. We both knew. Two young men together? That wouldn't work in a small town. That would only work in a place so big that nobody can keep track of anybody else. A place where you can be a stranger to the people all around you—the people living right next to you. It had to be a place where we could get lost and stay lost.

"Why New York?" I asked him.

"Why not New York?"

"It's so far."

"Not when you're there."

I laughed out loud. It felt good. It was hard to remember when I last had.

"What's funny?" he asked.

"Just the way you said it. It's not far when you're there."

"Well, it's not. It's only far from *here*. And if we go to New York, here won't matter anymore. And we'll stop measuring things by it."

"That's true, I guess. But we don't know the first thing about New York."

"I do. I was born there."

I tried to sit up. To look at him. But I didn't want to disturb the dog. I just craned my neck and looked over at the side of his face. "You were? I didn't know that. Why didn't I know that?"

"I don't know. I guess it just never came up. We didn't move out here to California till I was seven."

I uncraned my neck and rested the back of my head on my palm again. Stared up at the dirt ceiling with him.

"Well, I don't really care where we go," I said. "Just as long as we're together."

We lay quietly for a long time. Then I asked the question. Because the more time went by, the more not asking it felt more painful than asking it.

"When will you go?" I asked.

"Tonight."

"You don't have to move around in the dark anymore."

"I sort of do. Because we still don't want anyone to know you were hiding me."

"Oh. Okay. Will you at least come to the house and say goodbye?"

"I don't think I should. I don't want to get you in trouble. I think we need to say goodbye right here, right now. I have your address. I'll write and tell you how I'm doing."

"You better."

We fell silent, but did not end our meeting. Neither one of us seemed to want to rush that moment.

It was probably close to an hour later when he sat up suddenly. I sat up, too, holding Akira to my chest. Nick's face was close to mine. We looked into each other's eyes for what felt like a long time. It was deeply exhilarating and deeply awkward, all at once.

Then he kissed me on the lips. Brief. Firm. Sure.

"Go now," he said. "Trust me."

"Okay," I said. "I trust you."

I kissed the dog on the forehead and gave her back to Nick. Climbed the stairs. Looked both ways. Jogged home.

—

Pretty shortly after dark that night I packed some sandwiches and leftover chicken from the fridge for Nick and the dog. I put it in a bag with all the money I could scrape together. Every bit of allowance I had managed to save—which wasn't much because I'd been using it to buy extra food for them for months—and everything I'd earned doing farmwork since school let out. All the cash I had saved in my piggy bank. Dollar bills and quarters and nickels and dimes and pennies. I just dropped it all loose into the bag.

Then I walked out to the shed for what I knew would be the last time.

"Nick," I said from just inside the door.

I was afraid I had missed him.

"Steven, you really shouldn't—"

"I just brought you some things for the road. That's all. I'm not even coming down. I'm leaving them in a bag just inside the door. Don't go without them."

He might have said "thank you." I'm pretty sure he said something. But I had one more thing to say. I was halfway out the door, retreating as fast as I reasonably could. But I paused just long enough to say it.

"I love you."

"Love you, too, Steven." That came out loud and clear.

I trotted away, doing my best not to cry.

It was the beginning of a new era. An era for which I thought I was prepared.

Rarely in my life have I ever been so spectacularly wrong.

Part Four

Late Summer 1942

Chapter Sixteen

Kill Me Twice

I sat at the dinner table, watching my mother hover over my brother, Terrence, cutting his meat in a particularly fussy manner.

Yes, my brother was home. In mid-July he had returned from the war a changed man. Please believe me when I say none of those changes were toward the good.

He came home because he was seriously injured. It didn't look like much from the outside. It looked like five places on his cheek and forehead where shrapnel had cut through his skull and into his brain. Actually, it *was* bad to look at, in a very real way. It was hard to look at him without feeling that squeamishness brought on by imagining his pain. But it didn't look like something bad enough to earn him a ticket home.

It was, though. It was bad enough because those fragments in his brain could not be safely removed with even the most cutting-edge 1942 medicine. Not that soldiers in the field had that level of medicine available to them, but my mother had taken him into Fresno, then Los Angeles, then San Francisco to see all the best doctors. She got not only a second opinion but a third and fourth opinion. All the opinions were the same: leave well enough alone.

But well enough was not good.

His motor skills had been severely affected. He walked fairly well, though one of his feet did seem to drag ever so slightly. But he got from place to place. It was his hands. His hands had become only marginally within his control. It was painful to watch his right hand, loosely gripping a fork, try to stab a piece of meat. He would circle it hesitantly, like a helicopter coming in for a landing, before attempting a sudden poke. Sometimes he would miss. Sometimes he would drop his fork. Other times he managed it, but it seemed to have been by sheer luck more than anything else.

In the first few days my mother would jump up from the table after a couple of misses. I never got to watch long enough to see what she intended to do. Maybe feed him. My father quickly cured her of that bad habit, stating in no uncertain terms that Terrence was not to be treated like an infant.

He did not cure her of cutting his meat, and I suppose that was for the best, because there was no way he could have managed that on his own.

I worry that what I say next might sound cruel. I swear I don't mean it that way. His speech was left unaffected. And I suffered for that.

If I had thought my brother was aggravating before, I now learned I had known nothing of aggravation. He had come home fully insufferable. Where before he would shovel food into his mouth in silence, he now spoke constantly about the state of the world. Now that he had seen a glimpse of the world outside our rural valley, he considered himself an unimpeachable expert on everything.

"Here's the thing about Europe," he said. Which seemed absurd, because he had never been anywhere near the continent. But he was not about to let that stop him. "Now we're planning to send more and more of our guys to all these countries in Europe, or so they say, and I think it's stupid. It's just more American boys going to die. And for what? The South Pacific I can see, because the Japanese are so warlike. I mean, they attacked us, so we have to fight back. But what do we care what happens in Europe? What is it to us?"

Meanwhile my mother still hovered over him, cutting his meat into tiny dice. I worried that she was creating too small a target for his inexact stabs.

Nobody answered for a time. But after a while my father looked up and around, as though somebody had just wakened him. "They're our allies," he said. With not much conviction.

"So?" Terrence laid the word down immediately, like a fence he dared anyone to climb. "What does that even mean?"

"It means they would do the same for us," I said. Then I immediately regretted opening my mouth.

Terrence laughed like a mule braying. "And what do you know about wars, little man? You weren't there. I was there. Those countries don't even have big enough armies to pay us back. We'll always end up doing more for them than they could ever do for us."

I would have been smart to keep my mouth shut, but he had rankled me with that "little man" bull.

"You think we should just let Hitler take over the whole continent?" I asked.

My mother shot me a withering look. Nobody was supposed to challenge Terrence on his grand statements.

I ignored her.

"I don't see why not," Terrence shot back. "What's it to us?"

"He's putting people in camps," I said. "Thousands and thousands of people."

"So? We put Japanese people in camps."

I wanted to speak out quite thoroughly regarding my thoughts on Japanese internment. And I wasn't afraid to. It wasn't that. I just wasn't sure how to argue that Hitler should be stopped for doing something so similar to what we were doing. You see, it was only the summer of 1942, and we did not yet know what was happening inside those German camps. I don't know who all knew and who didn't. There was a wise old man in town who had a pretty good inkling, but I wouldn't meet him until the following day. At the dinner table that night, we had no idea.

"But they're Jewish people," I said. "And we're Jewish."

I had hit on a point that was true yet not much discussed in our family. Yes, Katz was a Jewish name, at least in our case. Yes, our ancestors were Jewish on our father's side. But we didn't live that way, or acknowledge it much. I'd bet money my father had never set foot in a synagogue, or his father before him. We seemed, as a family, determined to live as any other American family might, leaving that simple fact behind. And the sad thing was, it mostly worked for us. And that made me mad, because it did *not* work for Suki and his family.

I wondered if it was simply because our faces didn't give us away.

"So?" Terrence said again.

"If we were over there, he would put us in a camp."

"But we're not," Terrence said.

My mother returned to her seat at the table, and, on her way by, slapped me hard on the upper arm.

"Ow!" I said.

"Leave your brother alone." She sat politely and replaced her cloth napkin in her lap. "How many times have I told you to leave your brother alone? He has enough problems without you giving him a hard time."

We fell into that mealtime silence that was terrible but familiar. Then again, compared to Terrence's ranting, maybe silence wasn't the worst thing that could happen to a guy.

—

The following morning I ate breakfast while Terrence was still asleep. I hardly have words for how relieved I was.

I did a few quick chores around the farm, but by 9:00 a.m. or so the heat was beastly. It actually struck me as beast-like—as if it lived and grew. It felt like a fire-breathing dragon, moving closer. Opening its fiery mouth wider and wider.

I retired to my room and waited until my mom brought the mail into the house. I wasn't trying to be lazy by waiting for her to walk out to the road and get it. I just didn't want her to see how desperately I was waiting for news.

"Anything for me?" I called from my room when I heard her come back through the door.

"You always ask that," she called back. "And there never is."

I wasn't sure whether to take that as a hard no, so I pushed my luck a little further. "And today?" I shouted.

"Today is just like every other day."

I sighed. Pulled to my feet. Left the house to walk into town.

By that time it was probably about 11:00, and the heat shimmered up in waves over the horizon as I stepped out the front door. The house at least had the benefit of swamp coolers. From the inside of the house, you might swear and grumble that they barely helped at all. But stepping out the front door felt like stepping into a preheated oven.

I trudged out to the road and headed toward town, my shoes kicking up little puffs of dust in the perfectly dry road dirt. The sun beat down on my white shirt, and I rolled its short sleeves up higher to catch more of a breeze on my arms. Unfortunately, there was no breeze.

By the time I reached the board sidewalks of town, my head was throbbing in a way that signaled I was a phase or two short of heatstroke.

I stepped inside the general store and sighed.

I won't say it was cool in there. It wasn't. But at least the roof provided shade. The big double doors in both the front and back of the store had been propped open wide, and a massive and noisy fan was blowing. But of course there was nothing for it to blow but hot air. It felt like stepping from a regular oven into a convection oven, except I didn't think that thought at the time because we didn't have them back then. But it was a marginal improvement.

Mr. Barker stood behind the counter, mopping his sweaty brow with the hem of his white apron.

I stepped up to the very new, very modern chest freezer that stocked popsicles, Creamsicles, and ice cream sandwiches, but when I looked in, I saw nothing but the metal bottom of the display case.

My heart dropped into my belly. At least, it felt that way.

"Oh no," I said. "You're out of the frozen stuff?"

"Freezer motor blew out," he said. "Couldn't take the heat. You should've been here an hour and a half ago. I was giving ice cream away so it wouldn't go to waste."

"Darn," I said.

I wanted to say more, but I didn't want to fuss too much about it, because freezers were a modern invention, and a big deal, and I knew Mr. Barker had paid dearly for that one. Any reasonable person could see he was having a far worse day than I was.

"I have cold sodas in the Frigidaire," he said.

I got myself a Coca-Cola, pausing just a split second to feel the cold hit my face. I could've stood there for days, but I knew he wouldn't want the door left open long.

I left a nickel on Mr. Barker's counter and popped the cap with the bottle opener bolted to the front. Then I wandered over to watch the old men play checkers. There were only two old men that day, sitting at the board. On a cooler day there might have been another three or four or five waiting to play the winner.

I gulped deeply on the cold drink and savored the iciness of it going down.

One of the old men was George Stanley, a seventysomething recent widower who hung out at the general store because his home was too lonely. He hadn't said so out loud, but it was generally understood. The other was an elderly Chinese man whose face I knew, but whose name I could not produce in the moment, though I may have known it at one time. We had nodded at each other around town, but had never spoken as far as I could recall. Now I can tell you his name was Gordon Cho, but I didn't know that at the time.

Mr. Stanley never so much as glanced up at me. I might as well not have existed. But Gordon Cho nodded to me, and gave me a sort of salute of polite acknowledgment.

"You want to play me next?" he asked.

"He's supposed to play the winner," Mr. Stanley barked.

"True enough. And I will be the winner."

He shot me a wickedly delighted smile, complete with a couple of missing teeth, and I couldn't help smiling in return. I sat in a wicker chair and watched him. Not watched both of them. Just him. He had captured my fancy in some way I could not explain.

He had a narrow and wizened face and a long gray beard. The beard seemed to take a break under his lower lip, then roar back with a vengeance under his chin, leaving the apple of his chin bare. His head was almost completely bald, the skin of his scalp spotted.

I had barely made these observations when he proudly crowed, "King me!"

Mr. Stanley had no choice but to comply. Three moves later Mr. Stanley had lost his last piece, and the game.

"Damn it," Stanley said. Then he looked over his shoulder at me, a cloud of guilt in his eyes. "Sorry for the language, son," he added.

"I've heard worse."

"I'll bet you have," Gordon Cho said. "Step right up to play, son."

I sat across from him, and we considered each other briefly.

"Gordon Cho," he said, and reached his hand out to me.

I shook it.

"Steven Katz."

"Oh, I know exactly who you are."

"Meaning . . . ?"

"It's a small town."

As he spoke, he quickly set up the board, his spotted and wrinkled hands flashing. He put the white pieces on my side.

"Wait a minute," I said. "Do you play for money?"

"Sometimes I do and sometimes I don't. This time I don't. When some of these hotshot townies come around thinking they can beat me easy, I take 'em for all they're worth. But I don't need your money. You're a good boy. You get the first move, sonny."

I slid one of my pieces diagonally one space. It was the only move one could make to start.

"How do you know I'm a good boy?"

"Tell you later," he said, and made a move of his own.

For three games, we didn't speak. We were busy watching the board. He beat me three for three.

Then, as he was setting up the board for a fourth game, a couple of big farmhands came in and hovered over us, making it clear they wanted to play. I didn't like the look or the feel of them. They looked like the kind of guys who would dig up some trouble just for the entertainment value of watching the sparks fly.

Mr. Barker noticed.

"You know the rules, boys," he called over. "They get three games after you show up, and, after that, one of you can play winner."

"But we want to play each other," one of the big men whined.

"Well, that's not how it works," Barker said, his voice growing lower and harder. He was anything but a small man himself.

"Okay, fine," the other guy said. "We'll play winner."

"Nope," Mr. Cho said. His voice sounded upbeat. Perky. The very word seemed to delight him.

I froze, waiting for the reaction. The trouble.

"What d'you mean, no?" they both said, more or less at once.

"You can have the board. We're leaving. My friend and I are going to go outside and smoke a cigar."

He fairly leapt to his feet. He was surprisingly spry for a man his age, which I guessed to be over eighty.

I followed him out of the store.

There was a wooden bench in front of the general store, and it had blessedly fallen into the shade. He sat, and I sat next to him, pinning my hands under my thighs.

"I don't suppose you actually smoke cigars," he said. "But you're welcome to one if you want it." He held two gigantic stogies in my general direction.

"No thank you, Mr. Cho," I said.

"Call me Gordon."

I watched in fascination as he took a set of cigar accessories out of a fancy tooled leather case. One clipped off the end of the cigar. The other drilled a hole in its base. He lit a match and got the cigar lit and drawing well, puffing smoke out toward the passersby.

We sat a moment, him smoking, me watching, listening to the clatter of townspeople's boot heels on the wooden boards.

I opened my mouth to ask him how he knew who I was and why he thought I was a good boy, but I never got that far. I never needed to ask.

"Your brother just got back from the war," he said. "Injured. Your father owns one of the two biggest farms in the valley. The police thought you knew something about that bar fight that got so bad some months ago. We all knew it was Daniel to blame. I have no idea what made those detectives so easy to fool."

"And you know all that because . . . I know, it's a small town. You said that. But do you really know this much about everybody who lives here?"

"No," he said, quickly and surely. "No, I took a special interest in you."

"Why?"

"Because you were best friends with the Yamamoto boy. And, after Pearl Harbor, you didn't turn your back on him. And, after FDR's terrible order, you didn't turn your back on him. Those of us who are not in the good social graces of most of the town, we notice that."

"That's why you said I was a good boy."

"Correct."

"I liked him, though. I didn't do it just so people would think I was all noble."

"I know that. If you had done it just so people would think you were all noble, then you wouldn't be a good boy. Just a good actor. So tell me, Steven. How is your brother?"

"He's driving me crazy," I said. "Oh, I'm sorry. That sounded terrible. It's really hard to say anything against him, the way things are now. Makes me sound like a terrible person."

"Is he driving you crazy because he's injured and can't do things as well as before?"

"No, of course not. I wouldn't fault him for that."

"Then in what way is he driving you crazy?"

"He's just being a jerk."

"Then I wouldn't worry too much. So far you don't sound terrible."

"He just . . . he came back thinking he knows everything. He's just decided he's the complete authority on the entire world. Like last night at dinner. He starts talking about the war in Europe. He thinks it's none of our business. That we should just let Hitler take what he wants."

"Then he doesn't know everything," Gordon said. "And what do *you* think about Europe, Steven?"

"I think somebody needs to stop him. He's locking up Jews, and my family is Jewish. I told my brother he'd lock us up if we were there. But he just said we aren't there. Like that solves it. Like if it's not us, it doesn't matter."

"Ah, yes, that's a common disease. The dreaded 'If it's not us, it doesn't matter' disease. I'm glad you spoke your mind to him."

"I did, but every time I do, my mother tells me to leave him alone. But also, he said something, and I didn't know what to say back to him.

He said we can't really stop another country from locking its own people up in camps because we lock people up in camps, too."

For a few seconds he only smoked in silence. I watched the heavy smoke roll out into the street. The heat and complete lack of breeze seemed to trap it. Hold it together. It looked bluish, and smelled almost fruity.

"You have to know that I think the camps this country built for the Japanese are very, very bad," he said. "Very shameful. A national shame. But the camps Hitler built in Germany and Poland? They're different. They're a whole different kind of bad. Evil bad. You know he's not only locking up Jews, right?"

"No. I didn't know that. I only heard about Jews."

"The camps are plenty full of Jews, but also Poles and other kinds of Slavic peoples. Gypsies. And people who are . . . what's the word? Who are not . . . able. Physically or mentally fully able. And homosexuals." My blood froze at the word. I rarely heard it spoken out loud. "And Jehovah's Witnesses. And of course anyone who opposes him or even speaks against him. And I can't tell you absolutely and for a fact what goes on once they have them there. I just know that too many people are going in."

"Wait a minute," I said. "How do you know all this?"

"My great-grandson is in the army, and they sent him to Europe. He writes me a letter every day. Every day without fail. He says nobody really knows about the insides of the camps. It's a guarded secret. But so many people go in. Trainload after trainload after trainload of people. Hundreds of thousands of people are taken there, maybe more, but there's no way the camps are big enough to house all those people. There couldn't possibly be room. And yet no one is ever seen leaving again."

"Wait . . . ," I said again.

"All right. I'll wait."

We sat a moment. He smoked. My brain ran in circles.

"What are you saying happened to them?"

"I'm not saying what happened to them, because I don't know. I try only to say what I know. I'm just presenting a few facts. Far too many people go in. No one comes out."

The minute he mentioned people coming out, those two big farmhands stepped out of the general store and into the dirt of the street, shuffling their feet as they walked away.

"Ah, good," Gordon said. "I felt a bad cloud surrounding those two. Now that they're gone, shall we go in and play a few more games?"

"Okay," I said.

I stood, and got a good glimpse of myself in the store window. My shirt was soaked through with sweat. Under the armpits and right down to the waistband of my pants. Around and under the collar, with a big patch of sweat in the middle of my belly. My hair was plastered to my forehead with sweat. And my brow was furrowed into a puzzled and disturbed expression.

I looked at my own reflection and pictured myself being stared down by Adolf Hitler. Maybe he would decide to kill me. Maybe he would even want to kill me twice.

I followed Gordon back into the only slightly cooler store and lost four more games of checkers. I told myself it was because my thoughts were such a tangle. But because it was Gordon, I probably would have lost the four games anyway.

———

That night at dinner, I was the instigator. Why I sometimes felt the need to poke that gruff and dangerous bear during one of its rare naps might be hard to explain. But I was nursing a deep grievance toward my family after my talk with Gordon Cho that day. In fact, I was on fire with grievances. Burning to the ground inside. Some little piece of that turmoil needed to come up and out.

"I think Hitler's camps are worse than you think they are," I said.

Everyone had been eating in silence, heads down. I saw all three of their forks pause. Hang there in the air. As if the forks were more shocked by my outburst than the people holding them. But nobody looked up at me. And nobody spoke.

I poked harder.

"Hundreds of thousands of people are being forced into them. Trainload after trainload after trainload of people. More than could ever live in those places. More than could possibly fit. But nobody ever comes out again."

My brother, Terrence, was the only one to acknowledge me. "How'd you get to be the big expert all of a sudden?"

"I know a man whose great-grandson is in Europe, fighting. And he writes to him every day about what's going on in Europe. And it's bad. Nobody really exactly knows *how* bad, but bad. And it's not just Jews, either, even though they're rounding up plenty of those. It's Polish people and Slavic people and Gypsies and Jehovah's Witnesses." I opened my mouth to say the final part, but my voice, my brain, skipped like the needle on a phonograph record. But I tried again. Pushed harder this time. "And homosexuals."

I felt a collective wince around the table as the word struck them.

"Well, he can have the faggots," my father said.

My father. Not stupid, immature eighteen-year-old Terrence. My own father said that to me.

"Don't use words like that at the dinner table, Marv," my mother said.

"Right," I said. "Don't. It's a terrible way to talk about people."

"I don't mean because it's derogatory," my mom said, her voice casual. Her mouth full. "Some people deserve derogatory language. It's just such an ugly word. The whole idea of people like that is so ugly. We're trying to eat. I don't see why you'd bring up something like that at the dinner table."

"I didn't bring it up," my father said. "Steven did."

"Well, I'm talking to him, too," she said.

A silence fell around the table. I looked at them one by one. Nobody looked back. But I still had a flash of memory. Of staring at my reflection in the glass of the general store earlier that day. I had pictured Hitler looking back at me. Seeing someone he'd be perfectly happy to kill. But now I was looking at my own family, such as it was. A family dinner was a bizarre time to have that feeling come around again.

I couldn't let it sit. I had to know. It was too integral to my existence. I had to hear where I really stood in the eyes of the people I lived with every day.

"Are you saying that if somebody is a homosexual, you figure it's okay for them to be killed?"

"Whoa," my father said between bites. "Who said anything about killing?"

"All those people going in and never coming out again."

"Maybe they're just packed in really tight," my father said.

It struck me as a childlike way to look at the world. Twisting it around in your mind until it reached a shape you could live with, so as not to have to examine too many of your own beliefs too deeply.

"Or maybe they really are getting killed," I said. "Would that be okay?"

"Well, not for the Jews," my father said. "And not just for a person's nationality. That's not their fault. But if a person was a deviant like that . . . seems you're protecting the world from them. Protecting the children."

"How did children get into this?" I asked, trying to sound a tiny bit less aghast than I felt. I doubt I succeeded.

I couldn't stop. I could feel something burning inside me, and it had taken over. Like a house fire when the house is fully engulfed. When a fire is very small, say, at the end of a match, you have a chance of blowing it out. Once it takes over the whole house, there's not much one little person can do to fight it. It'll blow *you* out if you try to stop it.

"They prey on children," he said. "Try to convert them. You're too young to know about such things. But the world could use a little cleaning up in that regard."

Terrence took a stab at a pile of macaroni on his plate. In a pile the size of that one, it was hard to miss. "Hell, I'll take out a few with my own hands," he said.

The fact that his hands fell a good bit short of lethal did not help his words go down any easier. Not one bit easier.

"Language," my mother barked at him.

I took that to mean that the word "hell" was the only part of Terrence's sentence to trouble her.

I looked to my mother, who—remarkably—looked back. When she spoke, it was seemingly to my brother and father.

"I don't know why we're talking about this at the dinner table," she said. "It's disgusting. We're lucky that a thing like that isn't any part of our lives or our town, and I don't know why we're even letting it spoil our dinner."

No more was said about it that evening. No more was said at that dinner, period. But something had changed in me. The very thin thread of emotional connection to my family had snapped, and I could feel it. It felt the way I imagined being set adrift in space might feel. I was alone in that house, unrelated to these people in any way that could benefit me. I was stuck in a life with three people who would just as soon see me dead. It was only their ignorance of the real me that had kept this truth from me for so many years.

I made up my mind that as soon as I knew Nick's whereabouts, I would be out of there. No, not even "made up my mind." That suggests a chain of thoughts. It was just there, and true. It was more *revealed* to me than *created* by me.

I never poked the bear by trying to get through to my family again. You may say I learn slowly, but you can't say I never learn.

Chapter Seventeen

Things Are Incomplete

After a couple more days I grew so despondent regarding the mail that I didn't bother to ask my mother if there was anything for me. I just figured there still wasn't.

I heard her come back into the house, but I didn't make a sound.

I was lying on my back on the bed, fingers laced behind my head, my face up into the flow from the swamp cooler. Eyes squeezed shut. Almost as though I were praying to the swamp cooler to do better. To send me a little more relief. I was wearing a pair of shorts but nothing else—all the better to feel that tiny breath of coolness on my chest, belly, and legs.

I heard the door to my room open, and I knew it was my mom. I did not know it was mail.

"You could knock," I said.

"Sure, because it's so private, what you're doing in here. Which is exactly nothing."

I felt something light land on my stomach. Then I knew.

I sat up quickly, grabbing for the mail and missing, causing it to flutter off onto the floor. Correction: causing *them* to flutter off onto the floor.

There were two letters.

I looked to my mom to see how closely she was watching, but I saw only my bedroom door closing. She had already let herself out.

I sat on the edge of the bed, frozen, staring at the two letters. One had landed on the rag rug near my bed, the other had slid halfway under the nightstand.

The one on the rug was from Suki. I knew it immediately by its return address. It read:

> Yamamoto
> 32-8-1
> Manzanar, California

Just simple like that. Nothing more.

The one half under the nightstand was from Nick. I knew because I recognized his handwriting. It was one of those small white envelopes with the stamp printed right on it that you could buy for three cents at the post office. I jumped for it, and pulled it out, anxious to see the return address.

There was none.

I turned it over in my hands, thinking maybe he had written the return address on the back flap, as people sometimes did. Nothing.

I decided he had put his new address inside, on the letter, to guard it from prying eyes.

I decimated that envelope tearing it open. Absolutely ripped it to shreds.

Inside was a small single sheet of paper, written in loopy, messy script on both sides.

> *Dear Steven,*
> *Sorry it took me so long to write, but my mother doesn't give me any money. She also doesn't give me any food, so I have to earn whatever I can to buy something to eat for me and Akira. So I had to do that before I could buy postage.*

Don't tell anybody this, but I stole dog food for her. I've never stolen anything in my life, but I stole dog food for her from the market in town, because it was okay with me if I had to go hungry, but not if she did. But now I was able to get a couple of small jobs, so I don't expect to have to do it again. Thank goodness. I'm saving up to pay the store back for what I took.

My mom didn't exactly take me in. She said she would have, but she just got started with a new boyfriend, and she didn't want to scare him away. Not sure why I would be so scary, except I know some men don't want to think about being fathers to somebody else's kid. Also, I don't know this for a fact, but I think she's lying about her age to him. I think she doesn't want him to know she's old enough to have a 15-year-old son. The reason I think so is because she told the guy I'm her nephew—her older sister's boy. She doesn't even have a sister.

The place where she lives has a big yard with a big tree house, and she told me she wouldn't kick me out if I wanted to stay there. It's honestly not much better than a root cellar, except in another way it is, because there's lots of light, and I can come and go as I please. But if it's better than what I got from you, it's really not because she was trying to give me better. It's just nice to be free and not looking over my shoulder for the police.

I've been doing odd jobs for the neighbors to make enough to feed us (me and the dog). I think I'm going to try to go back to school in the fall.

I don't know if you can write letters to Suki at Manzanar, or if you figured out for a fact that it's where they put him. But if you do manage to get a

letter through to him, please tell him the dog is doing
great. I know he'll be happy to hear that, and he can
tell his grandmother.
   I hope you forgive me for waiting so long to write.
Love, Nick

I finished reading, then turned back to the front of the letter. Then back again to the flip side. I turned it over and over in my hands, as if a return address would simply appear. As if I could force one to materialize through my sheer will. But he had not given me his new address.

I sat on the edge of the bed for a time, holding that letter, my thoughts whirling through my poor tired brain like a dust devil in the dry valley dirt.

Maybe he had been afraid one of my parents would intercept the letter and read it. Maybe that's why he kept his new address a secret. But what could anyone do to hurt him now, anyway? Maybe he was still halfway afraid that law enforcement was tricking him by pretending there was no more warrant for his arrest. Maybe he forgot it. I just had no idea.

I picked up the mangled envelope, which I had to piece together like a jigsaw puzzle to make out the postmark. The letter had been stamped in Phoenix, Arizona. Which didn't tell me much. Maybe he mailed it from Mesa, and the mail was sent to Phoenix for postmarking.

I had no idea about anything.

It took a minute or two of whirling before I picked up Suki's letter, noting that Manzanar, California, had its own postmark. It seemed weird to think of that camp as a bigger, better-organized location than Mesa, Arizona.

I opened the envelope far more carefully. Far more respectfully. I tore the flap away, but did no more damage to it than that.

I held in my hands two sheets of unlined paper, filled with neat, careful block print.

Dear Steven,

I wrote to you before and never heard back, but maybe you didn't get it. They say some of the letters are slow to go through and some never do. I guess I choose to believe you wouldn't get a letter from me and not write back. Or maybe you wrote back and they never gave your letter to me. That happens, too. Anyway, I had to try again.

How are you and how is Akira? I guess it might sound rude to ask after her first thing like that, but my family would be very happy for any news. But also I have to tell you that if you kept her for a while but then couldn't keep her anymore, I won't judge. None of us will. If you gave her any extra days at all we'll be thankful to you for that. Otherwise it's just putting you in a terrible position. But of course I hope like crazy that you'll write back and tell me she's doing okay. My grandmother is not doing well. The weather is really extreme here, even compared to home. Very hot and very cold. She's old, and it's hard for her. And also I think just the very fact of being locked up in this place is taking a toll on her health. I worry she might die before we get out of here. I always knew my grandmother would die—everybody's grandmother will die sooner or later, that's just life—but it's really hard to think about the end of her life being here. It would mean the world to me if I could tell her Akira is happy and alive with somebody. In fact, if you tell me she's not, I'll probably lie and tell my grandmother she is. But if I could show her a real letter from you with good news about the dog, that would just mean everything.

I'm guessing your brother Terrence had to ship out since my family and I left. Is he okay? Do you get letters from him? I know you guys are not close. I just wondered.

I know you probably want to hear about life here. Someday I'll see you again and tell you all about it. But they say the letters get read and censored before they go out, so I'm not going to write about it now. It'll just get blacked out anyway.

I know you must be lonely there all on your own, unless you're somehow able to see Nick. Or maybe you have some new friends. I hope so. I wish I could be there to go camping up in the mountains with you. Those were some good times, and now I think I didn't appreciate them enough. I want to go back and do them over, knowing what I know now, so I can feel how lucky I am to be up there. But I guess that's not the way life works. Is it?

Please write back when you can.

Love, Suki

I read the closing three or four times, and it set my brain to spinning again. I had thought that Nick ending his letter with the word "love" was significant. And maybe it was. But then Suki reminded me that lots of people end their letters that way.

I lay on my back on the bed for a while, the letters on my belly, but the swamp cooler blew them onto the rug again. I didn't go after them. I just lay there and tried to make sense of the world. Everything I cared about felt so distant. It was all one step removed from me. Every bit of information was limited, leaving me to grasp for how I should interpret it.

In time I got up, got decently dressed, and walked into town to try to find Gordon Cho, the letters burning in my pocket.

———

I hung around the general store for a few minutes, running a cold, sweaty bottle of orange soda back and forth across my forehead and watching the old men play checkers.

I wanted to ask after Mr. Cho, but I wasn't sure how wise it would be to let everybody know I wanted to see him. It was all over town that Suki and I were friends, and that I had tried to assault a man for underpaying Mr. Yamamoto for his truck. I already had a reputation as something of a race traitor. Part of me didn't mind—considered it a badge of honor, in fact—but it depended how far I was from home, and how outnumbered I felt.

I decided Mr. Barker was okay, and that I could trust him not to make trouble for me on purpose. I wandered over to his counter and whispered my question.

"Has Mr. Cho been in today?"

"He was here all morning," he said, "but he left a couple of hours ago."

I sighed, and carried my nearly empty orange soda out onto the board sidewalks of town, where I looked around, sheltering my eyes from the sun with one arm. Then I sighed again, glugged down the last of the drink, and set off toward home, bracing myself for the long, hot walk, tossing my empty soda bottle into a public trash can as I walked by.

And then, like magic, I saw him. Somehow I was looking in just the right place at just the right time. There was a gap between the land office and one of the feed stores, and I happened to glance through it. And there he was, sitting on the tiny front stoop of his tiny house, under a carefully patched awning, fanning himself with a colorful silk fan.

He waved expansively to me, and I cut between the buildings and walked at an angle across the dirt lot to where he sat.

I felt as though the sun was pouring down on me in an entirely different way. I'm not sure if I can explain it. I felt as though the sky had split open and cast some much-needed light down all around me, like a blessing. Just for that moment I felt blessed. As though not everything in my life had to hurt all the time. It was a feeling like breathing easily, if that makes sense.

As I got closer, I saw he was sipping some kind of hot drink from an expensive-looking bone china cup with no handle. I don't mean the handle had been broken off. I mean it was clearly designed and made without one. I stood with the toes of my shoes right up against his little stoop, and nodded to him, and he nodded back with a broad, partially toothless smile.

"Can I get you a cup of tea, my friend Steven?" he asked.

It was nice to matter to someone again. To be someone's friend.

"Isn't it awfully hot today for tea?"

"It's better than you think to have a hot drink on a hot day. People can't bring themselves to do it, but they should. They wouldn't feel the heat so much. But if you don't want to try it, or you need to go, I'll understand."

"I don't need to go. Actually, I was hoping to get a chance to talk to you. I was hoping to get your advice on something."

"My advice?" he asked. He sounded genuinely surprised. It struck me that maybe he didn't know he was wise. "What makes you think I know enough to offer good advice?"

"Seems to me you know a lot."

"I don't know everything," he said.

"But that's just it. That's why I want your advice. Because you're smart enough to know you don't know everything."

"Unlike your brother."

"Exactly."

"Well, my friend, I can't say how helpful I'll be, but have a seat and we'll see how I do. What about the tea? Yes or no on that?"

"Yes," I said. "I'll give it a try. Thank you."

I sat in the shade of his awning on a hard wooden chair while he rattled around inside the little shack dwelling. When he emerged, he held my tea in another beautiful bone china cup. It was thin and fragile looking, with flowering tree designs around the outside of the rim.

I had to hold it by the very edge because of the lack of a handle, and because it was hot.

I sipped the tea. I don't think I'd ever had tea before. It was strong, and a little bitter. And yet, somehow, pleasing.

"What's on your mind, my friend Steven?"

"I'm just wondering about people."

He let loose a delightful bark of a laugh. "Who doesn't wonder about people? They give us so much to try to figure out! They are a never-ending mystery."

"I'll say."

"Can you be more specific?"

"I guess I'm wondering about what people do. And what they don't do. And whether, if you were expecting them to do something, and then they don't do it . . . I guess I'm wondering if that was on purpose or not."

He looked perplexed, and I realized it would be better if I stopped talking in riddles. I said more.

"Let's say a friend of yours went away. And for weeks you were waiting for them to write and tell you where they are now. Where you can find this person, or even just write a letter back to them." I wondered if he noticed how hard I was working to avoid male or female pronouns. It seemed painfully obvious to *me*. "But then this person finally writes but doesn't even give you a return address. I'm just wondering if people forget things like that or if they leave them out on purpose."

I took another sip of tea, waiting for him to answer. The steam rose into my face, and the hot drink was warming me up on the inside. And I remember thinking maybe he was right. Maybe it was making me suffer a tiny bit less from the heat.

"The problem here," Gordon Cho said, "is that nothing is absolute. I get the impression that you think I know all about the world, but nobody can really answer for human nature. I worry that you might give too much weight to what I say."

"I just want to know what you would think if that happened to you."

"If it happened to me," he repeated. "All right. I tend to think that people mostly do what it was their intention to do. They might tell you otherwise and really believe it themselves, but it seems people have reasons for doing what they do. And not doing what they don't do. But it's certainly possible to forget to include something until after you've mailed a letter. Nothing absolute, as I've said. Maybe there are three chances out of four that it was purposeful, conscious or not, and one chance that it was an honest mistake."

I sighed deeply. Watched a man walk by on the board sidewalk of town and stop and stare at us from the distance. I couldn't see the look on his face from Gordon Cho's porch, but I got the sense that he wanted me to notice how long he was staring. That he wanted to register his disapproval.

I ignored him as best I could.

"So I still don't know," I said.

He offered a cryptic smile. "I hope you didn't think I could tell you for a fact what your friend intended."

I sighed again. "I guess not."

We sipped in silence for a moment. I watched the distant passersby, braced for more disapproval. But then I noticed, in my peripheral vision, that Mr. Cho was staring at the side of my face. I looked over and connected with his eyes.

"Permission to offer advice you didn't ask me for," he said.

"Yes. Please. I need all the advice I can get."

"Good. Because clearly the world is making you very unhappy."

I felt a miniature lurch in my stomach. I wondered if he was reading my thoughts, and if he already knew more than I wanted anybody to know.

"How do you know that?"

"Do you think our pain is invisible to others? It's not. Yours is right there in your eyes and on your face. And now that you've told me you were waiting for something important and didn't get it . . . well . . .

let's just say it's very common to want to know how everything will be resolved. We have all these situations in our lives that have not yet wrapped up, and we want to know how they will end. It can drive us crazy, wanting to know. But life will always be incomplete. Our situations with people and things will always be in progress. By the time you find out where your friend lives now, there will be other situations in your life to trouble you, and you will be dying to know how they will resolve. But then you will always be dying to know something. And dying is not much of a way to live."

I breathed for a moment, trying to take in everything he'd said. It was a lot to process.

"I don't know how to do it any other way."

"I understand," he said. "Of course you don't. You're just a young boy. I've had eighty-six years to practice living. And you've had . . . ?"

"Fifteen years this month. But . . . practice what, exactly?"

"Enjoying the world just as it is. Understanding that many things are incomplete. Allowing it to be so. One day there will come a time in your life when you know how everything has ended, but, unfortunately, that will be the day you die. On that day, even if you are waiting for an answer to something, you will know how that story ended: you died before learning. But you don't want this to be the day you die. Nobody does. Those are your two choices. You can be alive and wondering, or you can die and know how everything turned out. Put that way, doesn't the living option sound better?"

"Yes," I said. "I guess it does. Still . . ."

"I know. Your problems don't go away just because I told you this. But you knew that. You knew you wouldn't come talk to me and walk away with your problem literally solved."

"That's true, I guess."

"Just practice, Steven. Practice accepting that things are incomplete. Practice accepting that the answer at the moment is that you don't know."

"I can't accept that. I hate it."

"You can accept something you hate."

I connected with his eyes again, and saw the patience there. Saw the way he cared about my turmoil.

"How do you figure? That makes no sense."

"Did you think to accept something means to like it?"

"Well. Yeah. I guess I did. Doesn't everybody?"

"No, my friend. To accept something means you stop trying to fight with what is. You stop trying to change things that are outside of your control to change. That's exhausting. You must be very tired. Some things are impossible for us to change, and any time we try to do something impossible, it's going to wear us out. It saps our life force. Our energy. Maybe you hate a thing more than anything. But it's what is. To accept it means to see that it *is* that way, and that it won't be another way no matter how much you hate it."

"Whoa." My head literally felt a little spinny. "That's a lot to take in."

"It is."

"I'm going to go home and think about that."

"You do."

"Thank you for the tea."

"Anytime. Drop by anytime, my friend Steven."

I would drop by many times in the months after that. Well into the following year. But in that moment I had to go home and settle my poor tired brain. And think. Think about what it meant to stop fighting the world. To let things be the way they were.

And I needed to write a letter to Suki, to tell him two hugely important things.

That Akira was with Nick and doing very well.

That I had indeed made new friends.

Well, *friend*. Singular. But one beats none any day.

Chapter Eighteen

Your Mother Was Right

My father drove me into Fresno for my court date. My mother not only wouldn't drive me, she wasn't speaking to either one of us.

We bounced along the dirt road in his truck, all the windows wide open. The truck didn't have air conditioning. No vehicles had air conditioning back then. Well . . . to be perfectly accurate, in the previous year or two we had seen shiny, exciting magazine ads for a Packard that was cooled by brand-new Frigidaire technology. But it wasn't like anybody I knew actually owned one.

My dad liked to joke that his truck had 2-40 air-conditioning, which meant you open both windows and drive forty miles per hour. But we were on a 25-mile-per-hour road, and the heat was stifling, even though it was barely nine in the morning.

I was wearing my brother's hand-me-down suit, the jacket on my lap. It was not a good fit. I tried to loosen the tie because it felt like I was being strangled, but my father was having none of it.

"Leave the tie be," he said.

I dropped my hands back into my lap and said nothing.

"If you're going to be a man, you're going to have to get used to things like that."

I didn't respond to that, either, but I remember thinking it was a strange way to phrase the thing. "If" I was going to be a man. As though I had lots of different options. Or maybe he had no confidence that a thing like that would ever happen.

We bounced along in silence for a few miles.

Then he knocked me out of my thoughts by speaking. "You've been awful quiet lately."

"I'm just a little tired," I said.

I was also nervous as hell, but for some reason I didn't feel I could say so without laying myself open to my father. Without offering up a vulnerability I did not trust him to handle.

"I don't mean just now," he said. "I mean for weeks. Something seems different about you."

"I don't know what you mean," I said.

I knew exactly what he meant.

"Hard to put my finger on it. It's like you're gone somehow. Like you're not in there."

"I have no idea what you're talking about," I said. "I'm right here."

If I could have explained the concept of retreat to my father, and expected him to hear and understand, no retreat would ever have been needed in the first place.

—

My father made me put on the suit jacket when we got out of the car.

"It's hot," I said.

"I know it's hot. You have to think about the impression you make. Everybody'll be wearing a suit jacket."

He was wearing one. In fact, he had worn it on the drive, as if someone were already judging him by his appearance as we motored down a fairly deserted road.

We stepped inside the courthouse, and I followed my father into a courtroom he seemed to know how to find. I think he had the room number written down.

Court was in session already, so we slipped in quietly and took a seat on one of the hard wooden benches in the back. There was no air conditioning. No swamp cooler. The windows were open, but there was no breeze, so they provided no relief. And no one was wearing a jacket. No one. The men had their shirtsleeves rolled up, and the ladies fanned themselves with newspapers or magazines or actual fans.

I glared briefly at my father and then took off the coat. At the corner of my eye I saw him slip out of his as well.

I could see the back of Nick's father. He was sitting at a table on what I could only assume was the defense side. It made my heart pound harder to see him, even if only from behind.

There was no jury. Apparently this was a trial in front of a judge only.

There was a man on the stand being questioned by one of the attorneys.

I didn't know who the man was until the attorney asked, "Why did you leave the hospital? You'd been the victim of a violent crime. Why didn't you stay and tell someone what happened?"

The man looked uncomfortable. He was a short, stocky guy in maybe his late forties, with hair parted down the middle and looking wet and shiny. He had an ugly scar over his left eyebrow. It had been stitched together in such a way that the eyebrow didn't match with itself anymore. I wondered if he'd gotten that scar from Nick's dad.

"You mean talk to the police?" he asked. He seemed hesitant about the whole line of questioning.

"Police. The detectives working on the case. Even the hospital staff. If you'd left some information with them, even that would have been helpful."

I could see the man swallow from where I sat. His Adam's apple jumped, then settled again.

"There might have been one or two *very minor* little incidents in my life that had me not so keen on talking to law enforcement. Sir."

"You just snuck away like a thief in the night and let Daniel Mattaliano's son take the blame for something he didn't do?"

An attorney sitting next to Nick's father jumped to his feet.

"Objection, Your Honor. It hasn't been established who committed the crime. That's what we're here to figure out."

The judge scowled and wiped his brow with a handkerchief. He looked down at the witness, his neck jowls folding and billowing. "Did you know when you ran away from the hospital that someone besides the defendant had been implicated in the crime?" he asked the witness directly.

"No, sir. How could I know that? I'd been in a coma."

The judge glared at the prosecuting attorney. The one doing the questioning. "Tread carefully," he said.

"Yes, Your Honor." Then, to the witness, "I just have one more question for you, Mr. Mulligan. The man who assaulted you on the morning of December seventh. Do you see him in the courtroom today?"

"Yes, sir."

"Can you point him out?"

Mulligan pointed to Nick's father.

"No more questions, Your Honor," the attorney said.

Edward Mulligan slid down off the stand.

The uniformed bailiff stepped into the middle of the courtroom and called another name. I thought it would be mine, and it made my throat feel as though it were closing up. Sealing off.

I was wrong. The name he called wasn't mine.

"Roger Steadman!"

Roger Steadman walked slowly up to the stand and took a seat. I hadn't seen him since that day I tracked him down at the tavern and confronted him. I could see him notice me as he was sworn in. He put his hand on the Bible and repeated the words, but his gaze was snagged on mine. He did not look happy to see me again. Not that I would have expected otherwise.

The defense attorney seated next to Nick's father stood up to approach the stand. The back of his white dress shirt was soaked through with a map of perspiration.

"Mr. Steadman," he said. "You told the detectives that you saw with your own eyes that it was *Nicolas* Mattaliano who viciously assaulted Mr. Mulligan. Is that correct?"

Steadman squirmed uncomfortably in his chair. "Yes and no," he said.

I could feel a tremor run through the small crowd. I could hear a few breaths suck in. I could see that the defense attorney was knocked off balance inside. I watched him open his mouth to speak and try to determine which direction to take the questioning, all in the same split second.

"You told the detectives it was Nicolas."

"I did, yeah. And that's what I thought. But it was dark, and I'd been doing some drinking. Now I'm not so sure if I was right."

It took the attorney a moment to rise up to a reply. It occurred to me that maybe the trial was more or less over. That the defense might just give up and tell the judge never mind about even trying to win. Without the testimony of Roger Steadman, what did they have? Just a man—a man who didn't want to go to prison—claiming innocence.

"Are you actually trying to tell the court, Mr. Steadman, that even after a couple of drinks you didn't know the difference between Daniel Mattaliano and his fourteen-year-old son?"

"It was more than a couple," he said. "But anyway, you never saw this Nick kid. He's a big kid. Tall as his father and probably just as heavy."

"So you really can't say for a fact which Mattaliano it was."

That was pretty much all the defense anybody had left, I figured.

"I think it was Daniel."

"But you said otherwise to the detectives investigating the case. You must know there are legal penalties for filing a false police report. You could go to jail for that."

"If I'd lied, I guess I could go to jail. But it was dark, and I'd been drinking. Can't see how you could put a guy in jail for just an honest mistake like that."

A long, uncomfortable silence fell. I could see the attorney wrestling inside his own head. I felt as though I could see his thoughts spinning, mirrored on his face.

"No more questions, Your Honor," he said after a time.

That was the moment I knew Daniel Mattaliano was cooked. In fact, I figured they wouldn't even call me up to testify. What was the need now?

But the bailiff stepped in front of the bench and called my name.

"Steven Katz!"

I walked up to the front of the room, feeling slightly dizzy and weak. It could have been the heat, but I'm sure fear factored in there somewhere.

I stepped onto the stand. Turned around. Sat. I saw the two detectives sitting in the front row of benches, just behind the wooden railing. Engel acknowledged me with a barely perceptible nod as I was sworn in.

I was careful never to look at Nick's father.

The prosecuting attorney stepped up to the stand.

"Don't be nervous, son," he said.

That surprised me, but in a pleasant way. I tried to breathe normally.

"Yes, sir," I said.

"Please tell the court where you were in the early morning hours of December seventh, 1941."

My brain flooded with the memory of that night up at the lake with Nick. Sitting under all those brilliant stars. Snowflakes landing on my eyelashes. His arm around my shoulder. It was the beginning of the most important era of my life, and deeply personal to me. And here I was being asked to discuss it in a court of law.

"I was on a camping trip in the mountains with three of my friends."

"Name the three friends, please."

I only paused for a split second. Maybe no one except me even noticed. Still, a lot happened in that tiny space of time. I could see my father in my peripheral vision. Watching. Listening. Waiting. I had no idea if he knew about my friendship with Suki. Frankly, I didn't care how he felt about it. I no longer craved his approval, because I had long ago accepted that it was out of reach. But I had to drive home with him. There might be punishment involved.

Yet it made no real difference. There was only one way to go. I had just vowed to tell the truth, the whole truth, and nothing but the truth.

"Nicolas Mattaliano. Oliver Franklin." Another micropause that likely no one noticed but me. My ears felt hot. "Itsuki Yamamoto."

I looked past the attorney to my father. I tried not to. I told myself not to. But it was a thing that seemed to do itself, rather than giving me the option to do it or not. I saw nothing on his face. He was a closed book. The cover was just what it had always been.

"The younger Mattaliano was with you."

"Yes, sir."

"Any chance he could have gone down into town in the night?"

"No, sir. No chance at all."

"Please tell the court why you say that."

"Because it took us hours to hike up there. It was probably more than an eight-hour round-trip hike. And besides, I woke up after midnight and couldn't get back to sleep, so I got out of the tent, and Nick was already awake, and we sat by the lake together and looked at the stars. The stars were really beautiful that night. And it had been snowing. I'd never seen snow before. Not close up."

During the end of that answer I felt some part of myself standing outside me, knocking on my brain and telling me to stop talking. This was one of the last moments in my life I wanted to share with anybody, and nobody needed to know it. They only cared that I saw Nick. Nothing about stars or snow. But in my fear and disorientation I just kept talking.

"You're sure Nicolas was up at the lake all night."

"Yes, sir. Positive."

"No more questions, Your Honor."

I stood, thinking I was done, but the judge shot me a stern look and indicated with a dip of his chin that I was to sit back down.

Of course, I did.

The defense attorney approached me, boring into me with his eyes. He was angry because everything had gone south for his client. I could see it in his face. In a disconnected thought, I remember it occurring to me that he would be a terrible poker player. He telegraphed everything he was thinking and feeling. At least, it struck me as everything. I couldn't imagine knowing more about the inside of someone just by looking.

I was his enemy. That came through, too.

"These other friends. Not Nicolas. Not you. The other two. Tell me their names again."

"Oliver Franklin. Itsuki Yamamoto."

"It seems awfully convenient that you're the only one who showed up to testify. Why aren't Oliver and Itsuki here to testify?"

"Ollie enlisted in the army and got killed on a supply ship headed for New Guinea. And Suki and his family were sent to Manzanar."

"Three people were supposedly up there with Nicolas, but you're conveniently the only one willing to provide an alibi for him?"

I opened my mouth, but the prosecuting attorney jumped to his feet and spoke before any words could come out of me.

"Objection, Your Honor. It's clearly been entered into the record that both Itsuki Yamamoto and Oliver Franklin were questioned at the time of the crime by detectives Bailey and Engel. And they both said the exact same thing the Katz boy just said. The detectives are here in the courtroom and can testify to that."

"Sustained," the judge barked. Then, to the defense attorney, "Counselor, move on. If you have other questions, get to them. If not . . ."

In the pause that followed, I watched the attorney fold inside. I saw that it hurt him to lose. I wondered if he was a paid attorney or a public defender assigned to the case. I wondered if he cared in the slightest about Nick's father. If he had any thoughts at all about his innocence or guilt, or if he simply tallied up his wins and was upset because he couldn't count this one in the right column.

"No more questions, Your Honor."

The judge peered down at me. "*Now* you may step down, son," he said.

I walked back to the spot where I'd left my father, but he wasn't in his seat. He was on his feet at the rear of the room, talking to a man in uniform. They had their heads together, speaking in hushed tones.

A minute later my dad turned back and walked to me, grabbing me by the sleeve and towing me out of the courtroom. Out into the courthouse hall.

"What?" I asked.

"We're going. I have to get back to the farm."

"Maybe they need me to stay."

"They don't. I asked. Now come on. We're going home."

"But I want to see how it turns out."

"We'll read about it in the paper. Now come on. I'm your ride. And your ride's leaving. You want to walk home from Fresno?"

I thought about my second good, long talk with Gordon Cho. How he had advised me to accept those things which were incomplete in my life.

I followed my father outside in silence. Out into the baking heat. Over to his truck, which was broiling in the full sunshine. There had been no parking places in the shade. It burned my palm to pull on the door handle.

I sat in that oven as he started up the engine and drove toward home.

For a few miles, he said nothing. He seemed lost in his own thoughts.

Then he said, "I don't say this often, Steven, but I think your mother was right. Heaven knows I love that woman, but she's notional as all hell, and wrong more than she's right. But this time I think she saw the truth sooner than I did."

I didn't answer. Just looked through the open window and watched the outskirts of Fresno flash by. Of course I could have asked him what she was so right about. But that would only have been inviting him to tell me.

I just wanted to get home with as little conversation as possible.

He didn't let it drop.

"I think you haven't been choosing your friends very wisely."

I looked over at the side of his face as he drove. Watched his jaw working as he ground his molars together. And I knew I was about to say something brave. Not because I felt big and courageous, but because I didn't care anymore.

I could feel the automatic fear reactions in my body—pounding heart, spinning head. Slight breathlessness. But I also felt removed from them, as though they were happening to someone else entirely.

"I don't really care what you and Mom think about Suki."

He seemed more surprised than furious.

"That's a hell of a way to talk to your father," he said.

"Maybe," I said. "Maybe it is. But I'm sorry, it's the truth."

I waited for his anger. Or for a calm declaration of the punishment he would mete out. Instead I got silence. Just silence. All the way home.

———

My mother continued to ignore my dad and me for the rest of the summer. That woman could grip the life out of a grudge.

Also my dad stopped trying to reach out to me, wherever I had gone. He just gave up and left me alone.

But I don't really say any of that like it was a bad thing. I had turned my back on them, and they simply returned the favor. It didn't even feel like a big change. It felt more like we went from pretending we were a real family to acknowledging the sad, simple truth that we were not.

And whether the truth is happy or sad, I've found there is value in acknowledging it.

Nick's dad was convicted and sentenced to six years in prison for attempted murder. I had to read about it in the paper, like a stranger.

Part Five

Spring 1943

Chapter Nineteen

Run

I stood in line at the bank, tapping my passbook against my thigh. The second letter from Nick had been stashed in my pants pocket on that side, and I could feel the bulk of it every time I tapped.

In front of me at the counter—this was a tiny one-teller bank branch—was an old lady counting out pennies from a jar. It was a jar so big I was surprised she'd been able to carry it in and set it on the counter. She was making a deposit entirely in pennies, nickels, and dimes.

I was worried about my own transaction, and worried about missing my bus. There was only one bus a day now, due to the war—the gasoline and rubber rations brought on by the war. All in all, suffice it to say I was quite worried.

When I finally stepped up to the window, the teller, a middle-aged woman with rheumy eyes, looked first down at my withdrawal slip and note, and then up at me.

I remembered what Suki had said about me. How I looked away and looked uncomfortable when I lied. I held her gaze with perfect, pasted-on confidence.

"I would have to have the manager approve this," she said.

"Okay," I said. "Go ahead and do that."

I thought she would walk away from the counter, but instead she just turned her head and called loudly toward the one office with a door that closed.

"Mr. Fredericks?" she shouted.

The door opened and Mr. Fredericks stepped out. I knew him. Not well, but I did. He had a son in my class. He looked first at his teller and then at me, reaching for a pair of glasses that sat on his receding hairline, and shifting them down to rest on his nose.

"What do we have here?" he asked, his eyes narrowing.

"This young man wants to withdraw all the money in his passbook account."

"Unless the customer can prove he's eighteen, which I happen to know this customer is not, he'll need his father's signature for that."

"He has his father's signature," she said.

She held up, and pointed to, my careful forgery.

"Then what's the problem?" he asked.

"No problem, I guess. It's just a big withdrawal." It was exactly forty-two dollars. But, in fairness to her, forty-two dollars was a good chunk of money in 1943. "And his father isn't physically here. I just wanted you to sign off on this."

He stepped up next to the teller, slid my forged note over so it rested directly in front of him, then scribbled his signature on it with a silver pen he pulled from the pocket of his suit jacket.

"Steven is a good young man," he said, sliding it back. "We trust that everything is what he says it is. All the young people in this little town are trustworthy, if only because they have to keep living here, and there's no place to hide. This is not Los Angeles."

He looked up and leveled me with a firm gaze, and I held his eyes steadily. I knew what he was saying. He was telling me that I would pay a price if I was doing anything underhanded.

I didn't care. I had someplace to hide.

I had Mesa, Arizona.

The teller counted out my cash in tens and ones and slid them across the counter to me. I folded it all into my pocket next to Nick's letter and stepped out onto the board sidewalk to catch my bus. I retrieved my two bags, which I had left outside the bank building so the people inside wouldn't know I was packed to leave town.

I just barely made it in time. And I do mean barely. The bus was pulling up to the stop as I walked out into the light. I was relieved, because it occurred to me that Mr. Fredericks might be back in his office calling my father.

I trotted up the steps and paid the driver, and the bus pulled away with a groan of gears and a belch of exhaust.

I turned to walk down the aisle to find a seat, and immediately saw Gordon Cho. He was one of only four passengers on the bus so far. He was sitting on the left-hand side, behind the driver, in a window seat. He waved enthusiastically to me, and smiled that gap-toothed smile I had come to love.

I lifted my heavy bags onto the overhead rack and sat down beside him.

"Where are you going?" I asked him.

"To visit my daughter in Pomona. Where are *you* going, friend?"

"Mesa, Arizona."

"Oh? That's quite a long trip."

"Yes. I guess it will be."

"What's in Mesa, Arizona? If it's all right to ask."

"I have a friend there."

"Is this the friend who wrote a letter with no return address?"

"The first time. Yes. But now I have a second letter. And it was just a mistake. It wasn't purposeful. I know because this time I have the address. It was right on the envelope."

Again, I was talking carefully to avoid male pronouns.

"How long will you stay?"

I didn't answer. I only stared past him out the window, watching the dusty valley slide by. It seemed so stark and unappealing. Just dirt and not much more. I felt as though I'd seen enough dirt to last me a lifetime. I never cared to see that forlorn place again. I was so glad to be getting out at last. It was even more of a relief than I had imagined it would be.

When it was clear I wasn't about to answer, he spoke again.

"Will you come back to us, Steven?"

"No."

"I see," he said. "You're young to strike out on your own. But young people do it all the time. I certainly wish you the best. Here, I'll write down my postal address, and maybe you'll see fit to send a letter and tell me how you're doing."

"I will. Definitely."

I watched him scribble his address on the corner of a newspaper that sat on his lap. He was using a pencil. I could see that the paper was open to the crossword puzzle, which was about one-third filled in.

He tore off the corner of the page and handed it to me, and I stuck it deep in my pocket with the money and Nick's letter.

"I hope you find what you're looking for," he said.

"Thank you."

"I know your life growing up with your family has not been a happy one."

"That's true."

At first I thought I would say no more. But then, a minute or two later, I found myself talking again.

"They just don't . . . they don't know the real me, and if they did, they couldn't possibly accept it."

"Do you know this for a fact?"

"Yes. They told me straight-out how they feel about people like me, without knowing that the people they were talking about were like me."

"Then maybe it's best you move along. Everybody has a right to be what they are."

I realized we were skirting close to a truth I did not discuss out loud with anyone. I guess I figured if he could catch on to hints like that, he already knew. And if not, he probably never would.

"Can I ask you a question?" I said. But I didn't wait for his answer. "Remember when you told me about all the people Hitler's putting in camps? And how maybe they're dying there, which you didn't say straight-out, but I think we both knew what you were saying. Of all those different kinds of people, are there any you think deserve to be killed?"

"Of course not," he said, without hesitation. He sounded a little shocked that I had even asked. "Nobody deserves that. Why would you ask such a thing?"

"Because my parents . . . and my brother . . . they didn't feel sorry for everybody you mentioned. They said the world was better off without some of them."

For a few seconds he just stroked his long, wispy beard. Part stroked, part tugged. It seemed to help him think.

Then he said, "Run, Steven. Run fast and far."

"I already am," I said.

———

Gordon Cho and I changed to a long-distance route in Fresno, and I rode with him all the way to Pomona, California. His route and my route happened to run together. Pomona was along a newly improved stretch of highway that was also the route to the southern parts of Arizona. Not that I had ever been to Arizona before, but I had looked at the whole thing on a library map in Fresno in the month before leaving.

I didn't get to meet his daughter, because Pomona was too quick a stop, with no break to allow any through travelers to get off the bus. I just waved to them from the window as they stood on the lit platform watching the bus pull away.

Yes, it was already dark. Partly because it was early spring. Partly because the many stops and breaks made bus travel a painfully slow way to move through California.

I don't think it was late, but I don't know for a fact, because I had sold my watch to get extra money for the trip.

Late or not, I fell asleep.

Next thing I knew, the driver was shaking me and telling me this was Phoenix and I had to get off the bus. I knew Phoenix was not the last stop, so I could only figure he kept track of how far everybody had paid to go.

He had turned on the overhead lights above the bus aisle, and I blinked into them miserably.

"What time is it?" I asked him.

"Little after eleven."

"Is there a bus from here to Mesa?"

"There's a bus to everywhere. But not at this hour. Local buses start running at seven in the morning."

I hauled my bags down from the overhead rack and carried them out into the night.

I was the only one getting off in Phoenix, and I stood on the platform in the dark with my bags and watched the bus pull away. The platform was pitch dark because the station was closed. I felt more lost than I had ever felt in my life. And if you count all the various definitions of lost I'd previously experienced, that's pretty damned lost.

I didn't miss my family or my house, but I missed Gordon Cho and other faces that I might not have been as deeply bonded with but at least were familiar to me. I missed being in a place where I knew how to find . . . well, anything.

I began to notice that there were gaps in my plan.

I knew from my library research that Mesa was around twenty miles from downtown Phoenix, so continuing on foot was out of the question, especially with my heavy bags.

I walked around downtown for a few minutes, hoping to find somebody who could direct me to a hotel, but there was no one around. The whole world seemed shut down and locked up.

In time I saw the word **HOTEL** flashing red on a neon sign.

I stood outside the locked door into its lobby and rang the bell as directed on the sign.

It took several minutes, and the desperate, lost feeling came charging back with a vengeance, but in time a man stumbled to the door. I had clearly rousted him from sleep. He opened the door and blinked too much in my general direction.

"Two dollars a night," he said. "In advance."

It seemed like a lot to me, but I was thin on options in that moment, so I paid it.

———

I woke in the morning, after only a couple hours of fitful sleep, with sunlight pouring through the dirty windows and into my eyes.

I rose and showered as best I could, but the water wasn't hot, and it was too much of a shock to my system. Still, I managed to wash off the dirty feel of public transportation and get myself decently clean.

I decided to leave my bags there at the hotel. It was a risky move, because I knew if I didn't get back to fetch them by noon, I could be on the hook for another day's two-dollar charge. But they were a lot to haul around. And, more to the point, I didn't want to face Nick—for the first time in all those months—looking like I was moving in. A guy who lived in a tree house with his dog wasn't ready to receive me and more or less everything I owned.

I walked down to the lobby, where the man who had let me in was sleeping sitting up on a stool, his back against the faded floral wallpaper behind him.

"Excuse me," I said.

He jumped awake.

"Sorry," I added. "Would you happen to have a map of this area?"

"Yeah. But you can't take it."

"I could write down directions if you had paper, and a pen or pencil."

He handed me a pad of stationery that said "Hotel Wallace" on top, and a yellow pencil that said nothing.

"I need the pencil back, too," he said.

I mapped out where I was going, so I could at least tell the bus driver, and I could at least be relatively assured of getting on the right bus.

It was beginning to dawn on me that I would see Nick soon. It was beginning to feel real. The excitement of it was building in my chest, feeling electric and deliciously scary. And yet at the same time I could feel myself nursing a sense of dread. Because anytime you get excited about what will happen soon, you run the risk that it won't happen, or won't happen the way you pictured it.

It's not like he'd told me to come ahead. I had written back to say I was coming, but I hadn't waited for the letter to be delivered, or for him to reply.

Still, I remembered him saying that as soon as I was willing to leave home, we could be together. I couldn't imagine how an offer like that had changed. I couldn't imagine his feelings had changed. Mine certainly hadn't.

Still, I had a lot riding on that day.

I walked to the bus station with all those feelings warring inside me. Between that battle and my lack of sleep, it left me feeling slightly ill.

—

When I finally got to Nick's mother's house, which involved several miles of walking, I stood in the yard and tried to decide whether to knock. After all, I knew Nick didn't live inside the house, and I wasn't sure how his mother and her new boyfriend would feel about visitors.

I just stood there like an idiot, frozen in my fear of deciding.

The yard was nothing but sandy dirt with a few scrubby desert plants growing here and there, apparently of their own accord. The house was one level, and no color at all. It seemed to be exactly the color of the dirt on which it sat. Only the front door provided any contrast at all. It had been painted a bright pumpkin orange, but now that paint was badly peeling.

I unstuck my feet and walked around to the back.

The house seemed to be on a huge lot, though I had no way of knowing where the property lines lay. But there were no neighbors anywhere nearby. Just a house sitting out in the desert by itself, looking lonely. But I did see the tree house immediately.

It had been built on a tree that had long since died. Only the dry, shrunken vestiges of its petrified branches remained. The platform had been shored up with wooden framing, as the tree was clearly no longer up to the task of supporting it.

I stopped for a moment, and stood looking, and I was hit with a shot of pity for poor Nick. I couldn't imagine why the powers that be had doomed him to such pitiful accommodations. First that damp root cellar and now this monstrosity. Didn't he deserve more of a home? Doesn't any kid?

I tried on the idea that the reason he had been slow to share his address might have been shame. Maybe he was ashamed to be seen in this place. Maybe he had already written back and told me not to come. Begged me to give him time to find a more suitable life before I came out and observed him living it.

Real a possibility though that was, I had come all this way. I was there. It was too late to go home.

It was just too late.

I shuffled through the sandy dirt to the bottom of the ladder and called up.

"Nick?"

Nothing.

"Akira?"

Still nothing.

The back door of the house flew open, startling me. I turned to see a man in the open doorway wearing nothing but polka-dotted boxer shorts. He was leveling a shotgun at me.

Every inch of my body, from the crown of my scalp to the tips of my toes, turned to tingling ice.

"Wait," I said. "Whoa."

I automatically raised my hands, the way people do when they're being held at gunpoint.

"Who's there?" he barked, still viewing me through the gun sights.

"I'm looking for Nick. I'm a friend of Nick's."

"He's not here," the man said, his voice still a harsh bark.

But, on the plus side, he did let the muzzle end of the shotgun droop down so it was no longer pointing directly at me. I breathed again, wondering when I last had.

"You know when he'll be back?"

"Never. He'll be back never. He doesn't live here anymore."

I stood still a moment, letting those words sink in.

Had he given me his address at his mother's and then immediately moved somewhere else? Had he even been here long enough to get my letter saying I was coming? Had he written back to me to tell me he was somewhere else now? And, if so, how would I ever know? It's not as if I could go home and check the mail.

"You're still here," the man said.

"I was hoping you were about to tell me where he lives now."

"Couldn't if I wanted to. He didn't say."

My heart inched down another notch in my chest. Or seemed to, anyway. It was already practically in my belly from the feel of it.

"Maybe his mother knows."

"She doesn't."

"Can I ask her?"

For a long few seconds, he said nothing at all. Did nothing at all. I was toying with the idea that he hadn't even heard me.

Then he turned toward the inside of the house and called a name over his shoulder.

"Laverne!"

He disappeared inside, taking the shotgun with him. I breathed more deeply, noticing that the cores of my arms and legs felt rubbery and weak in the aftermath of that fear.

While I was waiting, I moved a few steps closer to the dangerous house.

What felt like several minutes later a woman came to the door. She was wearing a men's terry cloth robe, and her hair was up in curlers. She held a lit cigarette drooping from the corner of her mouth. She narrowed her eyes against the smoke.

Or against *me*. It was hard to tell.

"What?" she asked me.

"I was hoping you knew where Nick was now."

"I don't," she said.

And she turned to go.

"Wait!" I said. I sounded desperate. I *was* desperate. "Wait, don't go yet. How long has he been gone?"

"Not sure. Might've taken us a couple days to notice."

"Maybe he's coming back."

"I doubt it. He left a note saying bye."

"Oh." I scrambled for more to say, because she was about to go back in the house and be done with me. And when I lost her, I'd lose everything. Any connection to anything that mattered. "Did he have the dog with him?"

"Of course he had the dog with him. He has that dog with him everywhere he goes. He even skipped going back to school in the fall because he didn't want to leave her alone. He loves that dog a lot more than he loves me, I can tell you that much."

It seemed like a strange thing to say. It was hard to imagine a mother leaving her only child with a dangerous father for years, then refusing to feed him or house him when he came to her for help, then bemoaning the fact that he didn't love her enough.

While I was thinking all that, she walked back inside and slammed the door. Hard.

I walked back to the bus stop. I had no other moves. No other plans.

———

I stayed one more night at that hotel in Phoenix and hatched a short-term plan. I would go see Suki, if such a thing was allowed. I had no idea if Manzanar accommodated visitors. But I planned to show up there and find out. Maybe I would even refuse to leave until they let me see him.

And after that, well . . . I had no idea. I couldn't go home. Nick was a needle in the proverbial haystack. I had no idea where I could live or how I could support myself. I did have a vague idea that I knew farmwork, and could get a job working somebody's land somewhere. But the "who" and the "where" were things not yet sorted out.

I think I came up with the plan to go see Suki as a way of disguising, even to myself, that I had no plan at all beyond that.

Chapter Twenty

With No Earth in Between

Getting to Manzanar was more of an adventure than I'd anticipated. I asked bus drivers, and I asked the ticketing agents at every stop. They all shook their heads at me and offered vague answers that seemed to suggest one couldn't get there from here—no matter where the "here" was in each given case. There was no bus route up that lonely and desolate Highway 395, which bisected the heart of the Owens Valley, challenging my first driver's assertion that there was a bus to everywhere.

Determined to defy the odds, I got off the bus in San Bernardino and started hitchhiking. It was around six in the morning, which was perfect, because people would be on their way to work.

The first short leg of that journey was looking easy enough. A lot of cars went by, their drivers apparently headed to Victorville or Hesperia.

The guy who offered me a ride was going all the way to Barstow, but that was well past my cutoff.

"Where you headed?" he asked me as I loaded my heavy bags into his back seat.

"I'm getting off at the junction with the 395."

He frowned, and furrowed his brow, but said nothing for the time being.

I jumped in and we rolled toward my destination. I was thinking this was going to be easy. I'm not sure why I thought so. Nothing in my life had been to that date. But I clearly remember the feeling. As if I had chosen wisely by doing what I was doing, and now everything would flow well.

"Not much up there," he said, still frowning. "What's up there that you need to get to?"

I looked over at him. Sized him up as best I could. He was an older guy. I took him to be in the fifty-to-sixty range. His waist was stout, his hair buzzed short. I decided confiding in him would be an unacceptable risk.

"I have an aunt in Bishop," I said.

"And she can't help you get up there?"

"She's at the end of her gas ration," I said, realizing I had grown more comfortable with lying to save my own skin. I had been practicing.

I think I may have mentioned earlier that gasoline and rubber products—think automobile tires—were rationed during the war. As a result, all travel was more or less essential travel. People didn't motor down the road for fun. People didn't motor down the road unless there was no good way to avoid doing so, and, even then, if their ration card was spent, it was just spent.

It was a reminder that hitchhiking in a remote area could be challenging.

"Well, good luck to you," he said. "You might have trouble catching a ride after I drop you off. Got any food with you?"

"I have a couple of candy bars."

In truth, I had one candy bar.

"Good," he said. "That might be all that stands between you and starving."

—

I sat in the sun on one of my bags for what I guessed to be two or three hours, waiting for even one soul to drive by. My forehead had begun to feel sunburned, so I had taken an extra shirt out of one of my bags and draped it over my head like a hood, casting shade onto my face.

I had eaten my only candy bar. There was no point in saving it, because it would only have melted in the heat. I wondered why the man who dropped me here hadn't thought to ask if I had water in addition to food. Then I wondered why I hadn't thought to ask myself the same question.

I was beginning to lose the feeling that this was going to go smoothly, and yet I was still determined that it was going to go.

I thought about walking.

I hadn't had a chance to chart it out directly on a map, but I had some sense of the area. If not for the mountains in between, this would be close to home. I knew roughly where things lay on a north-south grid compared to familiar spots in the valley where I grew up. I figured my destination was at least a hundred and fifty miles north.

I could ditch my bags, stash them somewhere—somewhere I could find them again when I was done. I could do fifteen miles a day, walking in the cool night after the sun went down. The road would keep me from getting lost.

Then it hit me that it would still be a ten-day journey. And I had no food or water.

I was in the early stages of considering backtracking the mile or two I'd walked from the highway and giving up, but just then I saw a Jeep in the distance. I jumped up, desperately pantomiming my hitchhiking gesture, my thumb wildly extended into the road. I knew this was it. If he stopped, great. If not, it could be hours before another car came by. It could be days.

By the time he pulled level with me, he had slowed down to take in my situation. I was practically jumping up and down on the shoulder of the highway. He stopped the Jeep and leaned closer, peering at me through narrow eyes.

"What the hell are you doing out here all by yourself?" he asked me.

He was a youngish guy. Late twenties, maybe. He had the haircut I associated with the armed services, and he had the army vehicle, but he was not in uniform. His eyes said he thought I was crazy.

"No buses out here," I said. "I have to get there somehow."

"Get where?"

"Independence," I said.

I wasn't ready to trust him with my real destination. If I had told him the truth, he might have driven off without me.

Manzanar was up that highway between Lone Pine to the south and Independence to the north. My lie about Independence took me just past the camp. That way I figured I could wait until we got level with Manzanar before I admitted it was where I was going. And then, what could he do? Put me out? I'd be getting out anyway.

"I can take you most of that way," he said. "Get in."

I threw my bags behind the seat and climbed in up front, and we rolled away.

I watched him tap his fingers on the steering wheel in rhythm, as if in time to some distant music only he could hear. I watched the California desert roll by through the dust in my eyes.

At first, we didn't talk at all.

Then, just to have something to say, I asked, "How far on this road do you go?"

"I'm going up to Manzanar," he said.

It made my stomach tingle and buzz. I was unsure as to whether it was time to give away the secret of my own destination.

"You're visiting somebody there?" I asked. It was a stupid question to ask a man driving an army Jeep.

He snorted laughter. Then he looked over at me briefly before turning his eyes back to the road. He seemed to be assessing me to see if I were utterly insane.

"I'm stationed there," he said.

"Oh."

"Once we get up there, it shouldn't be too hard to hitch a ride north. Lot of army guys there, and when they go off shift, they might be headed up to Bishop for the evening."

"Thanks," I said.

I remembered the look in his eyes when he glanced over at me, and I let it be the answer to my question: it was not the right time to tell him where I was going.

———

When I got my first look at the place, it changed me. I really don't know how to explain it better than that. It was like . . . I knew there was a war on, but suddenly, here it was. It had come home to me. It was right in front of my eyes. This was an army installation during wartime. It was something I had always known was happening, but was now able to see for myself, close up.

It's different when you see it for yourself, and close up.

The closer we got, the more I was able to take in details. The thing I remember best was the contrast. The stark, frightening-looking barracks lined up in rows. The workers picking in the fields in the hot sun. The big guns in the guard towers. Soldiers standing ramrod straight between rows with their weapons brandished over their shoulders, the long bayonets pointing up at an angle. And power poles. So many poles. So many lines. But, behind that, the ethereal mountain range. The blue sky shot through with clouds. For a split second I had the thought that I might be seeing Heaven and Hell pressed together with no earthly world in between.

I saw an American flag high on a pole, and it was flapping wildly in the wind. Viciously. But I don't remember feeling the wind on my face. I must have, but I don't remember it. I think I was disconnected from my surroundings.

"Sorry," my driver said, "but this is as far as I go."

"I'm not going to Independence," I said.

"Oh? Where're you going, then?"

"Here."

He pulled into the entrance without answering. I could tell that he was chewing over what I'd just told him.

We passed a sign. A slab of wood with uneven edges. It was suspended between two stout poles by chains secured at the four corners. The poles seemed to rise up from a pile of rocks at their bases.

The sign read, **MANZANAR WAR RELOCATION CENTER**, with a star on either side of the word *War*. As if that was the one word the sign didn't want you to forget.

I could see a little booth of a guard station up ahead. A place you had to stop before being allowed inside.

The driver spoke again, knocking me out of my thoughts.

"Why would you want to go here?"

"I want to visit somebody."

He had slowed almost to a stop now, and he was staring at the side of my face. I just kept looking at that amazing cloudy sky hovering over the mountains. Those mountains that had meant so much to my friends and me, back when I'd still had my friends around me.

"You mean somebody stationed here?"

"I mean somebody who was relocated here."

His Jeep was at a full stop now. He continued to stare at the side of my face.

"Why didn't you tell me that when you got in?"

"I thought if I did, you might make me get out again."

For another long moment he only stared. Then he shook his head. He stomped on the gas pedal, maybe harder than he'd meant to. When I looked up, we were at the guard booth.

A young man in an army uniform stepped out. He set his hands on the edge of the driver's door and leaned closer, staring at me.

It might sound bizarre to say, but I think that was the first moment I realized I might be bringing a lot of trouble onto my own head by being there.

"Hey, Rick," the guy said. "Who do we have here?"

"Not sure. He thinks he's a visitor."

"A visitor? Well, that's a good one. You just hear something new every day, don't you? What d'you plan to do with him?"

"I figured I'd take him to administration and let them sort him out."

"Okay," the guard said. "Good luck with that."

And we drove on through.

———

The man who questioned me was some kind of army officer. He had large and complex patches on his uniform sleeves, but I didn't know enough about the army to know his rank just by looking. He sat with the soles of his boots braced on the desk and his wooden chair pushed back at a wild angle. If there hadn't been a wall behind him, he would have fallen over. He had a clipboard against his knees, and he seemed prepared to write down what I said.

"Full name," he demanded.

He was easily in his forties, with a wide, misshapen nose and a face that reminded me of a bulldog.

"Steven Douglas Katz."

"And who is this internee you decided it would be fun to drop in on?"

"Itsuki Yamamoto." Then, suddenly worried I could get Suki in trouble, I added, "It wasn't his idea. He's written me a couple of letters, and I've written him a couple, but he didn't ever say I should come. That was totally my own plan. He doesn't even know about it. I was just passing through near here, and I decided all at once that I would do it."

I braved a look at his face. I got the impression that he found me amusing.

"What exactly do you mean by 'near here'? Where could you have been that's near here? Nothing is near here. That's the point of the whole thing."

"I was at the bottom end of the 395. Near Victorville."

"That's 175 miles from here."

"Yes, sir. If you say so. I guess that was close enough for me."

"Is that sass? Are you sassing me?"

"No, sir. Not at all. I was just telling you what I decided."

I waited, but he seemed to have no more to say on the subject. I got brave and asked a question of my own.

"Are visitors allowed here or not? Nobody's really told me. If it's no visitors allowed, then I guess I could just go, but nobody's said straight-out to me that it's no visitors allowed."

"It doesn't come up much," he said.

I waited. He didn't seem to want to elaborate.

"I don't know what that means."

"There's a war on, son," he said, his voice serious.

"I know there's a war on." I was irritated by his answer, and I wasn't doing a good job of disguising that. I could hear it in my own voice. "You don't have to tell me there's a war on. I lost one of my best friends in this war when his supply ship got hit by a torpedo. My brother came home with shrapnel in his brain from this war, and he'll never be the same. I don't need a lesson on the fact that we're in a war."

"I'm sorry about your brother," he said. It was the first break in his formal demeanor. "The United States thanks your family for its sacrifices to the war effort."

I sat a moment, hands in my lap, taking that in. I wondered why he wasn't sorry about Ollie. I figured maybe the United States only cared about losses from your blood family. Which in my case was getting it backward.

"You still never answered my question about visitors," I said.

"Hold on a second."

He dropped the front legs of his chair onto the floor and rose. He had a holstered pistol at his belt. He walked away, taking the clipboard with him.

I waited for what seemed like an hour. I suppose it could have been twenty minutes, but it really felt like an hour.

In time he came back. No clipboard.

He sat behind his desk, leaning forward, his elbows planted on the desktop. He drilled into my face with his gaze. I did not look away. I also didn't ask again if visitors were allowed, because it was so obvious that the question was still out there waiting for its answer.

"I think the important question," he said, "is not if we allow visitors, but why anyone would want to visit someone here."

"He's my friend," I said.

"That's problematic, son. Because of the war. Which I don't have to tell you about, because you know everything about it already. The United States armed forces and the people of California—of the whole Pacific coast region of the United States—we're on one side. The people locked up in this relocation center are on the other side. I guess my question is . . . which side are *you* on?"

I was surprised by the directness of his question, and by how small and helpless it makes a person feel to have his loyalty called into question.

"I'm on the side of the US. I was born here. So were a lot of the people you put in this camp. Loyal, I mean. Well. Both."

"Maybe they *are* loyal. Maybe they're not. We have some cause to doubt their loyalty. What I'm asking is . . . do we have any cause to doubt yours?"

"No, sir. You don't. And I don't think it's fair for you to even suggest that you do."

I was getting irritated again. And not hiding it well.

"It's my *job* to question that," he said, his voice hard.

I think it was dawning on me for the first time that my visit here would come to nothing. I would not be allowed to see Suki. I could feel that now. Maybe I should have felt it a lot sooner. But I had been attempting optimism. I thought maybe someone would take pity on me, and see that I had come so far.

Then I started worrying about the trip home. Maybe I would have to hitchhike north, toward Sacramento, just to get a shot at enough cars.

I didn't yet know that the transportation for my next leg of the journey would take care of itself.

My mouth was dry, and my stomach twisted into hunger pangs that I had been half ignoring.

"Excuse me," the officer said.

And he stood and disappeared again.

I waited another long ten or fifteen minutes.

I looked around at the various desks and people inside the big administration office, but they tended to look back at me. After a while I stopped looking around and stared into the corner. Waiting.

When the officer arrived back, he had an MP with him. I know because the MP was wearing an armband on his uniform shirt with those initials on it.

I reflexively stood, and faced them.

"Go like this," the officer said to me. He pantomimed holding his hands extended and close together.

I did as he ordered.

The MP silently clicked a pair of handcuffs onto my wrists.

I looked up into the officer's face in utter shock.

"You're *arresting* me?"

"That seems to be the long and short of it, kid."

"You're arresting me for trying to visit a friend?"

"No. There's no law against that. We're arresting you for being a runaway."

I stood a moment, letting that sink in. I felt myself teeter slightly with the shock of the thing.

"How do you know I'm a runaway?"

He shot me a look that made me feel pitiful. It was a look that said he'd originally given me credit for intelligence, but had just revoked it.

"It never occurred to you that your parents would report you to the police for running away?"

I didn't answer. I didn't say anything more to the army men of Manzanar that day, or ever. But the answer was no. It had never occurred to me. It had never crossed my mind that my parents would take official steps to try to get me back.

If I had thought about it at all, I would have figured my sudden departure had left them feeling relieved.

———

I had to wait almost six hours in a hard chair in that administration office, the MP towering silently over me, for one of my parents to show up to get me. I was given nothing to eat. I was given a glass of water, which I had to drink with both hands because I was still handcuffed.

Then, after all those hours of waiting, I looked up to see my father towering over me instead. I was not happy to see him by any means, but it was better than if my mother had come.

It was hard to read the look on his face. It wasn't positive, of course. That went without saying. It was bad, but I couldn't figure out what kind of bad. I couldn't tell if he was angry, or sad, or disgusted, or some combination of all three.

"Come on," he said. "We're going home."

The MP walked with us out to my father's truck.

The wind was just battering. All I could hear was the roar of it blowing by my ears. It forced sand into my eyes, and I tried to shield them with one arm. But then I realized I was showing off my handcuffs, and there were people around. Lots and lots of people.

It was evening, and the sun was down behind the mountains, lighting up the clouds that hung over the high Sierra peaks, making them look like some kind of magic. Below that, a long line of internees were moving from one place to another. Maybe moving back to their barracks at the end of a day's work. Maybe going to a mess hall to eat.

Almost every one of their heads were bowed. It looked almost like a gesture of shame, but I knew it was the wind. They were trying to keep sand out of their eyes, and noses, and lungs.

A teenage boy raised his head to look at me, and for a split second I was hopeful. But it was no one I knew. He was a stranger, a person clearly working hard to maintain his dignity against almost insurmountable odds. He quickly looked away again. Maybe not because he was embarrassed, though. More likely because he figured I would be.

I was the one in handcuffs.

I scanned the crowd as they passed, looking for Suki or some member of his family. Meanwhile I think my father was yelling at me to hurry up and get in the car. He was yelling something. But all I could hear was that brutal wind across my ears.

Finally the MP yanked on my arm to get my attention back. He unlocked the handcuffs with a key and removed them. I never saw Suki or anyone else I knew. I later learned that there were more than ten thousand Japanese internees there, so I really never had much of a chance of being in the right place at the right time.

I wondered if he would ever know I'd tried.

The MP put a hand on the top of my head and pushed me down into the passenger seat of my father's truck, slamming the door behind me.

My father and I drove away in silence.

He turned south onto the 395, which made sense. It was the shorter route around the mountain range. I watched the dim, heavenly eastern Sierras flash by outside his filthy truck window. We had the windows closed because it was getting dark, and growing cold in the desert spring. And because of all that blowing sand.

When he finally spoke, it surprised me. I had pretty much assumed he would never speak to me again.

"This is the last of my gas ration," he said. "I used up my whole gas ration coming to get you."

"You didn't have to come get me. That wasn't my idea."

He only grunted slightly. "Your mother will never know about this," he said.

"Which part of 'this'?"

"Don't be a smart aleck."

"I'm not. I really don't know which part you mean."

"The part about where I picked you up."

"Oh. She doesn't know that? I figured she must've been the one to answer the phone."

"Yeah, but they didn't tell her much. Just that they'd found you. They wanted to speak to the man of the house. I told her you were in the San Bernardino Valley, and you'd better not make a liar out of me. There'll be a price to pay if you go and do that."

"I won't," I said. "I don't want her to know, either."

We rode in silence for a time. I watched the mountains gradually disappear. Fading because the peaks grew lower as we moved south. Fading because night was coming on fast.

"I'm only going to say this once," my father said. "Listen up. The day you turn eighteen you're a man. On that day you belong to yourself. On that day your mother and I have no more say in your life. Until then we own you. You got that? We *own* your skinny behind. You do not belong to yourself. You belong to us. We are your family whether you like it or not. And you will live at home until that day. If you take off again, I won't come get you. I'll tell them to put you in reform school. I realize we have our differences, but that's just the way life is. Your family is your family until you grow up, and there's nothing you can do about that. Does that sound fair enough to you?"

I opened my mouth to answer, but he never let me get that far.

"No, I take back that last part—the rest of what I said still stands. I don't care if it sounds fair to you or not. I just want you to tell me whether or not you understand me."

"I do," I said.

We drove the rest of the way home in silence.

I stayed there until I was eighteen. Because I had no better options.

I won't say I never spoke to my parents in that time, or that they never spoke to me. That would be a convenient exaggeration. I will say that we spoke only when there seemed to be no way around speaking. We didn't try to pretend that I was there by choice, or that my status in that house was much better than that of a hostage.

Part Six

1945

Chapter Twenty-One

The Envelope

My birthday was August fifteenth. My eighteenth birthday fell on August 15, 1945, which just happened to have been the V-J Day celebrations. Victory over Japan. The end of the war.

I almost couldn't believe my good fortune. The day I came of age to go fight in the war, there was no more war. I began to breathe in a way that suggested I hadn't been fully, deeply breathing for years.

I know my parents expected me to leave home pretty much that day. But I didn't. Because I had promised, by letter, to pick up Suki and his family on whatever date they learned they were free to go. Of course, my parents knew nothing of that arrangement.

I'm sure it surprised them when I stayed. I could feel them watching me in a different way. But they never said a word about it one way or the other.

In the intervening two years and a few months since my stab at freedom, I had received five letters from Nick, all chatty and not terribly substantive. All bearing a New York City postmark. All with no return address.

But when the war ended, and I turned eighteen, he wrote me a very different kind of letter. It reached me six days later.

I ripped it open anxiously, thinking, because of the timing, that it might contain a plan for being together again. But as I began to read, my heart fell.

My world fell.

I won't say it was entirely unexpected, because I'm not a total idiot. I knew something wasn't quite right. But I had been veering back and forth from a state of qualified optimism. I vacillated, sometimes multiple times a day. I had excuses for his distance. He didn't want me to see him living the way he was living. He was putting a plan in place, and it was a surprise.

And then, at other times, I would think he just didn't care to see me again.

When I read that last letter, and learned the truth, it was almost a relief. I mean, no. It wasn't. It was terrible. But it was almost better to drop down to terrible than to ping-pong back and forth between terrible and hopeful. At least that way you know where you are. At least that way you know what to feel.

> *Dear Steven,*
> *This is hard, and I really don't want to write this, but I have to. I think it would be better if you just forgot all about me. You deserve to be with somebody wonderful who can be everything you want him to be. I'm sorry I can't be that person for you.*
> *Even though I hope you'll forget me, I'll never forget you. I'll never forget all the ways you helped me and how much you loved me.*
> *I love you, too.*
> *I'm sorry.*
> *Nick*

I held it in my hands for a long time, nursing a feeling in my chest like a long knife piercing downward from my throat. I felt like a sword swallower.

He had still offered me no return address. I couldn't have written back and given him my reaction to his words, even if I had known what to say.

———

It was November when I was finally able to go pick up Suki and his family.

I was late getting there.

When I finally arrived, they were standing on that desolate road with a few parcels of belongings stacked around them. They looked inordinately relieved to see me. I guess they weren't sure I was coming at all.

I pulled up and parked the car next to them, just off the road. Behind them, I saw people moving through the camp in a sort of disarray. Fewer soldiers, but some. No lines or order. I guess everybody was trying to get ready to go. I guess there was no order left.

The day was overcast and gray, and the mountain peaks were obscured by clouds. Nothing looked like magic. It was just Hell. And maybe Earth, but I saw nothing that looked like Heaven. There was no sense of contrast. It was all terrible.

I jumped out of the car.

"I'm really sorry I'm late," I said. "I know you must've worried. I had to stop three or four times to put oil in the engine. It leaks oil. Then I had to stop to buy more oil. And then it overheated coming up to the higher elevations, and I had to stop a couple of times to let it cool down. There's water in the radiator. It's not that. I just think it's an old, bad radiator."

I looked at Suki, and he looked at me. And, for a moment, we only took each other in and nothing more. He had changed so much. He looked like a man to me. And, technically, he was a man. He was eighteen, just like I was. But he didn't exactly look eighteen. He just looked like a young but grown man. At first I tried on the idea that life in the camp had aged him beyond his years. Then I wondered if I also looked like a man to someone who hadn't seen me for so long.

It was a hard thing to judge.

We began loading up the trunk of the big brown sedan.

Mr. and Mrs. Yamamoto handed us parcels, and we found a way to fit them all in. Mr. Yamamoto was wearing a crisp white short-sleeved shirt and a necktie, plus a derby hat that he had to hold with one hand to keep the wind from taking it away. Mrs. Yamamoto had on a flower-print dress and clean stockings, and her small, neat pillbox hat had several pearl hatpins holding it in place. They were dressed as if headed to church, but there was no one around to see them but me. They had sandy dust in their windblown hair.

"Whose car?" Suki asked. "Yours?"

"No, I still don't have one. It belongs to one of my dad's farmhands. I bribed him with a little money to let me borrow it."

"We can pay you back. Later. When we get where we're going."

They weren't coming back to our little valley to live. I had already known that. It wasn't quite that easy. Just because the war was over and the camps were closing didn't automatically make California a welcoming place for a Japanese family. Old hatreds die hard.

They had each been given twenty-five dollars and a one-way bus ticket. That's a clear message.

Suki's mother had an aunt in Oklahoma. I had no idea what was in Oklahoma in the way of opportunities, and I expected they didn't know much more than I did. But they were about to find out.

"You don't have to pay me back," I said. "It wasn't that much."

I was rearranging parcels in the trunk so the lid would have half a chance of closing.

"What about all the oil?"

"Don't worry about it," I said. "It's on me."

I felt a tug at my sleeve. I turned around to see Suki's mother standing right behind me.

"Thank you so much, Steven," she said.

And from a few steps behind her, Suki's father said, "Yes. Thank you, Steven."

"It's fine," I said. "I'm happy to do it. I'm just sorry I was late. I didn't mean to worry you."

I slammed the trunk lid. Then I stood a moment. There was nothing to do but drive away. But there was one thing on my mind, and it was a delicate issue.

In our letters back and forth, Suki had not mentioned his grandmother again. Not after that first letter, when he desperately wanted news about Akira to give her. He had been afraid his grandmother was going to die soon. I thought she probably had. But he hadn't offered more information about her, and I hadn't asked, because I thought it might be a sore subject.

I was still holding on to a thread of hope that she was waiting in a more comfortable location where she could sit down. But it was a thin thread, let me tell you.

"Is this . . . ," I began. I paused, but nobody rescued me. I think because nobody knew where I was going with it. "Is this everything? Everybody?"

"Yes," Suki said. "We can go now."

I just stood a minute, absorbing the blow. Even though I hadn't known his grandmother well. She spoke almost no English, so I had never had a conversation with her. Still, I knew the family, and I knew what she meant to them.

But Suki turned his face away from me. He didn't want to talk about it. I figured if he could keep his thoughts about it to himself, so could I.

We all piled into the car, Suki in the passenger seat beside me, his parents in the back. I made a U-turn on the deserted highway, and we headed south, toward the bus station in Bakersfield.

Suki was silent for a time, staring through the windshield as the Sierras slid by. Then, when he did speak to me, I could feel a hesitance surrounding his words.

"You still hear from Nick?"

I winced inwardly. At least, I hoped it was only inwardly.

"Yes and no," I said. "The last letter he wrote me . . . I think he's not going to write again." I waited, but he didn't answer. So I added, "He's in New York."

"Yes," Suki said. "He's in New York."

"Oh, he wrote to you, too?"

"Yes."

He still seemed hesitant to offer much information. I could feel the tension surrounding the subject. I tried to talk over it.

"He didn't mention Akira in his last couple of letters," I said. "I don't know. She'd be awfully old by now. I guess I was afraid to ask."

In the rearview mirror, I noticed Suki's parents perk up and give me their attention at the mention of the dog's name.

"She's still alive," Suki said. "He still has her. He said she doesn't see or hear very well, but she's still pretty healthy and she still gets around. He actually . . . after the war ended . . . after V-J Day, he wrote and offered her back to us. He said it would just about kill him to lose her, but he figured she was rightfully ours. But I talked it over with my parents, and we decided she'd be better off staying with Nick. It's too long a trip for her, and she's already had her life upended once."

I wanted to say that we'd all had our lives upended. That there was a lot of that going around. I didn't. Mostly because I figured it would sound as though I thought my life had been upended as badly as theirs, and I knew that wasn't objectively true.

I wanted to ask more questions, including the one most important, most burning question I had. I didn't. I said nothing at all.

——

Suki and I stood side by side at the grille of the car, staring into the engine, waiting for another quart of oil to empty out and drain down.

We hadn't made it far. Only down near the tiny town of Indian Wells, near Inyokern, which was close to the place where we could cut over to Bakersfield.

"Let me ask you a question," I said to Suki.

He said, "Okay." But his voice sounded a little tight.

"When you got those letters from Nick. From New York. Did they have a return address?"

He didn't answer for a time. I didn't look over at him to get a sense of why not. I didn't dare.

"You two had some kind of falling-out," he said. It didn't sound like a question.

"I don't know if I'd put it like that. Did he tell you anything about it?"

"Not much. He asked me not to share his address with you. Well. He said 'with anybody,' but there's no one I would share it with except you. But I don't know why he said that."

The news hit my gut like a flaming hardball, for a couple of reasons I could single out. And maybe more that I couldn't.

"And you have no idea why?"

I asked because I was entertaining the painful thought that Suki might have no idea about me and my situation. I always figured he suspected. And, in that case, he had gone on to be friends with me anyway. But if he really had no idea, then I had no idea what he would do if he knew. What he would think of me.

"Well . . . ," he said. ". . . some idea. I guess."

That made me breathe a little easier.

"You won't tell me where he's living?"

"That's hard," he said. "I'm not sure what to do about that."

The oil had long since drained out of the can, but we made no move to slam the hood and get back inside the car with his parents. We made no move to travel on.

"I guess my question," he said, "is why you would want to see him if he doesn't want you to."

"I just need to know *why*, Suki. I need to know what happened. That's all. I'm not going to try to get him to do anything he doesn't want to do. If his feelings have changed, or he's met somebody, there's nothing I can do about that. But he didn't tell me why. That's what's killing me. I can't go my whole life not even knowing why."

But I knew, as I said it, that you should never say you can't do something when you may have no other choice but to do it.

"That would be hard," he said. "I can understand how hard that would be."

I had no idea what to say to that, so I never answered.

In time we slammed the hood, got back into the car, and drove on.

I thought of the late Gordon Cho, who had died peacefully in his sleep in 1944, and, in his honor, I let the moment remain incomplete.

———

I stood on the bus platform with the family for a long time, waiting for the bus to come. Feeling as though my presence was somehow helpful.

Then I took a really good look at Mrs. Yamamoto's eyes.

She was standing in the warm wind, leaning forward from the waist, as if her impatience would hurry some nonexistent bus along. And in her eyes I saw . . . well, so much. I might even have trouble putting it all into words.

Here's my best shot at explaining it, I think: In that moment I realized Manzanar had devastated her twice. When she was thrown in, she lost everything, and had to start all over. When she was thrown out, she lost the little she'd had in the interim, and had to start all over. It was just all there in her eyes, and it was possibly even harder the second time, and it was . . . I'm sorry. I honestly don't have the words for what it was.

Just as I was thinking it couldn't possibly be as bad as it looked, her husband moved to her side and tried to put a comforting arm around her. And I saw tears well up in her eyes. She looked briefly over her shoulder at me, and I knew it was time for me to go. People don't really like onlookers to their sorrow. I never liked it much myself.

"I should get started on that long drive home," I said to Suki.

"Yeah," he said, and I knew I had read the moment correctly. "I'll walk you to your car."

"Aren't you afraid you'll miss your bus?"

"We'll be quick."

I shook Mr. Yamamoto's hand, and gave Mrs. Yamamoto's hand a squeeze. I figured I'd never see them again. And I was right.

Suki and I jogged out to the parking lot together, feeling the stress of his possibly being late for that one bus a day. In fact, I had no idea why he'd chosen to go with me until he spoke.

"I was just thinking," he said. His voice was breathy with exertion. "I was going to write to you and tell you our address in Oklahoma when we got settled somewhere. But then I thought . . . maybe you'll leave home now. And maybe I won't know where to write to you, either. And I don't want us to lose touch. I wrote my great-aunt's address down for you. On this *envelope*."

I noticed that he put a strange emphasis on the word "envelope," but I didn't attach much significance to it at the time.

"Thanks," I said, and slid it into my shirt pocket.

"If you can't decide where to go," he said, "maybe come to Oklahoma."

"Maybe," I said. "Maybe I will."

We embraced, which we had been too shy to do in front of his parents.

Then he ran back to the station.

I walked back to the terrible car, climbed in, and started her up.

While the engine warmed, I took the envelope out of my pocket and read the address. The aunt's name was Eleanor Henderson. A married name, maybe. The address was in a town called Enid.

I tossed it onto the passenger seat, and it landed upside down. I stared at it, suddenly understanding what Suki had been trying to tell me. Suddenly decoding his strange inflection on the word "envelope."

He had written the address on an envelope, all right. It was the envelope from one of Nick's recent letters to him. The postmark was September 19, 1945, and Nick's full return address was written in the upper left-hand corner, in that loopy handwriting I would have known anywhere.

———

When I arrived home, my father was back in the house after his day's labor—if one could call supervising a bunch of underpaid workers "labor." My mother was nowhere to be seen. Her car was gone, so she had driven somewhere, but I had no idea where. And it didn't feel worth asking.

My father was sitting in his easy chair reading the paper. He looked up when I walked in.

"I'm just going to pack my things," I said. "And then I'm leaving."

"I'm not surprised. I'm more surprised it took you as long as it did."

"I had something I had to do first."

"Don't even tell me what. I don't want to know."

"No," I said. "You don't."

I almost walked into my room and left it at that. I almost just moved on to the packing. I started to. Then I decided I had one more thing I wanted to say.

"Remember when we were talking about all the people Hitler was killing? And he did kill them. I was right about that. They weren't just 'packed in there really tight.'" By that time the Allies had liberated the Nazi concentration camps. By that time we knew what they had found. "And you figured that was unfair to everybody except—"

I would have finished. I would have said the word. I wasn't afraid to. Well, yes, I was afraid. But I would have said it anyway.

He cut me off.

"You don't have to say it. I already know. Your mother found those letters under your mattress."

I knew he was referring to the letters from Nick, because they were the only things under my mattress. I was surprised, because I hadn't thought of them as particularly incriminating. I couldn't remember anything being said that was less than tame. But something he'd written had prompted my parents to put two and two together.

Then I decided it must have been the last one.

It burned like dry ice to think about her reading such personal correspondence, but there was nothing I could do about that, so I tried to put it away again.

"Can you at least drive me to the bus station in Fresno?"

He returned his eyes to his newspaper, but in the split second before he did, I saw something in them. He was calm. Weirdly calm. Almost artificially so. But in his eyes I saw something like . . . the only word I can think to use is *contempt*. The sad part is that I was not especially surprised.

"Seems to me you found it just fine on your own when you were fifteen," he said.

I waited, expecting the sting of it to land. But then I realized it had all landed a long time ago.

I didn't answer. There was nothing more I needed to say.

———

In the morning I packed light. Lighter than I had the first time I left. Because I had learned how heavy bags can slow you down, and also that we don't need as much as we think we do.

I carried my things out into the road, and walked toward town, turning to stick my thumb out every time a car came by.

The war was over, and people were out driving for every reason under the sun, and maybe for no reason at all. Getting a ride was easy. All the way to Fresno, I just held out my thumb, and there was my ride.

For once in my life, I had made the right choice, and my way was clear.

I never spoke to, or in any way communicated with, my parents or brother again. I had no reason to think they were unhappy with the arrangement.

That part of my life was over, and I had nothing to gain by looking back, so I never did.

Chapter Twenty-Two

That Which Is Not Level

Five days later I woke up in a little hotel in Greenwich Village, on the west side of lower Manhattan.

I showered for what felt like an hour. The water was hot, and it stayed hot, and it just felt like heaven to have it run all over me on that cool November morning. I felt as though it could wash away everything. The past. Maybe even the pain.

I dressed in clean clothes, and set out to find Nick's address on foot.

I had actually located it the night before, purposely, on my walk between Grand Central station and whatever close-to-Nick's-apartment hotel I would choose for the night. But I hadn't gone anywhere near.

When I found the building again, I stood in front of it for a long time, just looking up.

The air was crisp with autumn, and the street was lined with trees, which I hadn't pictured when I thought of New York City. Their falling red and brown leaves swirled around me on circular breezes as I stood rooted to that sidewalk.

I wasn't sure what I was feeling until I unstuck my feet and walked closer. Either everything or nothing, but those can be hard categories to sort out.

While I stared, I thought about Nick, lying on his back on the pallet bed in that damp root cellar, talking about the places we could live. I could almost feel Akira curled on my belly as we shared those dreams. I had known even then that a big city was a friend to a boy like me. I knew why he suggested only the biggest cities in the country. And, whatever else I was feeling, I felt that safety as I stood there, trying to be ready to approach the door. I had escaped my small-town life, where everybody knew everything about everybody. And I could feel that. The relief of it was all around me. Nobody knew me here, and even if they did, they probably wouldn't care. How can you get deeply involved in the lives of your neighbors when there are just so damned many of them?

Without really thinking it out, without really talking to myself about it, I think I knew in that moment that I would land here, and stay here, no matter how the next few minutes of my life played out.

I unstuck my feet and moved to the door. That's when I knew exactly what I felt: fear. Heart-pounding, hands-shaking fear.

The building was an old brownstone that may have been a single-family home at one time. Now it was divided into two apartments at the street level and two on the second story. What could have been a basement apartment instead had an awning and a neon sign, unlit at that hour, that said **THE HIDEAWAY**, and several signs for the different kinds of beer they served there. Three or four stone steps led up to the stoop, and there was an outer door with glass windows that let into a foyer. Through the windows I could see a set of stairs leading to the second floor.

I stepped up onto the stoop and stood a minute. And almost lost my nerve.

I was fairly sure I wouldn't catch Nick at home on this first try. Because, even though the building was anything but fancy, it was an apartment in New York City, and there was rent to be paid on it. I figured Nick must be working a job.

Unless . . .

And this is where it really got bad in my brain. Unless he had moved in with somebody. Met another man who worked and paid the rent. I felt as though I might die, almost literally die, if a man opened the door. I'm not quite sure why I thought so, except that it just seemed like more pain than a body could take on all at once.

I turned around to walk away, but stopped.

Of course, Gordon Cho had been right. When you can't know a thing . . . when it's incomplete, and you can't make it complete, then you have to accept it. But I had a chance to know.

I turned around and faced the door again.

Through its windows I saw that a young woman had stepped out of one of the upstairs apartments, and was standing on the landing, watching me. In her arms was a bundle that I took to be a small baby. I couldn't see a baby, just the swaddling clothes and the bulk of a tiny body inside. But there's a certain way a woman holds a baby.

She had long, honey-colored hair that spilled around her shoulders, and a kind face.

She gave me a quizzical look, as though asking me from that distance, and through that glass, what I wanted or needed. But what I wanted and needed was nothing she could possibly have provided.

Or so I thought.

I pushed the door open and took one step into the foyer.

"Are you looking for somebody?" she asked. "I saw you staring at the building for a long time."

"I was looking for Nick Mattaliano."

"He's at work," she said.

I said nothing, because I didn't know what to say. I wanted to know who she was to Nick. Maybe just a neighbor? Maybe he had to share the apartment to be able to afford rent? After that, I ran out of ideas.

As these thoughts spun in my head, I saw the dog. She stepped out of the open doorway and onto the upstairs landing, as if only now realizing someone was here. Her eyes looked cloudy, and her whole head had gone gray. But it was unmistakably her. She offered a few gruff barks.

"Akira," I said.

I don't think she heard me. She barked a couple more times, her gray snout working the air. And then she got it. I think she was too deaf to get it by my voice. I think she got it by my scent.

She wagged her whole body almost violently, and her gruff barks morphed into whimpers and squeaks of excitement.

"She knows you," the young woman said.

"Yes," I said. I didn't know what else to say.

"You're Steven."

My head spun even harder.

"How did you know that?"

"Nick told me all about you. He told me so much about you that I feel like I know you. I just knew it must be you if Akira knows you."

"Yes," I said. "I'm Steven. And you are . . . ?"

"Beth," she said. "Nick's wife."

I took a moment to try to digest what was happening, but I could barely even swallow it. Of course, in my shock, I said nothing.

"Come upstairs," she said.

And, through a dreamlike fog of confusion, I did as she had invited me to do.

———

"My mother's name was Beth," I said as she handed me a cup of tea. "Is, I mean. Her name *is* Beth. I don't mean to talk about her like she's dead."

I was sitting on a floral-print couch, the light from the avenue-side window pouring over me. Pouring into my eyes. She sat down next to me with the bundle of sleeping baby resting in her lap.

Then I had no idea what else to say.

Meanwhile Akira was rubbing her back joyfully against my pant leg, as if scratching herself on me. Her tail whipped back and forth while her nose swung in the air, enjoying the scent of me. I reached down and scratched her behind the ears, and she wagged harder.

"Nick works as a janitor at the grade school down the block," she said. "He won't be home till three. He goes in at seven in the morning and comes home at three. But there's a phone at the school. I could call him and tell him you're here."

"No. Don't do that. Don't bother him at work. He doesn't know I'm coming. I can come back after three."

"Stay and have your tea, though," she said.

Amazingly, I did.

We talked about Ollie, and my father's farm. We talked about the valley where Nick and I grew up, and our camping trips in the mountains. And about Nick's dad, who was still in prison. I told her about the experience of testifying at his trial.

It was several minutes before my brain was working well enough to look around and take in the apartment. I hadn't even fully realized there was a coffee table right in front of me. And, on it, proudly displayed, was one big hardcover book.

It was the book about astronomy that I had given Nick, back when I thought we were together.

"He kept that all this time," I said, my eyes fixed on it.

"Oh yes," she said. "He loves it. He loves *you*. Very much."

"Are you sure?"

"Oh yes," she said. "I'm positive."

———

When I walked back to the apartment at a little after three, Nick was sitting on the outside steps, waiting for me.

He didn't look like any Nick I had known. He didn't look like the Nick I'd first met, because he was so much older. So utterly grown. And he didn't look like the Nick I'd said goodbye to, because he was fit and robust, and clearly in good health.

Still, I would have known him anywhere.

I walked up to where he sat, and we looked straight into each other's eyes for a long moment.

"I'm not going to stay," I said. "I'm not going to give you a hard time. I know I'm here more or less against your will, but I'm not forcing myself on you. I just . . ."

He took advantage of my slight pause and jumped in.

"No, you're right," he said.

"I am?"

"Yes. You're right and I'm wrong. I was being a coward. I didn't want to hurt you, and I thought anything I said might only make it worse. But I at least owe you some kind of explanation."

It was not what I had been expecting. After his last letter, I'd been expecting to have to fight my way back into his life, if only for as long as it took to ask him why.

It left me not knowing how to proceed or what to say.

"Come on," he said. "Let's go get a cup of coffee."

He stood, and took hold of my sleeve, and tugged me toward the bar downstairs.

We stepped into the dim place together. It was open, but there were no lights on. Just the light spilling in from the street above. There were no customers, which was not surprising at that hour of the afternoon. There was one lone bartender, a handsome young man with the sleeves of his white short-sleeved shirt rolled up high, and a careful puff of dark hair combed into the style I would later know to call a pompadour.

"Nick," the man said, by way of a greeting.

"Just coffee, Sid. Since it's three o'clock in the afternoon and all."

He poured us two mugs, and we carried them over to a table in the very front corner, where we could look up onto the street and watch the feet and knees of pedestrians passing by.

"You look good," he said.

"You look good, too."

A silence fell.

I watched the knees and feet, but from the corner of my vision I could see him gathering up to say whatever it was he needed to say.

When he seemed unable to begin on his own, I gave the conversation a push start.

"You were wrong about only making it worse," I said. "If you'd told me everything, that would have made it a little better. I was picturing you here with somebody else. Well, you are. Obviously. But I think you know what I mean. I was thinking . . ." I glanced over toward the bar, but the bartender had gone into the kitchen, leaving us utterly alone. "You know. Another . . . male. Person. That would have been bad. Because then I would always be wondering why it couldn't have been me. But if someone like Beth is really who you want, well . . . I know why I can't be *that*. And, I mean . . . it's not what I wanted. But I can't be mad at you because you want a girl. I wouldn't want you to be mad at me because I don't."

I stopped talking. Sipped at my coffee. Waited.

"I made a lot of mistakes," he said. "But I never lied to you."

"You really thought . . ." But I trailed off and never finished.

"Here's the thing I need to explain. The way it was with us, it's not natural. Oh, I don't mean that the way it sounds. I'm talking about . . . you were my savior. You saved me. In every possible way. And that's good, in one sense. And I know you had all the best intentions, and I'll always appreciate it. But it's not the way relationships are supposed to go."

I kept my eyes on the passing feet. It was easier that way.

"How are they supposed to go?"

"Like this," he said.

Then I had to look at him to see what he meant. He was holding both his hands out, flat, in front of his face. Palms down. Perfectly level with one another.

"It's supposed to be level. Two people are supposed to be level. But then one is doing all the saving." The hand I took to be me rose up above his head. The hand I took to be him dropped down to the table. "You were literally the only person in my world. I didn't see anybody else. I didn't even see the world, except for the stars at night. But that's not really our world—that's the world beyond us. All I had was you, and everything came from you. If I ate, the food came from you. I needed to drink water to survive, and you were the one handing it to me. When I needed medicine to keep from dying of pneumonia, you handed it to me. My whole world was you, saving me. I started to forget who I was before you. Whatever your world was, that was my world. And I was so grateful to you . . . and I still am, but . . . I do love you, Steven. I'll always love you. But it was such a completely . . . what's the word . . . *dependent* situation, that I thought I could love you the way you loved me. No. Not even thought I *could*. I thought I *did*."

"I didn't mean for it to be that way," I said.

I was staring at his hands, which were still demonstrating that which was not level.

"I know you didn't. I'm not blaming you. You didn't make this world, and it's not your fault that saving people goes wrong. People need to save themselves. If they're having trouble saving themselves, then maybe a little help is good. But it has to go both ways. Two people need to save each other."

I watched as his hands leveled out again.

"Does that make sense?" he asked. "I'm not sure I'm explaining it right at all."

"You're explaining it fine," I said.

He dropped his hands, and we drank our coffee in a strangely satisfied silence.

Only when our mugs were empty and the light of the day had begun to fade did he speak again.

"I'm sorry I can't be who you wanted me to be."

I shook my head at him. "If I'm not apologizing for who I am, you shouldn't have to, either."

"I'm not. I'm just saying I know I hurt you, and that was the last thing I ever wanted to do, and that's the part I'm sorry about."

"At least I got my answer. I came here to find out why. And now I know."

"And it's not anything about you."

"No."

"I have something I want you to do," he said.

He stood, and dug a few coins out of his pocket, and left them on the table. I tried to do the same, but he waved me away.

"No, I've got the coffees," he said.

"What do you want me to do?"

"I want you to meet me right here at ten o'clock tonight. And I want you to just do it, and not ask any questions about it. Okay?"

"*Ten o'clock?* I'm a farm boy. I'm in bed by ten o'clock."

"Make an exception tonight," he said.

"No questions at all?"

"None. Just trust me one more time."

We walked up the stairs to the street together, and stood a foot or two apart. Then he dove in and embraced me enthusiastically, and I held him in return.

"I love you, Nick," I said quietly into his ear.

"I love you, too, Steven," he said.

I believed him.

It wasn't everything I had wanted from him. Not even close. But it was something. It was better than what I'd had when I arrived.

—

When I showed up at a little after ten, the place was packed, and loud. Standing room only. Nick was sitting at the bar. I guessed he had been there for a while, since he'd been able to get a seat.

I walked up to him, prepared to just stand at his side, but a man on the barstool beside him jumped up immediately.

"I can move, honey," he said. "If you want to sit with your friend." It seemed odd, but I took the stool.

"You want a beer?" Nick asked me.

"Sure."

He signaled the bartender, and one arrived in front of me. I took a few sips, then spun my stool around and took in my surroundings. Really looked for the first time. There were maybe forty patrons packed into that tiny place. And every single one of them was male.

There was a jukebox playing a slow ballad. I still remember the song. It was the one about the sentimental reasons for loving somebody.

There was a dance floor, and on it men were swaying. They were dancing together. With each other.

I looked over at Nick, who had spun his own stool around and was watching me watch. I realized my jaw was hanging slightly open.

"You just happen to live above this place?"

"Not really 'just happen to,'" he said. "First of all, there are places like this all over the Village. When I first got to New York I found this place and came here on purpose. I wasn't trying to meet anybody. It was nothing like that. I just wanted to see about . . . you know . . . myself. I came here and hung out a couple of nights, and there was a 'For rent' sign out front. That's how I found that apartment. I just wanted to know whether I belonged here or not."

"But you don't."

"No. But you do."

He stood, and I knew he was about to leave. I stood, too, thinking I could somehow prevent it. I didn't want what I thought was my last moment with him to be over.

"I hope you stay in the city," he said, his hands on my shoulders. "There's a lot here for you. And I hope if you do, you'll get in touch and tell me how you're doing. I'd love it if we could even stay friends, but if that's too hard for you, I understand. If you don't get in touch, well . . . have a good life, Steven."

He kissed me on the forehead and walked away.

I sank back down onto my barstool and watched his legs trotting up the stairs. I watched until he was gone.

Then I looked over to see that a large older man had taken the barstool beside me.

"That looked painful," he said.

"That *was* painful."

He reached his hand out for me to shake. "Freddie," he said.

I shook the hand, but I was filled with a sudden sense of dread. He was trying to pick me up. He was easily fifty, with jowls and a bald pate. Of all the men in that place, he was the last one I would want coming on to me. I'm sorry to sound cruel, but that's how I felt.

"Steven," I said, and tried to concentrate on my sweaty beer bottle, as if reading the label required every ounce of my attention.

"How long have you been out, Steven?"

I had no idea what he was talking about.

"Out?"

He laughed a little to himself. "Oh, that long, eh?" He stood, and grabbed a piece of my sleeve, and gave it a little tug. "Bring your beer," he said. "Some people I want you to meet."

I followed him through the crowded dance floor to a table in the corner where four very young, mostly very attractive men sat together. They looked up at me, their faces clearly open to the idea of meeting me. They looked at me as though they thought I was a person worth meeting.

I realized for the first time that Freddie had not been hitting on me. He had been trying to help me. He was making sure I didn't leave that night without finding what I needed.

"John, Jeff, Levi, Clarence? This is Steven. Steven is *very new* here. So take extra good care of him, okay?"

And with that he disappeared.

"Sit," Levi said to me.

"Where?"

There were no extra chairs.

"Here," he said.

He scooted over so only one of his butt cheeks was resting on the chair. I sat beside him, my hip bumping up against his.

They convinced me to tell my life story, while one of them kept an eye on the door. I had told them just about everything I was willing to share about myself before I asked why the lookout. What were they watching for?

"Just in case the police make a visit," Levi said. He had deep blue eyes that looked so big he reminded me of a deer. He had hair the color of wheat that stood straight up on his head. "We're young and fast, so we always make it out the back door and get away without being arrested."

"That sounds scary," I said, sipping at my beer.

"Compared to what you just described in that tiny town where you grew up?"

"Well. No. I guess compared to that, it's a decent trade-off."

"We're going to an after-hours club after this," John said. "You want to come along?"

I thought about what I'd said to Nick about late hours. How ten was past my bedtime. But the farm boy in me had died. In that moment it was gone forever.

"Absolutely," I said. "I'd love to come along."

Part Seven

2019

Chapter Twenty-Three

My Life's Epilogue

I knew there would come a time in this tale when I would have to start making a long story short, and I feel as though I'm there.

My life, looking back, was most of all about Levi, the man I was living with by Christmas. The man I married the very month it became legal to do so. The man I've spent seventy-six years with to date. Seems impossible even to say it, but it's true. Seventy-six years. I have no idea where I learned enough about relationships to make one last this long, except that I never forgot the lesson I picked up from Nick. That things have to be level. That it's not as good as you think when one person saves another, but it's very good when two people save each other. I took that to heart and made sure Levi and I stayed level.

Still, if he seems like an afterthought, I have to stress that this wasn't a story about Levi. It was a story about Suki and Ollie and Nick, and maybe, just to a small degree, a story about fate.

I'm on the fence in some ways regarding my beliefs about fate. But still, when you think about it, something remarkable happened. The man I would spend my life with lived on the other side of the country. Three thousand miles away. I had no reason to go there, and no way to find him. And, besides, I was convinced that Nick was my fate. If you believe in the concept, you can only conclude that Nick was indeed my fate, because he found an apartment right above the bar Levi frequented, and led me down there, and left me.

How can all those complex logistics be a random accident? To me, it strains credulity.

Maybe in addition to a story about Suki and Ollie and Nick, maybe this was a story to explain the odd statement I made when I started: that I often wonder why we think we know anything at all.

I'm ninety-four years old, and the older I get, the less I know. I mean that in a good way. Seems most of the trouble in this world stems from the things we're so sure we know. Now that I'm old enough and experienced enough to know I know nothing, the world is a constant, pleasant surprise, and the things I allow life to bring me are consistently better than anything I might have sought—or even imagined—for myself.

I like to think Gordon Cho would be proud.

Or that he *is* proud. Depending on your beliefs about a thing like that.

—

Suki picked us up at baggage claim in San Francisco International Airport.

I noticed that he walked with a cane now—one of those aluminum canes with a tripod of three legs at the bottom. That was new. But, otherwise, he didn't look any different. He didn't look any older. We came out to visit about every other year, and he never looked any older. Then again, once you hit ninety-four, it's possible that your ability to look old has stalled at some kind of max point.

We stopped when we saw each other, and beamed from a few steps away, and shared that initial moment that was happy and sad all at the same time. It used to be all happy, but as the years and the visits have gone by, I think we become more and more aware that we're the only ones left.

Nick died at age eighty-two, his second wife two years later. His daughter is still alive, and sends us a card at Christmas, but I don't claim to see her much. Suki's wife is gone, and his children, grandchildren, and great-grandchildren still live in Oklahoma.

Suki and I embraced, then Suki and Levi, and we waited for our bags to come up, watching the moving belt spin in an empty, pointless pattern.

"I'm not sure how you'll feel about this," Suki said. "But I made a mistake. I didn't realize that tomorrow's the anniversary of my grandmother's death. I wasn't planning very well, and I didn't think about it until after we arranged your visit. But don't worry either way, because if you don't want to do it, it's not a problem. I can go later. I don't have to do it on the exact day. But since I've been in the Bay Area, I try to drive down to visit her grave every year."

"If you're inviting us to go," I said, "I'm honored. Where is she buried?"

He seemed surprised that I asked. I could see it on his face. "Manzanar," he said. "I thought you knew. You knew she died there, right?"

"I didn't know they buried people on the site. And the graveyard is still there?"

"Oh yes. Everything is preserved. It's a historical site now. Well, not everything. The barracks have all been torn down. But there's a visitors center. And the graveyard is kept up. I didn't know how you would feel about going back there."

"If you can go back there," I said, "so can I."

———

We left very early the following morning, headed due east through Manteca, and took the 120—the Tioga Road—through the upper elevations of Yosemite. Partly because it was a beautiful drive, partly because there were precious few places to cross over to the eastern Sierras.

"That sign said we need chains on this road," Levi said from his spot in the back seat of Suki's SUV. "Have we got chains?"

"We have chains," Suki said. "In the well with the spare tire. But I think the better question is, do you see any snow?"

It was early November, but still clear.

"I'm just telling you what the sign said," Levi told him.

"I think they put up those signs," I said, "because at this time of year it can start any minute."

"Then my next question," Suki said. "Do you see a single cloud in the sky?" He had that sardonic smile on his face that he tended to wear when he poked fun at me.

"You enjoy a good laugh at my expense," I said. "Don't you?"

"Speaking of which," he said, "remember your last visit? You said, 'We should go up to Yosemite next time, Suki.' And I was all, 'Next time? Seriously, Steven, next time? Ninety-two-year-old man says he'll do *what* in two years?' Leaving aside the very real possibility of death, my kids have been on me to stop driving since I was eighty."

"And after all that, we never did go."

"Well, we're going there now," he said.

"Then I was right."

We stopped at the entrance booth, and Suki flashed his senior national parks pass, and we drove on through.

We drove through Big Oak Flat, past Mount Hoffman. We got out at Olmstead Point to breathe in the view over Half Dome. Then we got back on the road and drove past Tenaya Lake. Just as we were coming into Tuolumne Meadows, a black bear skittered across the road in front of us, and Suki had to swerve to avoid a collision, even though the speed limit was only 25 and we were not speeding.

"Hey," I said as we straightened out and drove on. "Remember the first time we came down from camping in the mountains, and Nick's dad wasn't there to pick us up, so we were walking toward town, and that bear ran across the road in front of us?"

He seemed to chew on his bottom lip for a moment, thinking.

"I remember so very much about that night," he said, all seriousness now. "But I can't honestly say I remember that."

It's funny, the different things we remember. It's not always the most important parts.

———

We stopped for lunch in the little town of Lee Vining, which was on the eastern side of the Tioga Pass, where the 120 drops down off the mountain and intersects the 395. We chose a restaurant with a patio, and a view. The views were epic from Lee Vining, because it looked out over Mono Lake.

We sat on the patio to enjoy the view. It was only a hair after eleven, and there was nobody else there.

The waitress who came to bring our menus looked barely over twenty, and she noticed our matching rings. Levi's and mine. A lot of people do. They're easy to notice. They have jade insets and are quite distinct.

"Those are beautiful," she said. "Are you guys married?"

"We are," Levi said.

"How long have you been together?"

"Seventy-six years," I said.

Then we had to pretend we didn't think her reaction was funny. The drop-jawed, gaping-mouthed disbelief. She probably couldn't imagine *living* that long. Maintaining a relationship that long was doubtlessly out of range for her poor youthful brain.

"That's so *great*," she said. "You guys are so *cute*. Can I take your picture? We have a wall inside for couples who come through here, and you two are just so cute."

I'll admit she might have been influenced by our Magic-Shrinking-Old-Man Syndrome. When you get to be our age, gravity is not your friend, and it's hard not to end up looking like some kind of forest elf.

We leaned together, and she snapped us with her phone.

After she left us alone to read the menus, Levi leaned over and said into my ear, "Did you ever think we'd live long enough to be a cute couple?"

I was opening my mouth to say something witty when we saw it.

Tooling south on the 395, a 1937 Ford pickup motored by. Just like the one Suki's dad had used to own, only a deep, shimmering midnight blue instead of maroon. It was either perfectly maintained or meticulously restored. Either way it was perfect.

Suki and I both rose unsteadily to our feet, watching it go. As though that might somehow prevent it from dropping out of sight.

"Did you see that?" I asked him. But it was a stupid question, because it was obvious that he had.

"That looked just like it, except for the paint job."

"Maybe that *was* it," I said.

"Maybe. I mean, people buy them and sell them and restore them."

We sat back down and picked up our menus. But I couldn't shake the feeling that some wispy little trace of Mr. Yamamoto had just blown through. Even though I didn't ask Suki if he thought so, too, I figured he must. It was a hard thought not to have.

"I tried to buy it back, you know," I said.

"No. You never told me that."

"I did. In those years I was stuck home, I saved up a hundred dollars. And I found the guy who bought it and tried to buy it back. Nine hundred percent profit, I pointed out to him. But he told me the price was a thousand dollars. He was just being an ass because I took a swing at him when he showed me the bill of sale."

"*That* I heard about," he said. "What would you have done with it? Driven it? You could've gotten more truck for a hundred dollars back then. Especially if he'd beat it up or put miles on it."

"I would've given it back. I would have come tooling up the road in it on the day I came to pick you up. And then I would have handed your dad the keys, and you could've driven to Oklahoma."

"Except we wouldn't've all fit in it."

"Oh. I hadn't thought of that."

"Well, anyway. It was a very nice gesture. But it's too much. It hurt him to lose it, but that didn't make it your job to right the wrong. It would have been too much. You'd done enough already."

I went silent for a time, thinking yet again about my conversation with Nick about people being "level." I realized I did that a lot in my teen years. Tried to be the savior. It wasn't really the first time I'd made the observation, but it might have been the first time it occurred to me that *I* was probably the one I had really wished I could save. I wondered if all saviors were like that. Lost.

"What did I do?" I asked Suki. "You make it sound like I did so much. I don't remember doing much."

"Are you kidding? You took the dog."

"Nick took the dog."

"No, you did. I needed to get her somewhere *that day*, or else. You took the dog and got her set up with Nick. I couldn't have done that. I had no options but you. And then you agreed to come get us when it was over."

"Yeah. But that was pretty much it."

"You offered to hide me."

"I'm not sure that's the favor I thought it was."

"And you tried to come visit me."

I sat for a few seconds with my eyes open wide. Possibly my mouth as well.

"I didn't know you knew about that. You never said you knew, and I purposely didn't tell you because I was ashamed."

"I don't see why."

"Because it was so naïve. It was pretty stupid."

"Yeah, maybe," Suki said. "It was also pretty nice."

———

The sign at the road was exactly the same, and seeing it hit me like a lead pipe swung hard. It rocketed me back, and I reexperienced what I felt driving up in an army Jeep, wondering if they'd let me pass through the gate. The rocks that seemed to grow around the base of the sign's massive poles were still the same. There was still a star on either side of the word *War*. Just so we couldn't possibly forget.

I remembered that army officer telling me, "There's a war on." I remembered how mad it had made me.

The foundations of a few of the terrifying guard towers still stood, and one seemed to have been restored to what I originally saw that day.

I looked over at Suki's face, but it only looked impassive. Maybe because he came here every year. It might have socked him in the gut the first time he came back, but it didn't seem to be doing so now. Or maybe he was just better than me at keeping such things contained on the inside. Maybe he always had been.

Then again, I thought, he hadn't eaten ice cream for lunch, so he must have found some kind of peace with the thing.

We drove past the visitor center without stopping.

Suki knew the way to the cemetery without hesitation. Then again, no one could miss it. Paradoxically, it was the only alive-looking spot on the premises. The rest was more or less a giant vacant lot with the roads preserved, and newish signs labeling the areas. But the cemetery featured a marker that was hard to miss. A pure white obelisk, considerably taller than a man. It sat within a rectangle of dirt surrounded by a handmade wooden fence. It sat in front of that incredible mountain range. It sat under that perfect cloudless blue sky. It bore a vertical inscription in black Japanese characters. It was surrounded on three sides by low posts, strung together with drooping ropes. Its three layers of base had been strewn with colorful strands of origami cranes.

For something so awful, it was strangely beautiful.

We pulled up and parked outside the rustic fence, but there was someone else there. A family of tourists. There seemed to be about five of them, parked in a minivan, and it was impossible to tell if they had just arrived or were just about to drive away.

Suki turned off the engine. He seemed content to wait.

A few seconds later the family piled out of the car, all shorts and flip-flops and expensive cameras.

I powered down the window because it was warm in the car without the air-conditioning. Yes, even in November. Suki did the same.

We just waited.

"Please don't tell anybody I was an internee," Suki said quietly, to both of us. He turned his head slightly so Levi could hear as well. "It's not so good when the tourists know that. They want to get pictures with you. They want to hear all the stories. It really changes the experience for me."

I pantomimed zipping my lips.

Only seconds later the father of the family approached our SUV on the driver's side, but stayed a few respectful feet away.

"You gentlemen want to go in first?" he asked politely.

"No, thank you," Suki said. "We might take a little longer. You and your family go ahead. We're not in a hurry."

The man touched the brim of his baseball cap in a gesture of respect and headed toward his family, who were now milling inside the rough outer fence. Then he stopped. Turned back.

I braced for him to ask.

"You fellows veterans of the war?" he asked instead.

I breathed again. He was closer to my side of the car now, so I answered him.

"No, we were just a little bit too young for that. I turned eighteen on the day the war ended. This guy is the baby of the group." I indicated Levi in the back with a hooked thumb. "He's five months younger. Those of us up front are old."

He smiled, then joined his family.

I heard Suki breathe a sigh of relief.

We only had to wait for a minute or two. The family seemed aware that someone was waiting for them to leave. They seemed to be made restless by it. Either that or it simply wasn't as riveting an experience as they had hoped.

"Does it make you uncomfortable?" I asked Suki in a low voice. "All those people coming through and staring at your grandmother's grave?"

"No," he said. "They should know. I want them to know. Later than one would hope, for people to know, but at least they finally do."

The family piled back into their minivan and we piled out.

Levi handed Suki his cane from the back seat, and the flowers we had stopped to buy on the way home from the airport the previous day.

"Should we stay here?" I asked.

"No, you should come. You're one of her favorite people."

"Because I took the dog?"

"Because you took the dog."

"What about me?" Levi asked. "I'm not one of her favorite people."

"Oh, yes you are," Suki said. "Because any friend of Steven's is a friend of hers."

We walked together, slowly. With care, the way elderly gentlemen tend to do.

We stopped in front of the obelisk and just took in its beauty. I knew it must have been restored, because the white of it practically glowed in the midday sun.

"Do you mind if I ask what it says?" Levi whispered.

Suki didn't seem to mind. "It says, 'Monument to console the souls of the dead.' And you can't see it from here, but on the back it has a date in 1943, and that it was put up by the Manzanar Japanese."

"Is it weird to say that it's beautiful?" I stared at the monument as I spoke, and at my beloved Sierra Nevada range as its riveting backdrop. "That all of this is just hauntingly beautiful?"

"Not at all. It's a beautiful spot. Provided you have heating and air-conditioning. And given that you can turn around and leave any time you're ready."

We moved over to one of the individual graves. There weren't many. It was marked with a ring of stones, but with no granite grave marker to identify it.

Suki set the flowers inside the ring of stones, and we stood in silence.

I had grown curious the night before, and looked it up on my phone. I was able to learn that about a hundred and fifty people had died here, but most had been cremated and their ashes carried away when the families left the camp. Fifteen had been buried here, but only six remained. It said they were older men with no immediate family and . . . I couldn't really remember as I stood there, but possibly something about premature babies. It did not account for Suki's grandmother. Then again, the recording of history is imperfect. Especially history like this. The kind that people would just as soon leave in the dust and forget.

I remembered Suki telling me that Nick had offered Akira back, but the family had decided she was too old and frail for such a long journey. I didn't ask why his grandmother was never moved, because I knew it probably hadn't been his decision, and besides, *res ipsa loquitur*. The thing spoke for itself. As evidenced by their decision regarding the dog, there is dignity in letting things remain. Everybody had been uprooted enough.

I felt a little dizzy standing in the warm sun. I didn't tend to stand well anymore. My circulation didn't support it.

"Okay," Suki said. "Done."

"That was quick," Levi said.

"It doesn't need to be long," Suki said. "It just needs to be."

———

As we were driving out of the monument, back toward the 395, Levi spoke up. This time I was in the back seat, and he was up front with Suki.

"Don't you guys even want to drive through the old homestead?"

He knew once Suki started driving north the decision would more or less have been made. I wasn't sure if he knew how long a drive it was around the bottom of the mountain range. I supposed being from New York made it seem close, relatively speaking.

"Not even a little bit," I said immediately.

I waited for Suki to chime in, but he seemed to have nothing to add. At least not for the moment. He was also not driving toward the highway anymore. We were just holding still there, the SUV still in drive, his foot on the brake.

"I can't imagine you're not even vaguely curious about the farm," Levi said.

"Not even vaguely."

"You don't know if your brother still has it."

"My brother would be ninety-seven. I think it's safe to assume we're the oldest alumni from that era of that town still walking around on the planet."

"But you don't know if he married or had children," Levi said.

"Or care," I added, with a sardonic note in my voice. So no one would think I was literally angry.

"If it were me," Levi said, "I'd want to at least see what the old place looks like now."

I opened my mouth to speak, but in that moment Suki entered the conversation.

"That's a useless endeavor."

"You've been back there?" Levi asked him.

"About five years ago I drove through. It's unrecognizable. Not one building left from the old town, and no way to even see where they used to be. Steven's father's farm, and the one my father used to work, they don't seem to exist anymore. The land has all been subdivided. Fresno is built up halfway to the mountains. Half of what we think of as the valley is suburbs now. And beyond that, resorts and vacation homes. So many people go on vacation there up in the mountains that there are gas stations and inns and restaurants here and there all along the road. Some of that land never really could be built up, but if it could be, it pretty much is. I literally couldn't figure out where anything we knew used to be. It's like the ground just swallowed it up and it disappeared."

"Good," I said. "It deserved to disappear."

Suki took his foot off the brake, and we drove toward the highway again.

"*We* survived and *it* disappeared," I added, half under my breath. "How's that for justice? Pretty sure they meant for it to be the other way around."

He turned north on the 395, and we headed back toward San Francisco.

———

That was five days ago.

Now Levi and I are moving through the security line at the airport, and I'm watching Suki walk down the long hall with his cane. He's just a dot in the distance now, but I don't stop watching him. I can't. It might be the last time I ever see him.

Then again, I've thought that at every parting for the last twenty years, and here we still are.

We've never discussed it out loud, at least not that I can recall, but there's a sense of triumph in that. Levi and I have likely outlived every cop who ever burst into The Hideaway to try to make arrests. Suki has likely outlived all the guards who stood with their bayoneted rifles over their shoulders while he and his family were trying to have a life.

Maybe living long is the best revenge.

Or maybe it's not the length of our lives that counts the most. Maybe it's the fact that the waitress found us adorable, and the man at the monument never thought to ask if Suki had been interned. Despite some tough losses in more than a few ancient battles, it would be hard to believe we didn't go on to win our own personal wars.

Then he turns a corner and drops out of sight, and I think that, even though I don't know if I'll see him again or not, it feels okay that I don't know. I decide I can accept that our story is incomplete.

I allow it to be so.

BOOK CLUB QUESTIONS

1. In the beginning of the book Steven had a hard time feeling that he fit in anywhere. By the end of the book he has overcome those feelings and become a person who is happy with himself and his life. What are some of the major turning points that led him in this direction, and what are some of the primary obstacles that stood in his way?

2. The hike up into the mountains is an experience that permanently bonds Steven, Suki, Nick, and Ollie. When they come back down, the whole world has changed due to the bombing of Pearl Harbor. In what ways would each of their lives have been different if they had not had the support of each other's friendship?

3. Mr. Cho acts as a mentor to Steven, and imparts many invaluable lessons that Steven carries with him throughout his life. One piece of advice that made the most impact was when Mr. Cho said, "Enjoying the world just as it is. Understanding that many things are incomplete. Allowing it to be so." How do you think Steven applied this wisdom to his own situation?

4. Nick leaves his mom's place for New York City without telling Steven, leaving Steven unsure what to do when he shows up at Nick's mother's house in 1943. He only hears

sporadically from Nick over the rest of the war, and Nick never includes his return address. Then Nick sends him a letter saying it would be better for Steven to forget him. Do you think these were acts of cowardice on Nick's part, or acts of love?

5. During a particularly difficult time in his life, Steven makes his way to Manzanar to find Suki. He is greatly impacted by the conditions he sees there. How did the author's vivid details of the hardship of the internment camp and descriptions of the brutal wind and blowing sand affect you as a reader?

6. When Steven arrives to pick up the Yamamoto family at Manzanar, Suki's grandmother isn't with Suki and his parents, and he realizes that she must have passed away while interned. In another scene, at the bus stop, Steven reflects on letting the Yamamoto family go and allows them the little dignity they have left. In these scenes and others, as the author clearly pulls back the veil on this often unspoken-of time in history, what revelations or insights most stood out to you?

7. Despite his family's contempt and lack of support for his sexual orientation and choice of friends, Steven stays true to himself, even after he returns home to his family after running away and realizes the only thing he can see in his father's eyes is scorn. What does this say about his character as a person and his courage?

8. At the end of the book, Steven, with his lifelong partner, Levi, returns to California for a visit with Suki. Steven reflects on the challenges and losses they have all faced, and yet here they are after all these years, still friends. How do you think they held on to their friendship despite the different paths their lives took?

ABOUT THE AUTHOR

Photo © 2019 Douglas Sonders

Catherine Ryan Hyde is the *New York Times*, *Wall Street Journal*, and #1 Amazon Charts bestselling author of forty books (and counting). An avid traveler, equestrian, and amateur photographer, she shares her astrophotography with readers on her website.

Her novel *Pay It Forward* was adapted into a major motion picture, chosen by the American Library Association (ALA) for its Best Books for Young Adults list, and translated into more than twenty-three languages in over thirty countries. Both *Becoming Chloe* and *Jumpstart the World* were included on the ALA's Rainbow list, and *Jumpstart the World* was a finalist for two Lambda Literary Awards. *Where We Belong* won two Rainbow Awards in 2013, and *The Language of Hoofbeats* won a Rainbow Award in 2015.

More than fifty of her short stories have been published in the Antioch Review, Michigan Quarterly Review, Virginia Quarterly Review, Ploughshares, Glimmer Train, and many other journals; in the anthologies Santa Barbara Stories and California Shorts; and in the bestselling anthology Dog Is My Copilot. Her stories have been honored by the Raymond Carver Short Story Contest and the Tobias Wolff Award and have been nominated for Best American Short Stories, the

O. Henry Award, and the Pushcart Prize. Three have been cited in the annual Best American Short Stories anthology.

She is founder and former president (2000–2009) of the Pay It Forward Foundation and still serves on its board of directors. As a professional public speaker, she has addressed the National Conference on Education, twice spoken at Cornell University, met with AmeriCorps members at the White House, and shared a dais with Bill Clinton.

For more information, please visit the author at www.catherineryanhyde.com.